Berlin
Hotel

VICKI BAUM

◉

Berlin
Hotel

London
MICHAEL JOSEPH

First published by
MICHAEL JOSEPH LTD.
26 *Bloomsbury Street*
London
JUNE 1944

FIRST PUBLISHED IN THIS EDITION 1950

MADE AND PRINTED IN GREAT BRITAIN BY PURNELL AND SONS, LTD.
PAULTON (SOMERSET) AND LONDON

HERR SCHMIDT was trying to squeeze a stepladder into the narrow space behind the desk and hang up the picture that had come off the wall at the first faint rattling of flak.

"That's the third time he's fallen on his face in two weeks," he said, picking up the picture and brushing over the glass with his sleeve. It was an official and glorified portrait of the Fuehrer, on which the mean little smirk around the flabby mouth had been wiped off, the ordinary nose had been chiselled to nobler lines, and the puffy eyes had been filled with visionary fire. So popular had this version of the Fuehrer's face become all over Europe that people had forgotten how the real man looked. But this was an old trick, used by every ruler, from Caesar to Napoleon.

Schmidt looked at it somewhat disgustedly, climbed up his little ladder and began searching for a place to put the nail in. "The wall is so full of holes he won't stand another air raid," he mumbled. He had crooked nails in his mouth and was straightening out another crooked nail with the hammer. New nails were hard to get.

"They won't get through tonight; not with our magnificent new air defences," said assistant clerk Ahlsen; he wore the party badge and received his information from the editorials in Goebbels' *Das Reich*. Herr Kliebert came out from behind his glass partition to supervise the action. He was a great one at supervising others at work, was Kliebert. Formerly the mayor of a middle-sized town, he had resigned under the Weimar Republic and later on watched the rise of the Nazis with timid misgivings. Now that all younger men were called into the army, he had been taken out of the mothballs, he and his outmoded Prince Albert and his cumbersome dignity, and here he was now, pasted behind the desk of the hotel as a most inefficient reception clerk. Old men were scattered all over the hotel; old men and sick men and crippled men, unfit for the manly and ennobling business of winning the war. Schmidt was the only fairly young one, and upon him had fallen most of the duties of those who had gone. But now he, too, had been called for medical examination. He hammered his anger into the wall.

"At my father's time they had Bismarck hanging here,

and when I was a pageboy it was the Kaiser. After the other war came Hindenburg's photo—and now it's Hitler. I wonder who comes next," he grumbled.

The sirens had screamed at seven minutes to eight; the populace of Berlin had dutifully scrambled into basements and cellars, for the rules were strict and to stay out was punishable by a fine. In the hotel the guests had been herded into the well-equipped shelter that tried hard to look like a cosy rathskeller. There had been the distant rumbling of flak, and a few scattered detonations as if a giant had made a strike in his giant bowling alley; the windows had rattled and the picture had come off, and that was all. As always during an air alarm, the lobby seemed strangely dismal and deserted. The lights were dimmed, the radio was off the air, the telephone silent. The bench for pageboys was empty, as there were strict orders to keep them in the personnel shelter behind the wine cellar; the florist's shop was closed because its measly supply of flowers had been sold out early in the afternoon, and the moth-eaten widow from the newspaper stand had left her post in a panic. Everywhere in this lobby with its sumptuous marble pillars and gilded stucco were the hidden signs of decay. The elevator bore a sign: "Out of order." Some of the windowpanes were still shattered from the last air raid and the windows temporarily boarded up. Some of the heavy brocade curtains had tears in them, and the stuffing was coming out of several of the deep, luxurious chairs, for repairs were a grave problem in this worm-eaten country where even thread and needles had become a rare treasure. The raspberry-red carpet with its pineapple pattern was threadbare and had big holes in it over which Herr Kliebert had pushed potted palms that were now in everybody's way. There was hope, however, that some sort of new floor covering would be allotted soon, for it was very important to keep the hotel in presentable shape. Under the National Socialists it had become less a hotel for passing guests than a half-official branch of the government, a comfortable island set apart from the rest of the country. Here lived Hitler's élite; officials who spent the week in Berlin and only occasionally visited their families on the fine old country estates they had acquired with their new money; industrialists who were bombed out of their homes; privileged people who had to give up living in the residential districts that had become almost inaccessible for lack of cars or taxis and who could afford the exorbitant prices of the hotel. Here the upper crust of the Third Reich could meet and mingle and haggle and bargain with important foreign visitors; here were the headquarters of all the Quislings and collaborationists, of the big, important bankers and industrialists, and of the small, shady foreign agents too. This was the place where rumours were started and rumours were suppressed, where promises were given and broken, where satellites were threatened and terrorized and neutrals were wheedled and cajoled into doing business with the Third Reich. This fine old reputable hotel was used by the Nazis as a show window to put their new Germany on display; it was an important prop of propaganda, and therefore its wine cellars were well stocked with good wines while the rest of the country had had to give up even its small rations of thin beer. Into its kitchen still flowed a steady stream of game and fowl and fish, while years of undernourishment had stripped the people of all instincts except the scavengerlike urge to hunt up, dig up, chase, steal, grub for food. Yes, the hotel and its obsolete crew of old men still kept a patriotic stiff upper lip, even if there were holes in the carpet and a sharp, menacing wind was blowing through the city. . . .

"You know what happened after the last raid," Schmidt said, climbing down from the ladder. "The houses were so badly shaken that the Fuehrer's picture came flying out of the windows for hours afterwards. Heil Hitler."

Herr Kliebert dived swiftly back into his cubicle, pretending to have heard nothing. But Ahlsen said with a snap in his voice: "If you don't learn to hold your trap, someone is going to report you some day, and then you'll get yours." Schmidt followed the glance Ahlsen threw at the figure of a thickset man in a tight blue suit who was sitting next to one of the marble pillars near the revolving door. He was reading a newspaper and absent-mindedly drinking some thin beer; a permanent fixture of the hotel lobby, a comparatively harmless manifestation of the thousand-headed monster called Gestapo.

"Him?" said Schmidt. "Why, he's the one who always tells me the newest whisper-jokes. *Prosit*, Heinrich!"

"*Prosit*," said Heinrich. Schmidt picked up the ladder and stopped for a little confidential chat. "Say, Heinrich, what's up around here?"

"Why? What should be up?"

"You know what. That police detachment that's snooping around the place. They even turned over the coal in the furnace room."

"That so? Well, I suppose they're looking for Richter. Someone got a hunch he might be hiding somewhere in this block."

"Holy thunder! You think that's true?"

The Gestapo put down the paper, wiped the beer from his mouth and looked omniscient. "I don't go by hunches," he said. "I go by facts. The fact is that not a flea could be hiding in this hotel as long as I and my men are watching it."

"That's what I'd say, Heinrich. Where would a runaway convict hide in this place?"

"On the other hand," the Gestapo said importantly— "on the other hand, this house is a rabbit warren, and it's full of highly suspicious characters. It takes a sharp mind to keep control of all these foreigners running in and out all day. Take that Rumanian Military Mission; I don't trust them, even if they are officers. Or the Hungarian czardas band! What the hell does the hotel need a Hungarian czardas band for? Only makes our work harder!"

"Right you are! It's lucky we have a man like you posted here. If Richter were trying to hide in the hotel he wouldn't have a chance."

"Don't worry. We'll get him, wherever he may be hiding. Traitors of his kind must be stamped out."

"Absolutely. Well—I must run along. Heil Hitler," Schmidt said halfheartedly and trotted off to put the stepladder into the tool closet in the basement.

"Did you hear the news? The place is full of Gestapo. They think Richter might be hiding somewhere around here," he told the old electrician who was fiddling with the disrupted connections of the service elevator.

"I hope they don't get him," he said evenly.

"They say he was a soldier. Fought at Stalingrad, too. Seems a shame they've got to execute our own soldiers now."

"They can't execute him as long as they haven't got him," said the electrician.

Richter—that was only a name scrawled on walls; it was a whisper, a rumour, a fear, a threat, a thought during a sleepless night, a wish, a hope, a myth. "You can kill Richter

—but you can't kill his spirit!" was written on houses, on the cars of the crowded underground trains, on park benches, buses, on the pedestals of monuments. Police crews went around and wiped it off, and guards were posted to watch the exposed spots during the night. And the next morning there was the handwriting again: "You can kill Richter—but you can't kill his spirit!"

People read it without daring to stop, with a swift, sidelong dart of their frightened eyes. People hardly knew who Richter was because all news about him had been suppressed. And yet, through the grapevine system that thrives so abundantly in oppressed countries, everybody had learned that there had been a riot at the venerable old University of Leipzig; that the leaders of the revolt had been arrested and grilled for information about the organization of the spreading unrest among the German students; and that, refusing to oblige, they had been punished with death by the axe. All but their leader, Martin Richter, who had managed to escape during his transport from one prison to another and was now being searched for in the hotel. . . .

Returning from the tool closet, Schmidt meandered over to the small table in the corner of the lobby where the hotel doctor was playing solitaire. On the chair at his side he had laid out his first-aid kit, sedatives, morphine, and syringes —just in case some lady should get a fit during the alarm, or if things should yet turn out to be serious.

"Did you hear the news?" Schmidt said, stopping at his side. "Police are searching the hotel; they think Richter is hiding somewhere in this block."

"He'd be a fool if he did," the doctor said, uninterested. Schmidt shuffled his feet and sighed. "Yes?" asked the doctor, pushing his cards together.

"It's about my medical examination, Doctor. I have to be there at eight o'clock in the morning," said Schmidt.

"Congratulations," said the doctor. "I expect to be called any day now myself." He wore the ribbon of the Iron Cross from the first war in the buttonhole of his unassuming civilian coat. He also had a stiff, damaged leg, a slight limp, and a chip on his shoulder. The army had rejected him as an invalid this time. In other words, the doctor was a pacifist, a frustrated pacifist who wanted to be in the war.

"Congratulations nothing! I was in the other war and

I still have my nose full of it. I know what it's all about and I don't want to go to Russia and be made into hash. Listen, Doctor—I'm not fit. I'm having stitches in my left side all the time. I'm too old for this game. But you know how it is. Just when I'd want to show these stitches to the medical examiner they will be gone——"

"Yes?" said the doctor.

"I thought you might give me something. I don't want to be a soldier. I'm tired. Sometimes I'm so tired I could cry——"

He sounded desperate. Neurotics, all of them, the whole damned Herrenvolk, thought the doctor.

"No," he said. "No, my good man. No digitalis for you, no caffeine shot to give you nice strong stitches in your heart. This is your war, and you're going to fight it. Weren't you the one who shouted 'Heil Hitler' for ten years and longer? You were so full of Strength through Joy you almost burst out of yourself. Remember that nice trip to the Bavarian mountains you told me about? Now you've got to pay the bill for that trip."

"Yes—but that was different——"

"Yes, it was different. It's always different when you are the one to be shot at." The doctor ran the cards through his fingers as he glanced at the revolving door, through which a strange apparition was entering. It was an old woman wearing big, old, men's shoes, a crumpled, uniform, and a helmet like an air-raid warden's. She looked as if she had lain in a grave for several years and had just been exhumed. Shuffling up to the desk with an inhuman, machinelike motion, she put down a batch of telegrams and held up a pad for Kliebert to sign.

"What's news?" Schmidt asked her.

"They say the Tommies were turned back over the Luene-burger Heide; twenty or thirty were shot down. There's a revolution in New York. The Russians lost eighty thousand men yesterday; and they haven't got Richter yet," she said, completely apathetic. Thus, having delivered her ration of good tidings in a lugubrious monotone, she put her big shoes in motion again and disappeared. The doctor got up and stretched his stiff left leg. Walking past the big red arrows which pointed the way to the shelter, he arrived circuitously at the desk.

"Telegram for me?" he asked.

"Not yet, Herr Doctor," said Ahlsen.

"I'm expecting a telegram, you know."

"Yes, of course. You told me so," said Ahlsen, blowing his nose into a slightly soiled handkerchief.

"Expecting to be called into service," remarked the doctor. "The telegram should come any minute now."

"Yes, indeed."

"Don't forget to notify me at once when it arrives," the doctor said and returned to his table. The queen of spades stared at him with an insipid smile. . . . What's so important about this telegram? he asked himself and shrugged his sharp shoulders in answer. I was in that other war too; I, too, know what it's all about and, by God, I don't like it. But, dear Heaven, I want to be in it! Whatever you might say, it would be some sort of a decent exit—better than sitting in the lobby of this god-forsaken hotel and playing solitaire and waiting for the final bomb to come down on it. . . . And as he thought it, he could smell the sweetish, rotten smell of a front-line dressing-station and share the fever of perilous activity and feel the sweat run down his face while he operated and hear the shells whistling, and there were the warm young bodies of his comrades close around him and he wasn't alone and his leg was not stiff and he was not a cripple.

"Hello—and what do we have here?" he said to himself, and turned his eyes toward the blacked-out revolving door. The alarm was still on, and it was surprising that a guest should come in from the empty street. But the young flier who pushed through the door as if he were in a great hurry did not seem to be aware of the alarm at all. He marched up to the desk with a light, metallic clinking of his boots, a bit too rigid, as if he were slightly drunk.

"Room with private bath—and don't tell me there's no hot water," he said to Ahlsen. He was very young, rather under middle size, and his waistline was small as a girl's. What drew the doctor's attention was his face; it would have been handsome in a childish, unfinished way but for the fact that his eyebrows and lashes were singed off and some whitish cream covered his left cheek and his chin. It made his face look obscenely naked, and his eyes were polished to a bright glitter and yet were empty and almost white; they looked like a little boy's milky glass marbles. With his left hand the young flier slapped his gloves impatiently against his boots; the right one was sloppily bandaged.

"My deepest regret, Herr Oberleutnant," said Ahlsen. "But alas, all rooms are taken. There is not an empty hotel room in all of Berlin, what with the evacuees from the Ruhr——"

"Listen, you!" the flier said, leaning far over the desk and pushing his burned chin into Ahlsen's grey, slick face. "I want a room with bath, you understand? I'm Oberleutnant Otto Kauders, in case you don't remember me. Now step on it."

Oberleutnant Otto Kauders had been mentioned in the papers for downing a great number of enemy planes. He was decorated with the Iron Cross. "Yes, Herr Oberleutnant. I'll see what can be done—at once," Ahlsen said, intimidated, while Kliebert, muttering greetings, came from his cubicle.

"Herr Oberleutnant had Number 36, third floor, the last time," said Schmidt, fishing the information from his unfailing memory. "Monsieur Rougier has it now, but we could put him in the monkey cage on Fifth . . ."

There was on each floor one completely graceless room, squeezed in between the elevator on one side and the men's toilet on the other; the hotel called them the monkey cages. As for Monsieur Rougier, he was a little man of uncertain nationality who dashed back and forth between the Balkans, Berlin, and Paris and managed shady little deals for those who had much influence or paid high commissions. There was no reason for handling him with velvet gloves.

"There—that's better," Kauders said, pacified, as Ahlsen handed him the key and Schmidt picked up the small suitcase. He looked around with his glazed white eyes and whistled. "Say—what's the matter with this place?" he asked. "It's as dead as Tutankhamen's tomb."

"That's on account of the air raid," Ahlsen said.

"On account of *what*?"

"The air raid, sir."

Kauders opened his mouth to a wide gap, and then he threw himself over the desk and began to laugh. The doctor left his corner and approached the desk, sizing up the young flier's condition. Shock, he thought; nerves shot to pieces but doesn't know it. They never know it. Heroes never know anything. "An air raid!" Kauders cried, sobbing with breathless laughter. "So that's what Berlin calls an air raid! Why don't you wrap your air raid in pink tissue paper so that I can take it back with me to where I come from!"

"Where, then, do you come from, Herr Oberleutnant?" Herr Kliebert asked respectfully.

"None of your business, Papi," the flier said rudely and stopped laughing. "But I can tell you one thing. Where I come from we have air raids that are air raids."

"It's not a raid; it's only an alarm," Ahlsen said. "We turned them back tonight."

"*You* did? Well, that's fine," Kauders said brusquely. "Bar open?" he asked Schmidt, who had unconsciously snapped into his sergeant's manners from the other war. "Any girls around this hole? You know the one I mean—forgot her name—gay as a skylark—blonde and oho," he said, moulding some curves in the air.

"That's Fraulein Tilli, Herr Oberleutnant," Schmidt said, as if Kauders had shown him a passport photo of her. "Sure, Herr Oberleutnant, she'll be around as soon as they come up from the shelter, Herr Oberleutnant."

"Tilli—that's it. Wonderful girl. The fun we had last time I was on leave!" Gesticulating, he hit his bandaged hand against the edge of the desk. "Goddamn," he swore, staring at the painful object as if surprised to find it still there. The doctor had once more arrived at the desk. "Let me take care of this, Herr Oberleutnant," he said. "Your bandage is coming off. I'm the hotel doctor around here, but I'm expecting to be called into service any moment now. I was in the last war, too. . . . Does it hurt?"

"It's nothing," the flier said, but he turned white under his tan as the doctor loosened the bandage from the burns.

"Like a sedative? A sleeping powder perhaps, to get over it?"

"Sleeping powder hell! I have no time to be sleepy. Three days' leave! Man, Doctor, that's not much time. God Almighty," he said and looked suddenly like a very small, very hungry boy, "I want to *live* these three days! Not sleep."

"Aren't you tired?" the doctor said, with his fingers unobtrusively on the boy's pulse; it went irregularly, tack, tack, tack; tchk.

"Clear, I'm tired. Everyone is—at least everyone I know. Listen, Doctor, I don't need a sedative. I need some Pervitine or something. I used up my ration."

"Well . . ." the doctor said, stalling. All these youngsters were given Pervitine, Benzedrine, all sorts of drugs to keep them alert and aggressive during combat. Afterwards came the deep depressions, the indigo moods, the bottomless fatigue. . . . But who am I to spoil his three days' leave, the doctor thought as he poured a few white pills into the flier's sound hand. Suddenly Kauders straightened up with one sharp reflex, left hand at the trouser seam, the bandaged right one clumsily saluting, heels clicking, eyes straight ahead. For, coming from the staircase and approaching the desk, was the imposing figure of General Arnim von Dahnwitz, the Victor of Kharkov.

The general carried himself with the ease of a well-trained athlete, which made him appear taller than he actually was; his head, completely shaved, rested on the crimson collar of his tunic, and his face was lined and yet ageless. From his collar dangled the two highest decorations the country had to offer: the Pour le Mérite from the other war and the Knight's Cross with Oak Leaf of the Third Reich. The faint little sound of the two decorations clicking together accompanied each of the general's movements. In the arrogant high arch of his right eye sat the monocle as if it were part of his face. Kauders stared at it with envy. Secretly the young flier had tried to wear a monocle too, but the plebeian frame of his head did not lend itself to it, and it had been a failure. To the general, on the other hand, the monocle had become a minor nuisance. His eyes had begun to go back on him since he had passed fifty, and looking at the world with one eye sharpened by the lens while the other saw everything blurred and vague gave him occasional headaches and a generally distorted view of things. But only in the seclusion of his own room, when not even his aide was around, did the general permit himself the sloppy comfort of a pair of eyeglasses. He might as well have worn his bedroom slippers with his uniform as to let himself go and wear glasses in public. Not to wear glasses was only one little symptom of his daily fight not to give in. Not to let down the barriers. Not to admit even to himself that he was a tired, middle-aged man.

"Fraulein Dorn not returned from the theatre yet?"

the general asked with an unexpectedly gentle voice, and Herr Kliebert, pushing Ahlsen aside, assured him eagerly that Fraulein Dorn hadn't returned yet, that in all probability she had been delayed by the alarm, and that he would notify his excellency at once when Fraulein Dorn arrived.

"Thank you. Very good of you," the general said, scattering a few grains of charm around. "But don't tell her that I am here. It's a surprise, you understand?"

The general's gentle charm was proverbial in the army —except for the brief moments when he was overcome by attacks of a black, storming anger which left him and everyone around him weak and trembling. "It's the Tartar in him," his mother used to say, referring to the marriage of a certain Joachim von Dahnwitz, who had been ambassador to the Russian court from 1765 to 1772 and had brought a Russian wife back home to the Dahnwitz estate of Elgede near Hanover. Actually there was something Mongolian in the shape of the general's round skull, the slant of his eyes, the sensual pleasure he took in women, his passion for horses, and the spasmodic outbreaks of his dark, tempestuous anger; but it was all chained down and sharply controlled by the inheritance of his North German ancestors, by the laws of his caste and the unrelenting strictness of his upbringing.

Turning away from the desk, the general discovered the young flier, still saluting rigidly. "At ease, Oberleutnant," he said, raising two slack fingers to his cap, and Kauders relaxed respectfully and reported his name, rank, and troop.

"Jagdstaffel Luetzow? Did you happen to know my son, Captain von Dahnwitz?" the general asked. At which Kauders, almost cross-eyed with concentration, replied that indeed he had known the captain and had had the honour of making a few sorties with Dahnwitz as leader of his squadron. He was, however, slightly taken aback by the general's question. The mentioning of dead fliers was taboo, and he wondered why the general had broken the rules.

"Yes, Arnim was a fine boy. Well, he did no more than his duty," the general said in the prescribed tone of voice. "No more than his duty. I see you got wounded."

"It's nothing. A few blisters, Herr General."

"And where did you get these blisters?"

"Over Muelheim. My plane caught fire and I had to bail

out, Herr General," Kauders said, and as he said it the whole awful thing began to roll off in his brain again like a film. He was flying her through the crisscross of the tracers, keeping on the tail of the four-engined Lancaster, and he gave the big brute a good burst and the tail gunner gave it back to him: Zing, zing, zing came the bullets singing through his crate, and it got hot and it got hotter very quickly and there were the blue flames from his right wing carried into the cockpit by the air draught, and he thought. That's it, and he was suddenly so scared that it paralysed him and it took him an eternity to unbuckle the safety belt with his paralysed fingers while the blue flames licked his face, and he jumped, or he thought he jumped, but his legs got stuck in the hatch and he thought, "Good-bye," and there was an eternity of abject, nauseating fear, and then he got free and tumbled out into the bottomless hell full of flak and bullets and fighting, roaring, burning planes. . . .

"Ah yes—Muelheim," said the general. "And how does it look out there?" He said " out there " as if western Germany were another war front. Kauders pulled himself together.

"Very good, Herr General. Our FW-190s with the 20-mm guns top everything the Tommies have. They've suffered very great losses recently. We got twelve of their Lancasters yesterday alone. They won't be able to keep it up much longer at this rate."

"To be sure—to be sure," the general said, not listening. He kept his glance on the revolving door through which Lisa Dorn was to enter any moment now. The impatience with which he waited for her, sweet, tearing, and painful, made him feel very young.

"Major Kant promised us that we would soon be flying some of the new ME-109-G-2s; that should be the end of the Tommies. A 20-mm. gun firing through the propeller, Herr General, plus two 7.9-mm. guns mounted above the engine and, if desired, one 20-mm. gun under each wing, Herr General. If we could only get enough of those——"

"You will—you will," the general said absently. "Well, there goes the All Clear now. Good hunting, Oberleutnant Kauders."

All of a sudden the lobby came to life and was a bright, glamorous, elegant place again. The lights were turned on, people streamed back from the shelter, chatting and laughing.

Telephones rang and the radio played the Einzugsmarsch from *Tannhauser*, pageboys in their impractical sky-blue uniforms flitted to and fro, and the desk was in a lather of activity. The sign "Closed" disappeared from the high double doors to the bar, which swung open and let a volley of thirsty customers in. There were uniforms of every description— not only the greyish-green of the German, but also French and Italian and even Spanish ones, not to mention the all too decorative get-up of the Rumanian Military Mission and the sober field-grey of a lonely Finnish brigadier general. In great part the crowd consisted of members of the Central European Trade Commission in whose honour a reception was being given tonight. There were ladies too, some very pretty and very smartly dressed and some heavy, ugly, the stamp "Hausfrau" indelibly imprinted upon them. The heaviest, fattest, shrillest, most overdressed one was Frau Plottke, wife of Gauleiter Heinrich Plottke. Plottke himself, a rather obnoxious fellow, his hair, eyes, and freckles of the more rusty colour, his soft, flabby flesh stuffed tightly into a brown SA uniform, had buttonholed Mynheer Vanderstraaten, who represented the Vanderstraaten Commerz Bank in Amsterdam. Plottke did not like his wife; nobody did. But she belonged to the early guard of fawning Hitler admirers—the sort of females to which the old party horses referred as the Varicose Vein Brigade—and therefore she had the Fuehrer's ear and was useful to be married to.

"Are you staying in town tonight?" asked Gestapo Commissar Joachim Helm in passing him; he was thin-lipped, bald-headed, tall, and soft-spoken, wearing on his long face a permanent smile that never reached the eyes.

"I planned to drive out to Karinsee and stay there for a few days. Why?"

"I recommend that you remain in Berlin. I have to see you tomorrow at eleven-fifteen. In my office upstairs."

And who are you to give me orders? Plottke thought angrily but did not have the nerve to say it aloud. Helm scanned his furious face with obvious scorn and walked away from him toward Baron von Stetten.

"If you can arrange the affair Dahnwitz for us discreetly, I think I can put some pressure on Plottke for you," he said nonchalantly. Stetten looked past him as he answered: "Thanks. I wish the general hadn't left the front just now.

It will be rather difficult to avoid some sort of fuss now. Why have I always to pull someone's chestnuts from the fire?"

Baron von Stetten, slim and smart in his grey Foreign Office uniform with the swanky white lapel, was the host of the evening. He was responsible to Department W of the AA for the success of the reception, and it was a stroke of ill luck that it had been interrupted by the alarm. Such an occurrence must necessarily make a bad impression on his guests, just at a time when it was of uppermost importance to make a good impression on neutrals, allies, and satellites alike. Talking now to the Turkish economist Professor Mazhar Cevdet Onar, now to Herr Dahlin, who represented the Swedish Bolander Mines, now to Mynheer Vanderstraaten and now to Major Philippescu of the Rumanian Military Mission, he tried to smooth out wrinkles and prepare the ground for the serious sessions to come. And now he had been saddled with this most unpleasant affair Dahnwitz, too. He encountered Helm's ironic glance.

"Dahnwitz claims he has a toothache; I suppose he feels safer here than at General Headquarters," the commissar said.

"A man can die of a toothache," said Stetten.

"Yes; especially a general in disgrace," Helm said; in one of the wall mirrors he noticed that Plottke had come up behind him, trying to listen in on their conversation. Without turning around, the commissar raised his voice as he added: "But Gauleiters are susceptible to all sorts of ailments, too." And with that he walked on toward the stairs, where an SS man drew to attention and gave him some inaudible report.

Stetten looked around for the general; he found him at last, leaning against the desk and keeping his eyes on the revolving door.

"Ah, Dahnwitz—here you are. I was looking for you. How is your toothache now?"

"Thanks. Fischer opened the abscess this afternoon—he said it was high time. Our dentist at headquarters seems to have bungled the job from A to Z. It's ridiculous to have to leave the front for such nonsense—but then, generals with toothaches don't win battles."

"Napoleon did," said Plottke, who put his foot in his mouth whenever he opened it.

"Don't forget that I must see you after the reception," Stetten said to Dahnwitz and flitted on, to urge his guests back into the banquet room.

Monsieur Rougier tried to catch Gauleiter Plottke's eye, but Plottke did not care to converse with the dubious little fellow in public. Slowly and stickily, like lava, the crowd began to flow toward the stairs. "According to our statistics the health of the nation was never in better condition," Herr Plottke was heard to say. "My dear, I know a little man who still has some real silk stockings! Seventy-five marks a pair," Frau Plottke whispered to Frau Helm. "Not forgetting the successes we're having on the eastern front," Von Stetten said to Dahlin. "In London Danish 5½ per cent gold bonds went up five points last week," Rougier told Vanderstraaten, who knew it anyway and had drawn his own conclusions. "Yes, and in Switzerland the Reichsmark has tumbled seven points," he remarked.

"Nice mess you've got us into with that speech of yours in Leipzig," Helm said unceremoniously, as he came up against Plottke once more. "A student revolt is exactly the thing we need just now. As if there wasn't enough trouble!"

"If the Gestapo were more efficient there wouldn't be any student revolts; it's scandalous, that's what it is. Leaflets, pamphlets, riots; if we don't show these young scoundrels an iron fist while there's still time, we'll be stabbed in the back. If *I* had something to say in the Gestapo——"

"But you haven't. Thank Heaven and our Fuehrer!"

Poison and daggers and open, unmitigated hatred between these two pillars of the Reich. Their nerves had worn raw and their minds were a jelly of fear, trembling under the thin crust of power and security that was yet left to them.

"Some day you'll come down off your high horse, you mark my word!" Herr Plottke hissed.

"Maybe—but after you, long after you, Herr Gauleiter!" Helm hissed back.

There came a blast of trumpets from the loudspeaker of the radio; they snapped to attention and automatically raised their right arms in an abrupt, lovely unison. The voice of the radio announcer fervently demanded attention for a special communiqué. The guests at the reception stopped on their way to the banquet hall, the chatter and talk subsided. The pageboys froze in their tracks, and the old French waiter,

Gaston, balancing a tray with bottles and glasses high over-head, became motionless, like a figure in a halted film. "Atten-tion, please. Attention for a special communiqué from our eastern front," the radio commanded smartly.

"Our High Command reports from the eastern front that during the five days of our offensive in the Kiev salient our victorious divisions destroyed or captured 1,197 Russian planes and 1,709 tanks, against a loss of only 54 planes and 26 tanks on our side. Russian losses in dead, wounded, and prisoners are enormous, amounting to not less than 35,000 men. It can be safely stated that all Russian tank units, including their reserves, in this sector have been wiped out, their air force has been crippled, and any attempt at a counter-offensive has been nipped in the bud. Zhitomir is firmly in our hands."

Everybody stood at attention and listened, their bodies drawn up but their faces rather apathetic. There were exceptions, of course; Gauleiter Plottke listened with osten-tatious rapture, and assistant clerk Ahlsen pushed out a deter-mined chin and his eyes were filled with loyalty for this victorious Third Reich. Some of the foreign guests, too, exhibited signs of enthusiasm. Maybe they did not dare not to exhibit them. As the communiqué ended, there came another fanfare of trumpets and the radio burst into the Horst Wessel song. All right arms flew up in the Hitler salute and all faces turned automatically to the Fuehrer's picture while the staccato of three measured "Sieg-Heil, Sieg-Heil, Sieg-Heil" was dutifully pronounced. After that the radio went into "Deutschland ueber Alles," verse after verse, and the people had to listen, respectfully uncomfortable as people listen to national anthems all over the world.

It was at that moment, while the crowd in the lobby were still frozen in poses like the chorus at the curtain of a musical comedy, that Lisa Dorn came blowing in through the revolving door.

She was very young and very lovely, and it was no wonder that the whole country was in love with her. Her forehead was smooth, delicately rounded, leaving a wide space between her blonde eyebrows that always seemed to express surprise. Her hair, plaited in two braids and piled like a small crown on the top of her head, was the colour of freshly hewn pinewood; her eyelashes, too, were very light; it was a face such as the innocent, primitive Rhenish masters of the fifteenth century gave to their childlike and capricious madonnas. Lisa's body was small and so weightless that she always seemed to be blown by a gust of wind. Being an actress—and a very good actress at that—she was aware of this effect and emphasized it with every trick at her command. Right now her smallness was accentuated by the massive body and heavy leonine head of a white-haired man who had entered behind her and now let his watery blue eyes pass with a trace of irony over the people and their raised arms. This was Johannes Koenig, the Reich's great poet. Lisa Dorn, measuring with quick perception the scene into which she had blown, stood arrested, lifting up her hand, which looked very small and helpless, and fastening her eyes adoringly upon the Fuehrer's picture. It was the pose she had used in the fade-outs of several movies, and she fell into it quite naturally. But even before she did so, her surprised glance had picked out the general among the crowd and she had given him a swift gleaming shooting-star of a smile.

Dahnwitz had been the first to notice her entrance, for which, indeed, he had waited with so much impatience. He began to edge toward her, and with the last strains of the anthem he had come to stand almost behind her.

"Good evening, child. Good evening, my love," he whispered into her neck.

"Oh, Arnim! What a surprise! You should feel my heart —it goes like the big drum in a circus. Boom-boom-boom. When did you arrive? Why are you here?"

"I wanted to see you. I haven't seen you for more than two months. That's too long for any man."

"Nonsense, Arnim. And who takes care of your war while you're here?"

"The war takes care of itself."

The radio finished with another burst of trumpets and then glided abruptly into a waltz. The arms came down, the marionettes moved again. Gaston, the old waiter, proceeded with his tray balanced on his fingertips. Near the potted palm that Herr Kliebert had placed over a hole in the carpet he brushed past another old Frenchman; this was Philippe, the sommelier, the wine steward. The big key to the wine cellar was tied on a chain around his neck, and he was carrying a bottle of Burgundy in a cradle toward a table in the background.

In passing, the two old men exchanged a few words in French.

"Everything in order in your cellar, *mon vieux*?"

"Perfectly."

"Nobody trying to break in?"

"Nobody. The cellar is safe—so far."

"*Bon, très bon.*" And old Gaston went on with his tray.

"I leave you the centre of the stage," whispered Johannes Koenig to Lisa and steered toward the table, his table, where Philippe deposited the Burgundy. Lisa, with her inborn sense of the dramatic, played her next little scene with the general, leaning against the Venetian fountain in the centre of the lobby, with the crowd surging around her, smiling at her, curiously watching her: a little more and they would have applauded.

"You look even lovelier than I remembered you, child," the general said, kissing her hand. "Yes, lovelier." He had a habit of repeating points he wanted to drive home, a habit acquired through the life-long necessity of impressing important details upon his staff.

"You like me in this outfit? I bought it in Paris," said Lisa, sketching a little pirouette and flipping the skirt of her silver-grey suit; she always wore silvery colours, fine, misty shades that enhanced the pastel quality of her beauty. "Oh, Arnim, it's wonderful to have you here," she said. "I worry so much about you. Sometimes I worry so that I can't sleep all night long. Tell me—is it dangerous for you?" But she did not look at all worried.

The general smiled down at her. With Lisa at his side he always felt a few inches taller than otherwise, which was a most pleasant and flattering sensation. Lisa, for her part, was keenly conscious of the effect she made in the general's company. It gave her a very good entrance and made her look and feel twice as small and helpless as usual. She also knew that it was this very helplessness of her person, the contrast to the sturdy, cowlike quality bred and trained into the average Nazi woman, that made everyone love her. To be loved by everyone was as necessary to her as air and light. She put her arm through his and pulled him away from the crowd.

"Dangerous? No, child," the general said. "All the world knows that generals die in bed."

"In *whose* bed?" she asked with a quick, mischievous

urchin's grin. She had as many registers as a fine old organ, and she used them all for the benefit of the gazing lobby. Suddenly she dropped her gaiety to the floor and pulled a wide-eyed, sad expression over her face. "Oh, Arnim," she said softly, "I was so unhappy when I heard about your son. I wrote you a letter—and then I didn't send it off. Words are such poor little beggars, aren't they? But you must know how I felt—you do know, don't you?" Without any effort the tears had sprung to her eyes and her lower lip quivered a little. The general saw it with horror; to see Lisel cry made him feel like a lump of butter on a hot stove.

"Don't let's talk about it," he said, very Prussian. "He did his duty. That's all. Only his duty."

The crowd around them began pressing closer; on its periphery there was a fringe of reporters, foreign correspondents and press photographers, cynics all of them.

"Hello, Schnucki," said someone to Plottke as he was glaring at the disappearing back of Helm's black uniform. He turned around and faced the girl who had been plucking at his sleeve.

This was Tilli. This was the gayest of the gay butterflies who hung around the bar and lounged in the lobby of the hotel. She was not quite as young as she tried to appear, and her prettiness was a bit too obvious. Like the carved idols of certain primitive tribes, Tilli consisted of sex only. There were breasts and thighs, the white nape of the neck, the soft shadows where the skirt clung to her lap, the knees, the legs, everything flinging an invitation into every passing man's senses. Tilli had sex on tap and could turn it off and on at will. She turned it on for Heinrich Plottke now. "Schnucki," she whispered, letting a warm wave of perfume sweep over him, "you didn't forget your little girl, did you?"

"'l Hitler," Plottke said with an officious flip of his hand to his shoulder. "How do?"

"How do you like my new hair-do, Schnucki?" she asked, lifting her arms and crossing her hands at the back of her head, odalisque fashion. The movement brought her breasts directly under the Gauleiter's eyes.

"This is hardly the place and time to tell you," he said; she watched the blood bring a blush to the yellow, sick-looking fat of his cheeks.

"How about the thing you promised me?" she said, giving him her best smile.

"I didn't promise you anything."

"Oh yes, you did. You promised to get me new shoes; it's urgent. I need them, and you know it."

"Oh—that," the Gauleiter said. "Well, I've other worries than to think of your shoes."

"Oh, you have, have you?" Tilli said, getting ugly. "Well, if the Herr Gauleiter had to run around with no soles on his last pair of shoes he wouldn't forget. Listen, you," she said, getting angrier and angrier—"you've stalled about these shoes now for six weeks and I'm fed up with it. I need new shoes and you're going to get me some."

Plottke, too, got angry now. "The nerve!" he said. "If you would work in a factory, as is the duty of every patriotic German woman, you wouldn't ask for the sort of shoes you need for the sort of life you're leading——"

"Look here, Schnucki," Tilli said sweetly. "Do you want me to make trouble for you with your wife? I can go over right now and tell her a little thing or two."

"Go on; go and make trouble," the Gauleiter said, and the yellow fat on his cheeks quivered with suppressed fury. "Go and make trouble for me. And then wait and see what sort of trouble I'll make for you."

At which Tilli crumbled and shrunk and said no more. . . . Where will I get shoes now? she thought in despair. Maybe Helm would get me some. Next time he needs some little information from me I won't take money for it, I'll demand new shoes. . . . For Tilli the whole world had been blotted out by the urgent necessity for a pair of shoes. Let there be war, let there be an offensive in Russia, let Italy be invaded, the Ruhr bombed to pieces—it didn't concern her. What concerned her and hurt her and tortured her were those sloppy old shoes of hers whose soles she would soon have to tie to her feet with paper string if she couldn't get a new pair.

"Hurrah, I found you! I bet a month's wages with myself that I'd find you, and I've won!" somebody shouted at her. She turned around and encountered the young flier, slobbering at her like a hungry dog—or so, at least, she termed it to herself. But she put two fingers to her forehead in a smart salute, her humorous way of greeting all officers. "Hurrah, Schnucki is back from the war! How are you, Schnucki!" she cried gaily. Calling all males Schnucki simplified her life and protected her against unpleasant mix-ups.

"You remember me, don't you ? Didn't we have fun last time! Great God, didn't we have fun !"

"Do I remember you ! Why, I thought of you day and night, Schnucki !" cried Tilli, who did not remember him at all. "Did we have fun ! Boy, oh boy, did we have fun !"

"But that's nothing to the fun we're going to have tonight, my girl. I've briefed it all, and you'll be surprised at the fireworks I have in store for you !"

"At your command, Oberleutnant," Tilli said, saluting again. "Let's begin with a drink at the bar, no ?"

"Suggestion accepted," Kauders said with a Prussian snap in his squashy Saxonian voice. The Pervitin had pepped him up considerably, but also increased his sensibility, and he felt pains in his burns.

"Who's that dame they're making all the fuss about ?" he asked, coming up against a wall of people, all turned toward the girl in the centre.

"That ? That's her. Lisa Dorn," Tilli said bitterly. She was jealous of Lisa, and for many good reasons. Because Lisa was as young as she would have liked to be ; because Lisa Dorn had success and money and influential friends and all the advantages pull and connections could get you in this Third Reich. Lisa Dorn could go to Paris with a *billet de couturier* and buy herself all the new creations she wanted, while Tilli had to change and patch and fix her two old dresses over and over. Lisa Dorn had all the cigarettes she wanted and all the food, even milk and sometimes an orange to keep her skin fresh and her hair shining, while Tilli had to paste bad grease paint over her grey, anaemic, vitamin-hungry skin and to struggle with her bleached hair that screamed with brittleness for lack of nutrition. But most bitterly did Tilli hate Lisa Dorn because Lisa had all the shoes she might ever want and did not have to lie sleepless at night, thinking up complicated and humiliating schemes for getting one pair—just one single pair of decent shoes.

"Really ? The star ? The one and only Lisa Dorn ? Just imagine ! I'd like to meet her," the lieutenant said, his schoolboy's heart deeply impressed.

"She wouldn't even look at you, Schatzi ; she likes old men, can't you see ? Old men and rich men and men high up in the party who can give her anything she wants. As for me, I like them young."

"What did you say?" asked the lieutenant. He had not listened, but stared fascinatedly at the actress.

"I said give me a young flier any day, Schnucki, a sweet one like you," Tilli said, snuggling up to him. He shook off her soft, clinging curves and cut his way through the crowd until he arrived at the general's side. Dahnwitz met the imploring glance of the flier's glassy eyes and decided to be magnanimous.

"My dear, may I present Oberleutnant Kauders? He was a comrade of Arnim," he introduced him, and Kauders bowed from the waist and clicked his heels.

"I'm delighted, Oberleutnant Kauders," said Lisa and gave him the morale-building smile reserved for her tours to camps and hospitals. She held out her hand, and he grasped it; a joyful little tingling went through him, and feeling very much of a Don Juan he bent down and kissed that famous small warm hand.

"You are on leave, Oberleutnant?"

"Yes; for three days—not much, but better than nothing."

"Oh, I'm certain you can do a lot of mischief in three days," she said.

"It takes two to do the right kind of mischief, Fraulein," he answered boldly.

"Well—I wish you lots of fun, Oberleutnant," she said, still smiling.

. . . Wait till I tell the boys that I met Lisa Dorn, Kauders thought elatedly. He had the definite impression that he had made a conquest. Sometimes he felt like that. That he could have any woman he wanted. Especially after a few drinks and a few of the little white pills he felt like that.

The eddy of people around Lisa receded slowly as Von Stetten urged his guests back into the banquet room. "Won't you join us, Lisel?" he asked her with perfunctory politeness. Actually this was an official reception, and he didn't want pretty actresses around; Lisa would only distract the men's minds and make the women jealous. He felt relieved when she answered: "No, thank you, Baron. I had promised myself a nice quiet evening. I still have to study my part for tomorrow's rehearsal. *Merchant of Venice*."

"I'm so sorry, Lisel. But then you must permit me to kidnap the general for an hour or two——"

"Kidnap? Kidnap me, Stetten?" the general said, arching his brow higher over the monocle. Stetten looked very straight into his face.

"Yes, Dahnwitz," he said with almost imperceptible emphasis. "I need you at the reception—and I have to talk to you afterwards."

There was a small pause in which Lisel glanced from one to the other.

"How mean of you, Baron," she said with a little pout; but she was not really disappointed, and the general noticed it. He stiffened slightly, as he asked: "Is it an invitation or an order?"

"Whatever you want to make of it," Stetten answered with an uncomfortable smile. The general sighed. "Well, then—duty before pleasure," he said. "I'm coming, Stetten. May I try to 'phone you when this confounded reception is over, my dear?"

He bent over Lisa's hand to kiss it, and she looked down at his sunburned neck with its network of fine wrinkles. A few minutes before she had looked down at the smooth skin of the young flier. . . . Funny, she thought, all of a sudden. I don't know any young men. I've never been kissed by a young man. I suppose young men are crude and stupid.

"If it isn't too late after the reception," she heard herself say. "I'm tired—and you must be tired too, Arnim."

The general clicked his heels, trying hard not to look angry.

"At your command, my dear," he said with formality, as he took her to the foot of the stairs.

It was twenty minutes to nine; the czardas band was playing in the banquet room, the champagne bottles popped, the Central European Trade Commission toasted the New Order, the glorious future of Europe, and the ties of friendship that linked their countries to the Third Reich. The people in the hotel—this crude, flashy new aristocracy of Hitler's creation—were well fed, well dressed, well behaved. But outside there was a town full of desperate, tired, exhausted people, people with grey faces, decaying teeth, minds poisoned by worry and fear and hatred. Outside of this island of purposeful lies and pretensions, there was nude, sheer misery everywhere: all over the country, all over Europe. There were empty market stalls and a broken-down transportation system and a helpless bureaucracy that had grown like a malignant tumour and now was feeding on its own rotten cells. Outside there were prisons crowded with tortured ghosts, hospitals and hospital trains filled with the groans of the wounded and the silence of those who had died. There were burning towns and destroyed provinces, bursting dams and exploding factories. There were homeless populations shifted around without mercy, and slave workers breaking down under stress and shock. There was confusion, panic, terror, and the taste of doom everywhere. But in the hotel they ate their last reserves of pâté de foie gras and rinsed it down with champagne, the Hungarian czardas band fiddled, and the Fuehrer's picture looked heroically down from the crumbling wall.

And in the wine cellar, crouching behind the iron door that Philippe had locked with his big key, Martin Richter was hiding—the student who had escaped from the Gestapo the day before his execution was to have taken place.

It was cold down there, and the carefully prepared chill that hung under the high vaults poured shudder after shudder down Martin's back. For a while he had fallen asleep, for the strain of these last days had been great. In his sleep he had lived through many horrors again; vague, floating, faceless horrors, much different from the real ones he had experienced to the limit. At last the pain in his injured shoulder had waked him up, and later he had heard the wail of the sirens, the bottles had rattled on the shelves, and there had been a puny bit of flak in the distance.

For a while he concentrated his mind on fixing a certain address in his memory. Rittergasse 39, Berlin N, second stairway, fourth floor, apartment 78. Ask for Walter. Rittergasse 39, Berlin N, second stairway, fourth floor, apartment 78. Ask for Walter. That was the address the two old French-men had told him to remember; that's where he was to go in the morning.

"You're safe down here now; tomorrow morning we'll smuggle you out on the garbage truck, and Walter will help you on from there. The route is well organized, we've never had anything go wrong. You're safe now."

Martin did not believe in safety, and he hardly cared for it. Safety, after all, was something very relative and unimportant. It was not fear for his own safety that made his teeth chatter and his back tremble with chills. . . . They did not break me, he thought, and there was a great bitter pride in it. With all they did to me, they did not break me. They never will. . . . He was thirsty. He was very thirsty. His mouth was dry as the mouth of a man is dry in the zero hour. He tried to collect a drop of saliva in this dried-out mouth of his, but gave up. He tried to swallow, but couldn't.

Water, he thought. Water. Water. He held his breath, for it seemed to him that he had heard the lovely sound of a tap dripping. But when he stopped breathing, the sound stopped, too. The next few minutes he spent in a no-man's-land between being awake and the stupor of exhaustion, and during these minutes he seemed to get up, find the leaking tap, turn it on and press his mouth to it. The water came tumbling cold and fresh and rich into his parched throat; and then he woke up with a start to find himself still in his corner, thirstier than before. He gathered up his legs and somewhat dizzily began to search the cellar for the tap that wasn't there. His thirst had become unbearable. Suddenly he was overcome by the irony of his situation. There he was, surrounded by thousands and thousands of bottles, filled with wine—and dying of thirst. He stared at the shelves where the bottles were stacked up in neat rows. Farther down the aisle there were asbestos pipes in which the choice vintages were kept, like honey in a honeycomb. Martin touched one of the bottles, lifted it in both hands as if to crush it. Through the spider-webs and dust he could see the beautiful, beautiful liquid inside. He lifted the bottle up to the light bulb and looked through it. He held it close to his ear and shook it to listen to the bubbling sound. He was crazy with thirst. He carried the bottle to the iron door to break its neck on the handle and drink the wine. There were yellow circles dancing in front of his eyes now. He had not eaten anything for two days. He had not had a drink of water since yesterday morning. For a moment he was again lying flat at the edge of the lake, breathless after his escape, drinking the muddy water and washing his wound; then he was back in the cellar of the hotel, dying of thirst and with a bottle of white wine in his shaking hands.

"You idiot, what do you think you're doing?" he said aloud. "Getting drunk? Giving yourself up? Put down that bottle. *Put down that bottle.*"

. . . "Yes, I have to keep a clear head," he said, obeying the command. He carried the bottle down the aisle and carefully put it back in its place. He felt very weak and very proud. He crouched down in the corner next to the door again and waited for the morning.

Immediately on his arrival in the afternoon, the general had bought the last bunch of roses from the florist in the lobby and sent them to Lisa's room. Their scent, a little acrid and tired by now, leaped into her face from the dark as she opened the door. She put down her handbag, switched on the light and took their heavy, nodding heads in her hands. "Poor darlings," she said to the flowers. "You poor darlings, so sleepy? Thirsty, too, aren't you?"

Lisa constantly had conversations with inanimate objects which, to her, were vividly alive and had faces and personalities of their own. The truth was that this great actress, this famous star, this devastatingly popular Lisa Dorn, had never had time to grow up and still lived, so to speak, in the fairy-tale world of her childhood, where everything had a voice and a soul of its own, as if the sweet downy years of growing up had been cut out and stolen from her life.

She had been a grey mouse of a little girl, one of a poor schoolteacher's five children, living in a drab, industrial section of Vienna, and the only outlet for her drama-hungry little heart had been the conspiratory, secret, and romantic doings of the Ostmark Youth to which she belonged. Then there had come the intoxicating days of the Anschluss, roaring of planes, waving of flags, the roll of drums, the never-ending rhythm of marching feet, the fantastic sight of tanks and guns, trumpets and speeches and cheers, the whole frenzy of liberation climaxing in the triumph of that one dizzy, piercing moment when the Fuehrer's car stopped and he bent down to receive a bunch of flowers from her moist, tremblinghands. The Fuehrer's smile, his voice, cameras, flashbulbs, the crowd tearing at her: "What did he say to you? You lucky girl!" Her picture in the papers with the sun on her hair and the Fuehrer smiling down at her, her picture in the newsreels, her picture on a poster, her first movie contract. Then Johannes Koenig had discovered her, had taught her in a great hurry how to walk, to talk, to laugh, to dress, to read, to act, to make love, to cry. Only three months after the Fuehrer's victorious entrance into Vienna, Lisa found herself on the venerable stage of the State Theatre in Berlin, playing the leading part in a revival of Koenig's drama, *Valiant Heart*. The Fuehrer was in his box, he applauded her, and the next morning Lisa Dorn woke up, the toast of the town. Sometimes she still felt as if she had been flung into the lap of success by an explosion. She wondered if all that had happened to her was what Johannes Koenig called "the dynamic of revolution."

Lisa switched off the light for a moment, opened the black-out curtains, and after giving the roses fresh water from the tap in her bathroom she carried them out on to her small balcony. . . . One dozen red roses, she thought. That's what it always is. Everyone sends the same, every time: one dozen red roses. . . . She stood for a little while in the evening air on her balcony, flexing her fingers; they felt empty and dissatisfied, although Lisa did not know what it was these restless fingers were craving. Different flowers, she decided. A great bunch of them, all sorts of them, a basket full of them. Wild flowers, wet after a rain, and grass and weed tied in with them. Poor Arnim, she thought with a little sigh as she returned to her room, secured the curtains, and switched on the light. One dozen red roses. Not fifteen and not eleven. One dozen, bought and paid for. Poor Arnim.

The general's photo, standing in a silver frame on her night table, seemed to watch her coldly. No doubt she had been pleased by his unexpected visit from the front, because she was very fond of him. "Yes, I'm very fond of you," she told the photo with some violence, as if it had questioned the sincerity of her emotions. But her first reaction on seeing the general in the lobby had been: There goes my nice, quiet evening ! And only after pushing away this untoward thought had she begun to smile and be radiant for him.

It was early yet, hardly nine o'clock. Since air raids had become more frequent, the theatres played several matinées a week and closed at night. Lisa had not yet been able to re-adjust her nerves to the new schedule, because she was a nocturnal creature and began to live and vibrate only in the evening. It was hard work to produce sweep and gusto in the soberness of an afternoon, and she often came home with a great discontent about her own performance. However, tonight she had been looking forward to being home early and alone. Because tonight she had promised herself to try on every one of the new dresses she had brought from Paris. It was as exciting as a secret love date. At least that's what Lisa, who had never had a secret date but whose attachments all took place rather publicly, thought of it. . . . Bless Von Stetten, she thought gaily, for taking the general off my hands and letting me have my nice quiet evening after all. ("Do you know what is the highest luxury in the life of a woman?" Maria asked in *Valiant Heart*. "It's the right to sleep alone.")

Happily she pushed back the sliding doors of the wardrobe that took up one whole wall and dived into the lovely, lovely abundance that fell in folds, floated, glittered, cascaded from the hangers. Silk and velvet and laces and chiffon. Greys and blues and pink mauves and the faint green of unripe apples. Street dresses, afternoon dresses, tea gowns, pyjamas, négligées, and the galaxy of evening dresses. She stepped out of the little silver grey outfit and into dress after dress. There were two mirrors in front of her, reflecting the mirrored door of the bathroom at her back. She got a little drunk with it all. She was Cinderella under the little tree that poured gold and silver over her. She sighed and sang and turned and moved and even tried a few timid dance steps. From the banquet room she could hear the *voom-voom* of the czardas band bass and sometimes the melancholy complaint of a fiddle. At last she chose a négligée the colour of hydrangeas and carried a blue chiffon nightgown to the broad bed in the alcove. She crumpled it in her hands and held it hungrily up to her face as if she wanted to eat it. She was madly in love with silk and chiffon, with thin, sheer stockings and caressing lingerie. Nothing gave her such peculiar gladness as the touch of fine materials. "Lisel is a fetishist," Johannes Koenig had said of her. "Other women live with their hearts or their minds or their eyes. Lisel lives with the tips of her fingers. She is Braille-reading life." "What do you know about me?" she had answered teasingly. Certainly he didn't know what it meant to grow up in poverty, sleep in a lumpy, creaking divan together with a pushy little sister. Share one limp, old, soiled towel with that sister and make it last a week.

Wear the ugly hand-me-downs her mother patched up for her
after the two older girls of the family were through with them.
Have one's skin fight scratchy cotton stockings and horrible
grey hostile underwear all the time, and dream of finer things,
beautiful, lovely, spider-webbed dreams. It was unfortunate
that just when her rise to fame and popularity began, the
luxurious things for which she had been yearning so shamefully vanished from the life of the average woman in Germany.
But then, Lisa Dorn was not an average woman. The Fuehrer
still smiled at her and applauded her, and the Third Reich
officially and generously acknowledged her exceptional status
by showering her with rare privileges.

Suddenly Lisa remembered the part she had wanted to
learn during this nice quiet evening of hers. Hastily she
pushed all her new dresses back into the wardrobe and
slammed the door shut to get them out of sight. A frown
appeared in the broad space between her eyes as she reached
for the small lemon-coloured, paper-bound book on her
secretary and put a finger between the pages that had so far
refused to become a part of her.

> *One half of me is yours, the other half yours—*
> *Mine own, I would say ; but if mine, then yours,*
> *And so all yours. O! these naughty times*
> *Put bars between the owners and their rights ;*
> *And so, though yours, not yours.*

Damn these lines, they had a way of getting tangled up in
themselves like a box full of angleworms. Lisa kicked off
her shoes and began padding up and down the room.

One half of me is yours, the other half yours . . . There
was too much coyness in it, it was disgusting, cloying. . . .

Mine own, I would say; but if mine, then yours. . . .
Impossible to bring any emotion into this. Wait, perhaps if
I could get a little laugh ?

One half of me is yours, the other half yours . . . Clap
one hand to my mouth, so, and they might laugh. The
poor darlings in the audience, they are so grateful when I
make them laugh. That's our share in the fight for victory.
They stand in line for hours to get into the theatre, and after
the performance they are full of courage and determination.
Germans are wonderful. Tell me another country where the

B

theatres are sold out during a war—— Lisa meditated in her happy ignorance. She skipped to another page, to some lines she liked better:

> *. . . the full sum of me*
> *Is sum of something, which, to term in gross,*
> *Is an unlesson'd girl, unschool'd, unpractis'd;*
> *Happy in this, she is not yet so old*
> *But she may learn;*

Still memorizing, she picked up the telephone on her night-stand and called room service.

> *. . . and happier than this,*
> *She is not bred so dull but she can learn;*

"Hello, room service? . . . Yes, will you please tell Gaston that he can bring up my supper now? . . . Yes, whatever you have. . . . No orange tonight? It doesn't matter, really."

> *Happiest of all is, that her gentle spirit*
> *Commits itself to yours to be directed.*

She put the book down and went, murmuring, into the bathroom to let the water run into the tub, memorizing while she brushed her hair. She liked her hair almost as much as she liked her new dresses, although the general used to tease her and call it baby hair. It was good hair for getting effects on the stage, in any case.

> *. . . her gentle spirit*
> *Commit itself . . . to be directed.*

This was the root from which to develop Portia's character. Her gentle spirit. No nonsense of a strident emancipation, even if she disguised herself as a man. How sweet and *innig* these Shakespearean women were. Not English at all. English women had enormous feet and buck teeth. Also, Lisa had heard that the English hardly knew who Shakespeare was, while in Germany every schoolchild knew his plays by heart.

But then, she had recently read a book in which it was proven that Shakespeare belonged by blood and heritage to the Teutonic race.

> . . . *her gentle spirit*
> *Commits itself . . . to be directed*

she murmured happily and let herself plump into the bathtub. Tonight the water was really warm, and on the glass shelf there were bottles of eau de cologne and perfume and bath salts; there was even a precious piece of French soap, Roger & Gallet, Gardenia. It was part of the loot she had brought from Paris. She sighed with pleasure. She was always happy to be alive and to be alive in the greatest time Germany had ever experienced; but rarely had the world seemed to her as perfect as just now. *Voom-voom* came the Hungarian bass through the walls. Lisa was just playing that her knees were icebergs and she was sailing around them adventurously with the soap-dish, when she heard the waiter roll the supper table into her room and there was the pleasant clinking of glass and china. Suddenly she felt enormously hungry.

"Wait a moment, Gaston," she called through the door. "I have something for you!" There was no answer, and she laughed softly to herself. Quickly she emerged from the tub, dried herself carelessly, and slipped on the new négligée. "Now I have seen your Paris, Gaston," she said happily. "And I didn't forget you. Guess what I brought you."

She took a little parcel from the shelf and held it out to the waiter as she came into the room. "Oh——" she said, startled, and stopped in her tracks. "I thought it was Gaston."

She had never seen the young waiter who was bent attentively over the covered dish under which he was trying to light the burner. The négligée clung to her moist body, and she felt unaccountably nude all of a sudden. Even her toes felt nude and embarrassed. It was different with Gaston; Gaston was an old man who served her every evening and she was used to him. Disappointed, she put the parcel down. It contained an album of views of Paris and a certain French patent medicine for which Gaston had lamented several times.

"Where's Gaston?" she asked the waiter. He moistened

his lips before answering: "Gaston has to help serving downstairs. There's a reception——"

"Yes, I know. Are you new here?" Lisa asked when he struck the third match without success.

"Yes, madame. I'm only helping out tonight," he said without lifting his head.

"Are you French too?"

The waiter shook his head. All she could see of him was his coarse dark hair and his nervous fingers struggling with the match. "Let me do it," she said, taking the match from him and lighting the burner. "There. And roll the table over to the window, please." The black-out curtains were drawn together, but the window was open and she was hungry for some air. Just as the waiter dropped a spoon, there was a timid knock at the door. That's the general, she thought (for even in her thoughts she seldom felt intimate enough with him to call him by his name), and there was a slight disappointment in her voice as she said: "Come in." . . . There goes my nice quiet evening, after all, she thought. . . . The door opened hesitantly, and there stood two men in uniform. Lisa got up.

"If the Fraulein will excuse us. We're the police," one of them said.

"Police?" Lisa said, astonished. "What do you want?"

"We're sorry to disturb the Fraulein," the taller one said. "But orders are orders. We have to search every room in the hotel."

"Of course, in your case that's only a routine, Fraulein Dorn," added the other one.

"Well—make yourselves at home, gentlemen," Lisa said, rather amused by the obvious embarrassment of the policemen. "Do you mind if I eat my supper before it gets cold? Maybe you'd like a cigarette?"

"Thank you, Fraulein," said the taller one. "Thank you, Fraulein," said the shorter one, as they helped themselves greedily from the golden cigarette case. "Excuse us," they said in unison, and began to walk around the room. Lisa watched them while she held her cup out for the waiter to pour into it the brown liquid that was called coffee. This was as good as a show on the stage. The taller one approached the bed in the alcove as if it might explode in his face any moment. He had not much control over his bulging eyes and his smirk as he ogled the nightgown of blue chiffon. The other man had got lost somewhere in the depths of the wardrobe among her new dresses, throwing curious side glances at her all the while. They took a perfunctory peep at the balcony and then they marched into the bathroom. It all took barely two minutes.

"Excuse us," they said, popping up again. The shorter one took heart and expressed what was on his mind. "I didn't dream I would have the honour of making the personal acquaintance of Lisa Dorn," he said. "Will my wife be surprised when I tell her! And my little girl—would it be asking too much if I begged you for an autograph ? My girl collects them. Thank you most obediently, Fraulein Dorn. You're very kind."

"I saw you in *Love on a String*, Fraulein Dorn," said the other one. "I don't see many pictures, but I certainly enjoyed that one." His eyes took a promenade up and down her négligée. Suddenly Lisa had had enough of them. "Good night, gentlemen," she said. "I hope you'll find whatever it is you're looking for."

"Excuse us," they chorused, stumbling over each other to the door. "We're only doing our duty. Excuse the disturbance. Heil Hitler."

As the door closed behind them, Lisa was struck by an unpleasant idea. She rushed into the bathroom. Her precious Roger & Gallet soap was still there, thank heavens. But the small grey piece of rationed soap had disappeared from the washbasin. While she was still wondering whether to laugh or to get angry, there came a dull noise from her room. She pushed the door open.

The waiter had fainted.

For a few confused moments Lisa did not know what to do. Everything she had learned in her Red Cross training had left her altogether. Kneeling down, she lifted his head from the floor, poured some water on her napkin and washed his face. She slapped his cheeks and rubbed his wrists. At last she remembered to loosen his collar and open his shirt. She broke her nail in the attempt and stared helplessly at the unfamiliar mechanism. Suddenly the shirt made itself independent and came loose with a snap. It was nothing but a stiff white shirt-front with a black tie and a celluloid collar grown to it. Lisa stared amazed at the comical contraption;

she had always thought such shirt-fronts were used only for funny effects in slapstick comedies. Hesitatingly she put her hand upon the man's bare chest to feel for his heart. His skin was hot and damp. Her reluctant fingers encountered a strange, dark, dry, crusty pad near his left shoulder, and as she moved it a thin, red line began to run down over the small, terribly unfamiliar nipple of his left breast and disappeared into the crumpled black tailcoat.

On the stage and in pictures Lisa had experienced innumerable strange situations which had solved themselves according to the strict and effective laws of drama, but now she was seized by panic. She brushed the waiter's head from her lap, so that it hit the floor with a dull bump. Stumbling over the hem of her négligée she rushed to the alcove, grabbed the phone on her night stand, and shouted hoarsely for the operator.

"Put that phone down," the man on the floor said suddenly. It was as if the dead began to speak. Lisa gasped. "*Put that phone down*," he said.

Lisa stared at him, the phone poised in her hand, her heart fluttering with fear. He had come to a sitting position but was rocking with dizziness. To Lisa all this was like one of those dreams in which she was standing on the stage and acting in a play she had never heard of, playing a part of which she did not know a single line. In the second it took her to regain a shred of her composure, the man flung himself across the length of the room and yanked the phone plug from the wall. This, suddenly, seemed familiar (*River People*, second act, third scene), and her mind opened up and released a cue.

"If you make another move I'll shoot," she said with a voice gone small and miserable.

"All right. Shoot. Go on and shoot. I don't care," Martin whispered. He was so weak, so spent, that for a moment he was willing to give up the struggle. Close his eyes, give up the struggle and be done with. . . .

Lisa did not shoot. She had no gun, in the first place, and she wouldn't have known how to pull the trigger in any case. Her panic subsided and she felt curiously sorry for the intruder. He looked so thin and desperate. He had a tanned, badly shaven face, but his lips were almost white now. He had burning blue eyes, set into the black shadows of deep sockets, and heavy black brows. He also looked funny with

his bare chest sticking out of the formal tailcoat. The blood
had stopped running.

"Who are you? What do you want here? You frightened
me," she said petulantly. Martin tried to focus his eyes on
her, but everything was still blurred and wavery, as though he
were swimming under water. At last the dizziness ebbed away
and he could see her clearly. She was sitting on her bed, her
knees pulled up to her chin; she was small and expensive and
rich and shameless, and she smelled of perfume and he hated
every inch of her.

"Give me a cigarette," he demanded roughly. She pointed
to the table where her golden cigarette case was lying. There
was only one lonely cigarette left in it. With the automatic
grip of a front-line soldier he broke it in two, put one half
into his own mouth and held the other out to her.

"Thanks," she said, and, keeping her eyes on him, she
began to smoke. As soon as the bitter smoke streamed
into his lungs, Martin realized that the peak of danger had
passed. "I'm sorry I frightened you, Fraulein," he said,
trying to sound rational. "I'm subject to these fainting spells—
and I didn't want you to make a big fuss about it. I didn't
want to lose my job, you see," he added with a pale,
cramped smile.

"Are you sick?" Lisa asked.

"Not sick exactly. A little damaged maybe. Got a bullet
in my chest. In Stalingrad that was. They stitched me up
and collapsed the lung; did a good job of it, the Russians did.
When I got away and home they gave me the Frozen Meat
Medal and an honourable discharge. But that's a long story."
Keep on talking, you fool, he told himself. Stall for time.
Make her ask questions, make her feel sorry for you. . . .

"Your mother must be very proud of you," Lisa said.
"*Dulce et decorum est pro patria mori.*"

Where did you get that blab, Fraulein Dorn? he thought.
Aloud he said: "My mother is dead."

Lisa kept on looking at him speculatively. On the whole she
was not displeased with the situation. It was some diver-
sion. The dramatic quality in it appealed to her, and she felt
safe now. She decided to play with it a little longer and
end it whenever it pleased her.

"What did you do that the police are looking for you?"
she asked him.

"The police aren't after me! God knows for whom they are looking, but it's not I. Believe me, Fraulein Dorn."

"You seem to think me more stupid than I am. It's obvious that you are not a waiter and that they are after you."

"If that is what you think, why don't you hand me over to them?" Martin said. It was sheer foolhardiness, but he said it. . . . I can still get away by the balcony and over the roof, he thought; but he didn't believe it. He waited.

"I'm not a Gestapo agent," Lisa said after a silence. She put her bare feet on the floor, folded her hands in her lap and smiled at him. Martin went over to the small supper table and began to pile up the empty dishes. Lisa watched him intently.

"If the Fraulein has finished her supper I shall take the table out now," he said politely. Her eyes followed him as he rolled the little contraption to the door. He held the door open with his foot and looked out, up and down the corridor. An SS man was loitering near the hall desk, not one of the two police inspectors who had searched the room. Martin quickly ducked back from the door. . . . I'm trapped, he thought in despair. This is the end. They've got me after all. Wheel this table past the guard—and what then? Wheel it where? I'd be caught at the first turn. . . . He had been chased from one trap to another, ever since his escape. Trapped at every step, trapped on the road, in the reeds of the lake, trapped behind the market stalls, trapped in the furnace room, in the wine cellar. He had known that he was trapped when Gaston had whisked him out of the cellar and in a panic had forced him into this clumsy disguise and pushed him into this perfumed room just as Gestapo men were coming up the stairs. Now there were guards posted outside, on every corridor, every staircase, at every door and every exit. The Gestapo was terrifyingly efficient, and there was no shortage of men in its ranks yet. His brain raced through every avenue of escape, sorting out, discarding, selecting. If he could only stay in this room, Gaston might find some way to get him out. Rittergasse 39, ask for Walter. It seemed as far away as Saturn.

"If you give me away I'll kill you," he whispered desperately. His mouth had gone dry again, and he could hardly speak. This was another line Lisa knew from the stage, and therefore it didn't frighten her at all. On the contrary, she had to smile as she said, not without sympathy: "Why are you so scared of me? I'm as quiet as a mouse."

The tension suddenly went out of him and left him limp. "You were right," he said. "They're after me. I'm trapped. If you give me away, my head will be under the axe tomorrow."

It is doubtful whether Lisa understood the full import of these words, because she was used to a world of make-believe dangers and big-mouthed passions without reality; she kept on smiling as if he had spoken his line well. . . . I'd better tie her up and gag her, Martin thought while she seemed to contemplate her answer. The *voom-voom* of the czardas bass knocked in the silence.

There had never been a conflict in Lisa's life. Her career had been swift and without hardship; her colleagues liked her, audiences adored her. The simple people on the street, the truck drivers, the soldiers in the camps called her "Our Lisel." She played the best parts in the best plays on the best stage in Germany. That was all that counted. Since she was happy and successful the whole universe seemed in the best of order. Possibly Lisa had never known a conflict because she had never been in love. The men who ruled the country were her friends, and she was proud of it. It had been no sacrifice at all to become the companion of the few of them she had known intimately in her young life. She had been fond of every one of them, had respected and admired them as she was respectfully and admiringly fond of the general now. Secretly she was even a little sorry for those men into whose mechanism she had gained some fleeting insight. Because men like the general were old, and old men were tired and always worried; even if they had all the power and the world trembled before them, when old men were in love with youth they were oddly humble and sensitive. It was a great satisfaction to be kind and generous to a powerful old man like the general. Thus the bitter conflict between love and duty had never entered Lisa's life.

Neither had the convulsions that tore at the roots of the world touched her mind more than superficially. She loved her country and had never questioned its supremacy. She was convinced that everything that was fine and noble in this

world was German. German music and German poetry,
German science, German philosophy, the German stage, the
German films, the German roads, the German landscape to
which she was bound with a deep and intimate attachment.
Lisa was completely and innocently and ignorantly a child
of the Third Reich and believed without a qualm or doubt in
the gospel of the New Order. It had been dinned into her
ears that it was Germany's solemn mission to spread this
New Order to the rest of the world; if she ever thought about
that at all, it made her happy to know that some day the whole
world would partake of its blessings. Her perception of this
outside world was one of chaos and disorder, of selfish grab-
bing and barbaric cruelty. As for the enemies of the Reich,
all those Bolsheviks, Americans, Jews, and Democrats, she
had fashioned them after the images of propaganda posters;
they were deformed, crippled, cross-eyed, hook-nosed, utterly
repulsive and cowardly, ripe only for annihilation.

"More foes, more honour," said the old German proverb.
Of course, there was the war. There were inevitable losses,
and some of Lisa's friends had died the glorious death on
the field of honour. But even this had never touched the core
of her being. To fall in battle was heroic and beautiful and
not quite real; it was somewhat like being killed on the stage.
After the play was over, the dead of the stage were alive
again and went out and had supper at Kranzler's. Somehow, the people who died in the war were not really dead for
Lisa. As if, surely, after the war they would all be alive
again. . . .

There had never been a conflict in Lisa's life, and there
was no conflict now. Not for a second did she question how
to act in this situation. She had never known of a play in
which the heroine would have delivered a fugitive to the
henchmen. It would, indeed, have made for a very bad play and a
very bad part. Also, while Lisa's mind was warped and twisted
by Nazi preachings, her immature heart had remained intact.

"Don't be scared," she said again, and there was a trace
of mockery mixed with her pity. "If things are as bad as all
that, you may stay here for a few minutes."

"Thanks," Martin said, watching her with his burning,
seared eyes. He was not sure he could trust her.

"Go in the bathroom, wash yourself, and take off this
ridiculous get-up of yours," she said with a little laughter

deep down in her throat. She seemed to take it all as a joke. He hesitated a moment and then went into the bathroom, but he left the door open and kept watching her in the mirror. If she tried to plug in the phone, if she tried to call the guards—— But she did nothing of the kind. She leaned back on the bed, crossed her arms behind her head and hummed a little tune. Martin permitted himself to relax. Suddenly he encountered his own reflection in the bathroom mirror, and it gave him a shock to see how terrible he looked: haggard and unshaven, his hair stiff with cold sweat, his bare chest with its smudge of dry blood sticking ludicrously out of Gaston's tailcoat. Quickly he flung off the coat, filled the washbasin with cold water and plunged his head into it. It was wonderful, like diving into a cold green mountain lake on a hot parched day. He drank half the basinful, more like a thirsty animal than like a man, and filled it again and splashed the good cold water over his chest and rubbed his arms with it until they glowed. He loosened the blood-crusted pad he had made of his socks and examined the wound on his shoulder. It was a nasty wound with jagged, gaping edges, and there was an ugly throb in it. He had forgotten about the girl for a few seconds, but when he looked at her once more in the mirror she was still lying on her bed, smiling up at the ceiling as if she had no idea that it was dangerous to hide him. He found a bottle of iodine in the cabinet over the basin, and, sucking in his breath, he painted the wound. The shoulder was wrenched, besides. As he put back the iodine he came across a little gem of a razor. He turned the tiny thing in his fingers, wondering what the girl might use it for. Then he proceeded in great concentration to rub some soap on his face and shave his stubble. He felt better now. He felt much better. He flung a wet towel over his shoulders and returned to the room. Lisa acknowledged the metamorphosis with a quick glance of amusement.

"Sit down," she said. "You look tired. And what is the matter with your shoulder?"

"I cut it on a rock. The police truck was doing eighty kilometres when I jumped off, and my hands were tied. It makes one clumsy."

Lisa digested this bit of information. "Now tell me why they're after you," she asked. "You don't look like a criminal."

"You don't have to be a criminal to have the Gestapo after you—or don't you know that, Fraulein Dorn? It's the other way round. The criminals are with the Gestapo," he said brusquely. Lisa remembered that the general in one of his rages had shouted something to the same effect; but it had made no impression on her at the time.

"How do you expect me to help you if you don't tell me who you are?" she said, almost timidly.

Martin surveyed all the possibilities and decided that telling the truth might be the best. "I am Martin Richter," he said.

"Yes? And who is Martin Richter?" she asked, unimpressed. "I've never heard his name before."

"No. You wouldn't have heard of me—nor of the others— of my friends, of my sister. Not you," he said bitterly. It stung Lisa. Here she was helping him, but he seemed neither grateful nor humble.

"I may be ignorant, but I'm always willing to learn," she said, a little angry. (. . . an unlesson'd girl, unschool'd, unpractis'd; happy in this, she is not yet so old but she may learn—the line from Portia's part sprang up in her mind, uninvited.)

"What's the use? If I were to tell you the truth you wouldn't believe me. Good. I'll tell you. One of the party bosses treated my sister like a prostitute, and I defended her. That's all it amounts to. That's my capital crime."

"Did you kill him?" asked Lisa, who had been reared on Schiller's dramas. He gave a grim little laugh. "Kill him? No. I wish I had. It didn't occur to our class of good little medical students that we could kill a Gauleiter. All we did was to boo at him. It has cost most fourteen of us their heads so far, and mine isn't too steady either. Now I know that we were just playing at being revolutionaries. A little printshop and a little pamphlet and a little demonstration and a little protest and a little riot—and fourteen of us dead. We didn't think of killing, but we are learning fast. If I get out of this alive I will know better what must be done."

Lisa watched the excited boy in silence. She was a bit afraid of him now, but not much. It was a prickling, exhilarating sensation which she had never before experienced in life, but only in climax scenes on the stage. . . . I can call for help whenever I have had enough of this, she told herself. . . . Martin had begun to circle the room on soundless feet, making himself acquainted with the locale, as had become second nature to him during the Russian campaign. Carefully he checked in his mind all the possibilities of attack and defence.

"Where does the balcony go?"

"It's over the main entrance, toward the street."

"The window in the bathroom?"

"Toward the courtyard."

"What's next door to the bathroom?"

"Nothing. I think the men's room, if you don't mind." Martin examined the bathroom. There was no second exit. . . . This is bad, he thought. . . . He turned off the light and raised the black blind and the small window. The courtyard was blacked out, but in the gleam of the rising moon he could see that the bottom of it consisted of a glass roof. This, too, was blacked out with some paint, but Martin assumed that it covered the lobby. The music from the banquet room became a little louder. He also discerned faintly some crisscross along the walls, as if of kitchen balconies or fire escapes. At the worst there might be a toehold on one of these, he noted, groping out into the dark and feeling along the edge of the window. He left the bathroom dark and the window open and returned to the other room.

"What's next to the men's room?"

"I don't know. I didn't build this hotel. I think it's where that sick English writer lives. Geoffrey Nichols. He's some sort of a war prisoner, you know."

Martin pushed back the sliding doors of the wardrobe. He thrust his hand through the rustling of the dresses and touched the wall at the back. No exit there, but in an emergency it was deep enough to serve as a hiding place. There were four sliding panels and one that only looked like one.

"What's this here?"

"A door. It's locked."

"Who lives in the next room?"

"There is no room. It gives on the little landing of the service elevator."

"Where's the key?"

"I don't know. I never use that door. It's for the chambermaids." Martin went to the table where Lisa had put down the key together with her purse. It was a clumsy thing chained to a big wooden disc. Number 69. He tried it on the second door, and after some coaxing it worked. Lisa watched him with bright, interested eyes.

"Why do you want this door open?"

"In case I have to get out."

"If you can get out, so can anyone get in," she said intelligently. He gave her a quick grin that changed his face completely. But it was gone like a flash of lightning that lifts a landscape out of the night and drops it into darkness again.

"You're clever, Fraulein Dorn," he said as he locked both doors and kept the key in his fingers.

"Better lock the bolt if you want to be on the safe side," Lisa said with a chuckle. She had suddenly remembered that the general had a key to her room and might walk in on the idyll any moment. But there was still the music, louder now that the bathroom window was open, reassuring her that the banquet was not yet over. Martin locked the bolts of both doors and then, leaning his back to the wall, gave her a speculative and surprised glance.

"You are not afraid of me?"

"Not half as afraid as you are of me, I assure you," Lisa said archly. "Now stop prowling like a caged tiger, sit down and get hold of your nerves. Breathe deeply; that's what I do when I have stage fright. And now tell me the whole story. What you said before doesn't make sense. Tell it to me from the beginning."

Why doesn't Gaston come? Martin asked himself desperately. How much longer can I hide here? Will this bundle of caprice get tired of her whim and throw me out? Tell her a story, you fool, and it had better be good. A funny sort of Scheherazade you're turning out to be, my boy. . . . He folded his hands between his knees and bent his head over them, the better to concentrate.

"I don't know how the whole story began or when or where. I think it must have been in Stalingrad. Whenever I try to remember the things that happened to us I come back to that night in Stalingrad when Kurt died. Kurt was my friend, we had been through a lot together. It took him five hours to die. A shell fragment in his abdomen. He was clutching the bloody mess that came out of the hole in his belly as if he were trying to stuff it back; you see that often

in a war. Boys hanging on to their smashed legs and arms as
if they thought they could be made whole again. It looks
funny when they do that. He screamed five hours long like
a stuck pig. They tell you the wounded don't cry—but they
do, and how they cry, Fraulein Dorn! After midnight he had
no more strength left for screaming, and then he died. We
couldn't see it because it was pitch dark in the cellar where we
had dug ourselves in, but we knew he was dead. We took his
uniform to wrap the pieces around ourselves. It was so cold
that the cold sometimes felt like fire. We couldn't bury
Kurt because the earth was frozen. We just piled the bodies
of our dead up along the wall, like frozen meat. It made no
sense when Kurt died. He was such a nice boy, and he wanted
so much to live. He worried a lot because we were missing
life while we were fighting. When he talked of life it sounded
like a train he was afraid to miss. He had a girl at home;
he wanted to become an architect. Sometimes he would go
on for hours thinking up all the things he was going to do
when the war was over. Like in a fever. We all talked like
that at times.

"When we had dug ourselves in in that cellar we had
been twelve, but after Kurt stopped screaming there were
only four of us left. The hell of it was that the Bolshies
had dug themselves in in the same house—upstairs. The roof
had been blown off before we got there. That stench of
explosions and burning things! I don't think I'll ever get it
out of my nostrils. We were out of everything. Out of food,
out of cigarettes, out of matches, in the end we were out of
ammunition and had to fight with bayonets alone. The
batteries in our flashlights were burned out or frozen. Once
in a while one of us went out foraging, and once we found the
frozen carcass of a horse on the street; that kept us alive for
a week. We had a few battles with the Bolshies every day.
They came down and killed a few of us and we killed a few
of them. They had hand grenades and we had bayonets.
We were waiting for the Sixth to bring up reinforcements, and
the Bolshies were waiting for their troops to come and help
them. Meanwhile we killed each other off. It didn't make
sense, once you began to think about it. Either the Bolsheviks
were our enemies or they were not. Either this war had been
forced upon Germany—or Germany had forced it upon the
others. Remember what the Fuehrer said when the war began,

September 2nd, 1939 ? It will never happen again that Germany and Russia will meet in battle. And there we were, croaking by the thousands in Stalingrad. It set us off thinking. We talked about it and came back to it in a circle. Once you had begun to unravel one thread, the whole thing went to pieces. Yes, that's how it began. You don't know what Stalingrad was, and no one can tell you if you weren't in it. It wasn't one hell, it was ten burning, freezing, screaming, starving hells, one piled on top of the other. At first we were sure we would get the city and later we weren't so sure, and then we were still sure some of our divisions would come and shoot us out of it and we waited and we got orders and we obeyed orders and we still believed in that blab the radio told us and still later we only waited for our planes to come and throw some food down for us and in the end we knew that they had given us up. You people at home never heard of it, you were fed the same old mush. All you heard was that our brave troops fought some delaying action. Well, we in that cellar were the brave troops and we fought the delaying action. We croaked in our little hell while our generals got away and threw us to the wolves so that they had time to save their precious skins. Yes—I think that's the beginning of the story. Once you begin to think, you can't help finding out that everything was lies and swindles."

He stopped, his voice rough with the old grief, the old, grim fury.

"Go on," Lisa whispered, revolted and yet fascinated. "Go on—go on."

"I had a lot of time for thinking," he said. He had fastened his eyes on the general's photo, but his mind was racing through the frozen steppes of the past. "The day I got that shot in my lung there were only two of us left in that cellar. The Bolshies took me prisoner while I was unconscious. They could easily have killed me then, but they took me prisoner. When I came to, it was because the Russian doctor who was operating on me hadn't given me enough anaesthetic. They did a good job, though. When I began to get better they gave me books, too. German books. Of course it was all propaganda and it didn't change me much. I didn't know how much of the stuff they told me had taken root in my mind. I was still a good German soldier then. I was so homesick for Germany I would have bitten off my own hands if it would

have helped me to get back. All I could think of was:
Deutschland, Deutschland, Deutschland. I've never been
crazy about a girl, but that's how it must feel. Every nerve
screaming and aching for just that one thing: Deutschland."

"But you came back to Deutschland," Lisa said with
shining eyes.

"Yes, I came back. Don't ask me how, because I don't
know how we ever made it; there were three of us, and it was
spring, our own troops were advancing again. They must
have thought that we were still too weak to escape from their
hospital. But we did it. I can't tell you much about that,
because most of the time during that escape I must have been
delirious; there are only patches of memory in my brain.
Like killing an old Russian couple in a hut where we were
hiding. Or hearing their guerrillas sing at the edge of a little
shell-splintered wood where we were lying under the mulch and
leaves. I'd like to get back to that part of the country some day
when this war is over and look at it. In the end we were picked
up by one of our own advance mechanized patrols. I was too
weak to realize what happened; I missed being happy about it.

"They sent me to Rumania with one of the transports
of wounded and patched me up in a hospital near Galatz.
They didn't let me go home until I looked halfway respectable.
Would have been bad for the home morale to let a sick soldier
go home to his mother. Of course, if a few thousand sick
soldiers should get home all at once and begin telling their
folks what they saw out there and what they thought about
the whole swinish mess our Fuehrer had got us into, it wouldn't
be so good for the morale, after all. And so I was home.
And so that was Deutschland. That was my own Deutschland
for which Kurt had died in a screaming horror and for which
we had fought and for which I had been eating my heart out.
It was as if somebody had thrown away my old eyes and put
a new pair of them into my head. I could see through everything as if I had X-rays in these new eyes. My mother had
died, waiting for me. My father was a crushed little worm,
living in mortal fear of every neighbour and of the house-
warden and the block-warden and the SS man at the corner
and of anyone who could get him into trouble if he didn't
knuckle under. They all were like that, every spark of pluck
or character stamped out of them. My older sister went
around with a big belly, she didn't even know who was the

father of her baby. She had done her patriotic duty and slept with a good part of our brave troops. 'What of it?' she said. 'All I have to do is to pick the name of some dead soldier and the little bastard will have a father.' But why am I telling you all this?"

"It isn't a nice story," Lisa said. The pupils of her grey eyes stood dilated and dark with excitement and confusion and—yes—a hot searing pity. "No wonder the Gestapo doesn't like that sort of talk. I don't think I like it myself."

"Listen—I didn't want to tell you all this," he said fervently, because everything depended on gaining time, keeping her quiet, maybe even making her see his side of it. Surely, Gaston or Philippe would somehow get him out of this cursed room if only he kept on talking and made her keep on listening. "I wanted to tell you about Annemarie," he said urgently. "You must listen. I want you to understand the whole thing. Annemarie was my twin sister. It's funny the way one feels about such a little twin sister. My mother used to tell me that when she had us in the perambulator— an extra wide one—I would have Annemarie's big toe in my mouth and she would have mine in hers and we were completely happy and contented. As if we were not two different babies but two halves of one and the same. It was that all along. School, sport, Hitler Youth, hikes, swimming, studying, being silly, growing up; Annemarie was the only one who didn't ask me questions when I came back the way I came back. She knew. She felt, she understood.

"'What are you planning to do now?' she asked me when I got my discharge. I had thought it over carefully while I was in that hospital in Rumania. 'I want to study medicine,' I told her. I don't know how to explain it—but before the war I had always thought I would be a lawyer, maybe go in for politics. But that had changed with everything else. There comes a time when you have done so much killing and seen so much slaughter that you feel like vomiting; to get rid of it, vomiting your own soul out of yourself. I wanted to cure and heal and patch and make well; be an obstetrician, maybe, help bring children into the world. 'I thought so; I want to study medicine too,' Annemarie said. She was in love with a boy who had lost a leg in Libya in 1941, Wilhelm Schott. He was at the university too; he was a serious sort of fellow, didn't want to marry her until he had got his doctor's degree. They had lowered the standards

for the examination, and we passed it together and registered
for the summer term. We soon found out there were many
students just as sober and disillusioned as I. All of us in our
old faded uniforms, and most of us had the Iron Cross and
one part or the other missing, and the same sort of experiences
behind us. We had come a long way from that glorious frenzy
of before the war. God in Heaven, when I think of that
Nuernberg Parteitag in 1934. I was one of the drummers,
and I'll never forget what it did to us when the Fuehrer came
up that long, long *via triumphalis* and when he stopped to
talk to us and the wind was flapping the banners over our
heads. They had certainly got us so drunk with it all that it
took a Stalingrad to sober us up. Do you know what I am
talking about, Fraulein Dorn? Or are you still on the crest
of that crazy binge?"

Lisa gave no answer. She was back in the shabby quarters
of her childhood, in Floridsdorf, a suburb on the wrong side
of the tracks. In the factories, on the street, in school, there
was that unkempt crowd of workers' children, alien and loud
and dark, Poles, Czechs, Jews, spiteful all of them. And then
the glory and romantic relief of belonging to the Ostmark
Youth. More than once the leader of their group had been
arrested, and once they had hidden him in the ruins of a
burned-out mill and at night they had brought him food;
they had rowed across a dead-end arm of the Danube in a
boat, with a little lantern, and little owls with red eyes had
been sitting on the willow trees. . . .

Martin did not understand the dreamy smile on Lisa's face.
But she was thinking just then: I'm incurable. I'm still
hiding men from the police.

"Does Annemarie look like you?" she asked softly.

"She did when she was alive," he said. It was like a guillotine
dropping. Lisa turned a little pale.

"That is another story that isn't quite nice, Fraulein Dorn,"
he said harshly, because the pain and the horror were still
too fresh in his mind. "I'll tell you how it happened. Some of
us felt that it was our responsibility to tell people the truth
as we saw it; we listened to the clandestine radio stations and
printed little bulletins and circulated them among the students.
We rummaged in the libraries of our parents and found some
of the books that were forbidden and organized an illegal
library service. We were students, after all. We were of an

inquisitive mind and we wanted to know and think for ourselves. We were tired of lapping up the cud Goebbels chewed
for us. It all came about quite spontaneously, not only in our
university but in many of them. You can't take back war
veterans who have seen what we had seen and treat them like
morons again. When they had the unfortunate idea of sending
us Herr Gauleiter Plottke to give us a talk and the Herr
Gauleiter began by insulting the girl students, we booed.
He treated the girls like streetwalkers and told them that
they were useless and lazy and that they had better start at
once sleeping with soldiers and bearing children. We didn't
like that, and the girls didn't like it either. When we booed,
the Herr Gauleiter got hysterical and threatened to have the
university closed and all of us arrested. The rumour spread
among the students, and that afternoon we assembled in front
of the university; we were a big crowd. No meeting had been
called; it was a spontaneous combustion. Then came the
police and wanted to arrest the girls, and we boys formed
a circle around them and tried to protect them. Most of us
had been through the war, and it seemed rather silly to have to
fight off some police bulls; I don't think any one of us took
the whole thing seriously. Wilhelm Schott and I, we stood
in front of Annemarie and prevented the policemen from
pushing her and kicking her around. It was what you would
call a little riot, and in the end we gave in and eighteen of us
were taken to police headquarters. We thought they would
keep us there for a few hours and send us home. But that
isn't how justice works in the Reich."

He stopped speaking because he felt his voice break. Lisa
was sitting on the edge of her bed now, her face in her hands,
as if she were afraid to look at him.

"For three days and nights they kept grilling us; they
wanted us to give away the names of the members of our
organization and how it worked. But not one of us gave an
answer. It is not easy to go through a grilling and not break,
Fraulein Dorn. But not one of us broke. I am proud of that.
The fourth day they shipped us to Berlin and shoved us before
a tribunal of their Volksgericht. Swastikas and flags and
judges and a statue of Justicia over the door and a big show.
It worked as fast and as simply as an automatic meat grinder.
As enemies of the State we were convicted and sentenced to
die under the axe. They took us to Ploetzensee, and every

morning we were taken out into the prison yard and stood up in a row. We boys, twelve of us, on one side, the six girls on the other, an SS squad between us. In the centre of the yard was the scaffold with the block. It looked new, as if they had erected it especially for us, and it smelled of freshly chopped wood. Every day one of us was executed while the others had to watch. And never did we know whose turn it was when they took us out into the yard. I think they thought we would go crazy and begin to fight among ourselves and give away whatever we knew to save ourselves. But we didn't. In a way I was grateful during that week that I had been a soldier and gone through a stiff training. But what about the girls?

"On the third day they executed Wilhelm Schott. I knew how Annemarie felt when she saw the axe come down on him. It is easier to die than to watch it. She tried to cover her face with her hands, but one of the guards pulled them down and pinned them behind her back. I broke out of line and rushed over to her and held my fingers over her eyes, and then she buckled up and fainted. They beat the soles of my feet for it until they were raw and then made me stand up on them all night.

"On the ninth day they killed Annemarie. I don't think she was fully conscious. Maybe the prison doctor had been merciful and given her a shot of scopolamine or something. There was that funny smell of the prison yard. Carbolic and dishwater and chopped wood and the foul smell of fear. Annemarie laughed when they took her up to the scaffold; she didn't smile, she laughed out loud as if she were drunk. When it was over they made us give the Hitler salute and sing the Horst Wessel Lied."

"Be quiet! I don't want to hear it! I don't believe it! I don't believe a word of it!" Lisa cried out; she leaped from her bed and clutched his shoulders as if she could force him to make it all unsaid. It gave him a sharp, stabbing pain in his wound, but also a grim satisfaction. . . . Have I waked you up at last, Fraulein Dorn? he thought. . . . He caught her hands in a hard grip and shoved them away from his body. She stared at him for another moment and then she began to pace up and down the room on her small, bare feet, beating her right fist into her left palm, as if to suppress a scream.

"Look at this," said Martin, and let the towel drop from his back.

"Go away—go!" Lisa whispered. "I don't want to hear another word. I don't want to see you. You can't force me to hear and see such things——"

Martin got up and stood close in front of her. "Look at this," he said and turned his back toward her. It was a mass of welts and sores and bruises. It made Lisa sick to see this tortured back so close to her eyes. The marks of prison and torture superseded the scar where the bullet had gone through his lung. Poor young, thin back, all muscles and sinews and hard, brave living. The sick sensation became a cramp in her throat and then it broke into a sob and a stream of hard, aching, burning tears. She let her forehead drop against that mangled back, clamping her hands into the belt that held his black trousers, and cried. Martin stood motionless and let her cry. . . . I gave her a shock, he thought; maybe this will be her Stalingrad. Maybe she, too, will begin to think now. . . . The salt of her tears burned into the open welts of his back, but he did not mind. He waited till she was through crying. . . . I would give anything for a cigarette now, he thought. . . . At last she pushed him away. But her crying over his sores had left something behind; a strange, new intimacy in his nerves and in hers too. As if they had come from very far and had been very close for a few moments.

"I'm sorry I made a spectacle of myself," Lisa said, trying to slip back into her former self. "It's foolish. I think you must leave now. I can't keep you here forever. I'm expecting somebody."

"Oh, naturally," he said, catching the frightened and unconscious glance she had passed over the general's stern photo. "I forgot for a moment that Fraulein Dorn is having a love affair with this whole rotten National Socialistic Government. I must have been crazy to hope that I could make you see the other side."

"I don't blame you for being bitter after what you've gone through," Lisa said; he had hurt her very deeply now. "But you are wrong, every word you say is wrong. Have you forgotten how things stood with us before the Fuehrer lifted us up and made Germany what she is now? We were miserable, downtrodden, poor. Now we are strong, victorious, powerful. We've conquered all of Europe—forever. It is men like the general who have got us to the top where we belong. Why should I not be proud if he honours me with his friendship?"

"Well spoken, little parrot," he said. "I, too, was brought up on those phrases. It took a few hard blows to shake them out of me. They will be shaken out of you, too. Oh, my dear God," he said with desperate urgency as it suddenly seemed to him that nothing counted if he could not make this small bundle of a girl see the truth. "Strong? Victorious? Powerful? Don't you know that we have lost the war already? Don't you feel the ground tremble under the feet of your great men, because they know what is ahead of them? There was a time when I believed in the Fuehrer as if he were the Messiah. If this man should ever be found lying to us, I could never laugh; I could not stay alive if he let us down; that's what I thought and what we all thought. Well, he let us down and he has lied and he has driven us all into an abyss—and I can still laugh and I'm still alive. And I want to stay alive for the fight that is ahead of us. What happened on the battlefields is nothing compared to what is coming when the German people ask for a reckoning. Victory! That's how all our victories end: Germans coming down on Germans and tearing each other to pieces!"

He had raised his voice in his excitement. There was a knock at the door, and he froze. The hair at the nape of his neck stood up, and every gland in his body poured out the signals: Danger! Danger! Danger!

"Yes? Who is it?" Lisa called; she was a good actress, and she had her voice fairly well under control.

"The chambermaid. Fresh towels, Fraulein Dorn," came from the corridor.

"Just a second," said Lisa. Martin vanished into the folds of the curtains, and Lisa opened a slit of the door. The towels appeared in the slit, together with the tousled curious head of the maid. "Thank you, Katrine," Lisa said. "I don't need anything else. Good night."

With the towels over her arm, she came back and stood over Martin, who, overcome by a sudden weakness, had dropped on her bed. Cold sweat covered his face and chest, and his teeth were chattering. He did not want them to chatter, but they chattered anyway.

"You are not frightened?" she asked with a trace of her old mockery.

"Yes, very frightened," he said.

"Such a hero ! Such big words ! And frightened by a chambermaid ?" she said; she wanted to hurt him and to make him small. She was struggling against something that had caught her as in a web, against her will, and was growing strong as a rope.

"Only fools are not frightened," he said. Lisa stood another moment bent over him, and then she gave in to her fingers that had a will of their own. She put her hands cautiously into his coarse, dark hair. It was lively and electric. His teeth stopped chattering and his eyes closed. There was for a moment the queer, purely physical remembrance of the general's shaved round head in her fingertips and of the criss-cross pattern of wrinkles on his neck. She began to stroke Martin's hair.

"Do you really care so much for living ?" she asked gently. "Is it really so important to you ?"

He seemed to ponder the question seriously before he gave an answer. "I don't know how important it is that I live. I don't think it is very important, not even to myself. But it is important that someone live. Someone must stay alive and carry on. We are still so few—such a pitiful, small group—if they kill every one of us, what will happen to Germany ?"

"Who are 'we' ? What is it that you want to carry on?"

"It's not as clear-cut as all that. We are not a 'Verein' with statutes. We are just a handful of young people who love the things Germany has lost. We want to bring them back if we can. But we must stay alive to do so."

"What things?"

Martin caught her hand and held it in his as he said: "You are an actress. Do you remember what the people demand in Goethe's *Egmont?* Peace, Security, Order and Freedom. But you wouldn't know what freedom is. You wouldn't recognize it if you met it on the street, and if you found it hiding in your room you wouldn't know what to do about it."

Lisa kept on studying the lines of his face. An hour ago she had not known this face; it was amazing how familiar she had become with it in such a brief span of time. The pattern of welts and sores and scars on his back, too, was engraved

on her eyes and her mind as a pain and a challenge. . . .
Freedom? she thought. Freedom has blue eyes and dark
hair that comes down in big ringlets, and a lean, stretched body
with every rib standing out, and a bleeding shoulder and a bullet
in the chest and scars everywhere. Freedom is hard and bitter
and has suffered much and is frightened and must hide and
is in danger every second. Is that freedom? Do I recognize
it now? . . . Freedom was a word that had a magnificent
ring to it; in classical plays it rang up to the galleries and
the galleries applauded. "Give us freedom of thought, sir,"
said Marquis Posa in Schiller's *Don Carlos*, and the galleries
had stamped and applauded and then the play had quietly
disappeared from the repertory. The actor Max Wildermann
who had killed his Jewish wife and his children and himself
rather than see them sent to Poland—had he meant freedom?
Suddenly a cataract of memories came tumbling down on her,
things she had forgotten, repressed, things she had not wanted
to see or to know because they would have disturbed the
comfort of her life. So few—such a handful—but they knew
freedom. There had always been a few in Germany who knew
freedom and fought for it. Luther and Hutten, and later the
young officers who had fought Napoleon and the revolutionaries of 1848. So few, such a handful. . . .

"Why did you have to come here?" she asked desperately.
"Why did you have to pick on me? Why didn't you hide in
some other room? I was happy. Why did you have to come
and tell me your dreadful stories and show me your sores?
What am I going to do with you now? You can't stay here all
night. But I can't send you away—I can't. If anything should
happen to you I would never have another good moment in
my life. You and your freedom—how I hate you! Why
are you staring at me as if you wanted to burn holes in
me?"

Martin was staring at her because he had just then, only
that very minute, discovered that she was a woman and he was
a man. It was a bitter-sweet revelation in the midst of pain
and fever and fear. It was like drinking strong wine on an
empty stomach. He took his burning eyes away from her.

"I'm hungry," he said. "I haven't eaten anything for
two days."

"Oh!" said Lisa. She had expected something different.
"Why didn't you tell me? Come—sit down and eat. There

must be some coffee left—and a sardine or two and a crust of bread."

She rolled the table over to the bed on which he was sitting and lighted the little flame under the chafing dish. He watched her over the rim of the coffee cup. The brew was tepid and bitter but it made him feel good. . . . Now a cigarette and I would be fine, he thought. . . . He said: "Do you realize that you are giving aid and comfort to an enemy of the Third Reich ?"

"Don't talk nonsense. Eat," she said. "Eat."

"Do you know that from now on you are in danger too ?"

Lisa looked away over his head with the floating, fleeting, weightless smile that enraptured her audiences every time at the second-act curtain of *House Without Windows*.

"Really ? Am I ?" she said, soaring into a clouded firmament full of lightning and thunder. "And all I wanted was a nice quiet evening."

WITH streams of French champagne and mutual goodwill the reception for the Central European Trade Commission approached its end. Every crumb of the cold buffet had been eaten up by the undernourished Central Europeans. Every toast had been spoken, every assurance of friendship had been given, every drop of propaganda had been squeezed from the special communiqués from the eastern front and from the bombers downed over the Lueneburger Heide.

"Thank God, this is over," sighed Baron von Stetten when he had patted the last back and kissed the last hand—Frau Plottke's padded, stubby hand, incidentally. "I thought they would never go. My dear Dahnwitz, dancing on volcanoes is a very tiresome occupation."

"Well, good night, Stetten. Glad I could help out," the general said at the door of the banquet room that looked now as if a swarm of locusts had gone through it.

"Wait till I get my coat," Stetten said. "I must talk with you. Confidentially."

"Can't that wait until tomorrow ?"

"No, it can't wait," Stetten said, and something in his tone made Dahnwitz straighten up and say: "*Bon*. Let's go to my room then; I think I still have some cognac left."

The general's room was on the first floor because he would have thought it poor taste to have his room close to that of Lisa on the fourth. He disliked ostentation of any kind. His orderly had laid out everything in that military order that seemed to be measured with a ruler. A map of Europe was pinned to the wall together with a large-scale contour map of the Zhitomir sector. There was a cool and manly whiff of leather, menthol, and rubbing alcohol in the air. The photo of the general's wife who had died seven years before stood on the writing desk. Although the general never looked at the photo and, in fact, had not much cared for his wife while she was alive, he was in the habit of carrying it with him wherever he went.

"If you'll pardon me, Stetten—I must make a phone call before we go *in medias res*," he said after he had poured some cognac into the water glasses he found on the dresser. Stetten disappeared discreetly into the bathroom to give Dahnwitz an opportunity to talk to Lisa Dorn undisturbed. Sitting on his bed, the general picked up the phone. He smiled in anticipation as he did so. "Operator, give me Number 69," he said and waited. "Ring again, if you please," he said when the operator reported that there was no answer. "Fräulein Dorn still doesn't answer," said the operator, and the general put the receiver back on the hook. . . . She has gone to sleep, he thought, a bit disappointed. Well, I can visit her in the morning. . . . It was a pleasant thought that sent a warm wave through his body. A lifetime in the army had made it impossible for him to sleep later than five a.m. But it was a bore to wake up before dawn in a hotel, in a town where nobody was up at that hour but the garbage collectors and the street sweepers. However, if he could spend the morning with Lisa, every hour was a gain. Lisa was never lovelier than when she woke up. Young women, warm with sleep, rubbing their eyes and smiling from their pillows, were a rare gift of the gods. But the Lord preserve us from the old ones before they have put themselves in harness, thought the general.

Stetten came back from the bathroom the moment Dahnwitz had put down the receiver. "*Prosit*," he said and "*Prosit*," said the general as they lifted their glasses and touched each other's little finger.

"Well, what was it you had to tell me?" asked Dahnwitz, when Stetten seemed to be having trouble in opening the conversation.

"I was sorry—about your son, I mean," Stetten said uneasily.

"Yes—now they are gone; both of them," said the general. "My nephew, Juergen, too. I had adopted him, you know. There's no one left now to take over Elgede. Well, these youngsters only did their duty."

It was the prescribed answer. Stetten, whose two younger brothers too had been killed in combat, understood. There had never been a war in which the leading officers' families had not lost almost all their young men. He got up and with an automatic gesture pulled the plug of the telephone from its socket. He also pondered the connection of the lamp on the night-stand, but seemed to decide that it was harmless.

"These Rumanians have become hard to handle recently," he said conversationally as he sat down again.

"Of course," said the general. "What else can you expect when we had to pull out three divisions and send them to Russia."

"How are things at G.H.Q. ?"

The general shrugged and filled the glasses again. "Remember how it was in August 1918 ? Except our spring offensive didn't come off so well this time as it did then."

"There was trouble in Krug's division, wasn't there ?"

"I wouldn't know," the general said, cutting off the discussion. Stetten came from his own caste and they had been officers of the same regiment, but now he had crept under with the Piefkes and the general didn't think it quite correct to discuss military matters with him. According to his own unbending standards, Stetten had lost caste by siding with the Piefkes. Piefke was what the general called anybody who was not a soldier. All civilians, all bureaucrats, all the small fry that in the Nazi lingo was addressed as the Sacred German Nation or even the Master Race. Piefkes, all of them. But above all, the leading Nazis were Piefkes; low-class rabble without discipline or principles or virtues. Piefkes gone wild. Stampeding, obnoxious Piefkes in all the high places. Piefkes, all of them, down from the man the general, in his own mind, never called anything but "this corporal Schickelgruber."

"I understand some of the companies gave up fighting," Von Stetten said. Although the telephone was disconnected, he threw an anxious side-glance over his shoulder—the characteristic side-glance of the Third Reich.

"Oh, they are fighting all right," the general said, indifferently. "Maybe their hearts are not in it. But show me the German soldier who wouldn't fight to the last wherever you put him."

There was a little silence while Stetten contemplated how to approach what he had to say.

"Seen Keith recently?" he asked.

The general put his glass down and looked at him with great attention. "Not recently," he answered. "No, not recently."

"Did you know that Fredendorff was court-martialled?"

"No. Was he?"

"Yes. As for Keith—he had an accident."

The general sat up very stiffly; he felt his pulse throb in the sore where Fischer had scraped out the abscess. He swallowed the taste of disinfectant and clove. Stetten could see his adam's apple move as he opened the stiff crimson collar; the two decorations clicked faintly in the dead quiet of the room.

"What happened to him?"

"Some sort of shooting accident. This morning. We have no details."

"That's bad. One fine strategist the less."

"Von Meyring took up his plane and crashed last night," said Stetten. Then there was a silence.

Berlin lay strangely muffled in the blacked-out night. Not a light, not a horn hooting, no cries of newspaper boys, not a whistle, not a voice, not a sound. Stifling. The general got up and went to the window and pulled the curtain back. A white moon shone over the roofs and the black skeletons of the scaffolds that hid some bombed buildings from view. A bomb crater farther down the street was filled with thick, inky shadows.

"Sounds like an epidemic," the general said at last, his back turned to Baron Stetten.

"Yes, and a dangerous one," Stetten said to his back.

The general kept on looking out, but he saw nothing. . . . So we lost, he thought. We took a risk and we lost and we have to take the consequences. . . . He was not frightened or surprised. As far back as he could remember he had learned that there were only two sides to every problem. In Gross-Lichterfelde in the cadet school, as a young lieutenant with the Koenigsulanen, in the military academy, on the staff, in manœuvres,

as commander of the Eleventh Military District, in war—you
won or lost. There was no other choice. With every move,
every operation, every battle it was the same—you won or
you lost. That was all there was to it. You knew the rules
of the game, you weighed the chances, you calculated the risks,
you made your plans, you laid out your strategy to the best
of your talent and knowledge. After that the game was out of
your hands. You won or you lost. When he and a small
group of high officers had entered into a conspiracy for over-
throwing the present High Command they had planned well,
and he could see no fault in their strategy. But they had lost
all the same. Keith and Fredendorff had taken the consequences, and now it was his turn. His tongue played mechanically with the sore spot on his gum; he almost enjoyed the
little pain. He pulled the curtain to, went back to the table
and poured the rest of the cognac into his glass. It pleased
him to notice that his hand was steady. Stetten looked pale,
and a fine film of perspiration covered his face. It made
Dahnwitz, suddenly and quite inappropriately, remember the
midwife in Elgede who had helped to bring his two sons into
the world; she had sweated and fretted and suffered much
more than his wife. He couldn't help smiling at the memory
of good, fat, busy Frau Kettel. Stetten, who saw his smile,
wondered whether the general had understood the full im-
plication of their conversation.

"Thanks, Stetten," Dahnwitz said politely. "Very good
of you to warn me. Very good, indeed. How did they find
out?"

"You trusted Mattoni too much. He was planted by the
Gestapo."

Mattoni had been one of the middlemen the conspiring
generals had used in their dealings with corresponding groups
in the Balkans. Dahnwitz had known him for many years;
Mattoni came from a good Tyrolean noble family and had been
liaison officer on his staff in the last war. Never trust a mongrel
or an Austrian, Dahnwitz's grandfather had always said. As
a young *Faehnrich*, his grandfather had fought in the Prussian-
Austrian war.

"It's very, very good of you to warn me," he said again.
"I realize that you're putting yourself in danger."

Baron von Stetten brushed it aside. "Pshaw, danger!
What is and what isn't dangerous, as matters stand today?

We're all frying in the same stew. I can understand your trying to get out of it while there is still time."

"*Sauve qui peut?* No, I don't believe we were thinking of ourselves when we tried to bring off a coup. Not of ourselves, Stetten. It was the best way we could see to save our country. Simple, sober mathematics. The war is lost, it's been lost since the winter of 1941. It is madness to go on feeding our divisions to the enemy. Madness. The only trump we hold is an intact army—and how long can we keep it intact? Once the army is broken up, what do we have to throw into the scales at the conference table? As a gentleman and an officer I know when it is time to count my chips and stop the game and go home. Only a bloody dilettante, an adventurer, a gambler like our little corporal will keep on gambling until he has lost his shirt and his pants—and our country to boot. I don't need to assure you that not one of us had selfish motives, none of us. All we thought of was Germany. We have clean hands and a clean conscience. But this is not the sort of war we were brought up to fight; this isn't a nice war, Stetten. The things we had to see and to watch and to cover with our names, in Poland, in the Ukraine—no, it's not a nice war. All we did was to keep our oath to serve our country. Yes. Serve the country, Stetten. We were stupid, unforgivably stupid, to stumble into Himmler's trap. But we weren't instructed at the Military Academy how to deal with scoundrels of Himmler's colour."

The general had started with his usual reserve, but as he spoke he felt his temper rise and the blood beat in his temples as if they would burst, and there was a roaring in his ears that made him deaf and he shouted louder and louder in order to hear himself. Stetten listened, patient but unimpressed. Dear Heaven, how used he had got to hysterical outbursts and nervous breakdowns during his career under the Third Reich! He was sorry for Dahnwitz, who was a fine strategist and a brave man but also a blundering fool. They had been young officers in the same regiment, had courted the same plump widow, played the same pranks in the officers' casino, and after being wounded in the last war they had recuperated in the same hospital in Baden-Baden. With faint sentimentality he remembered that Dahnwitz had once paid some gambling debt for him in their youth, thus saving him from disgrace. Now he was returning the favour. Poor Dahnwitz.

"Maybe history will justify you," he said politely. "Meanwhile I thought you would like to know where you stand and make your arrangements."

The general gave him a friendly, resigned grin. "History doesn't take notice of a *putsch* that doesn't come off. A dud. No explosion. Finished. How much time do I have to make my—er—arrangements?"

"Not much time, Dahnwitz, I'm afraid. Twenty-four hours at the most, I should say. That is, if you don't want the Gestapo to intervene."

"Not much of a choice, eh ?"

"No. Of course you know what has to be done."

The general gave him a grin. "In other words, it's your mission to give me a gun, one bullet, and a cigarette and leave me alone with them."

"Not quite so melodramatic and old-fashioned. But I'm sorry, Dahnwitz. You'll have to toe the line."

"To be sure. Toe the line. Toe the line."

The general folded his hands on the table and looked at his fingers in deep concentration. . . . I'm tired, he thought. I'm damnably tired. Why didn't I retire and go to Elgede and plant my rye before it came to this ? . . . Nostalgia for the old country seat swept over him in a great, warm surge. The wood crackling in the huge tile stove, the stuffed heads of stags with their proud crowns of antlers adorning the hall, the rifles well oiled on their racks in the rifle-chamber, the stables, the fields, the good brown smell of potatoes roasting in open fires at harvest time, the jolly noise of the battue. And his horses, Windmill, Crown Prince, and Attack. He had always wanted to teach Lisa to ride horseback. He had wanted to read some of the old books in his mother's room, too, and plant poplars along the driveway and have a little brick wall built off the south wing. . . .

"I could hand in my resignation and retire," he said, half to himself.

Stetten saw his own tiny reflection in the disc of the general's monocle. He did not like himself at that moment.

"No. No, Dahnwitz. I don't think that would be considered sufficient," he said.

"I see. Well. Twenty-four hours, what ? Good. Well then, I think I won't detain you any longer. I'll have to look after my affairs. Thanks again. Very decent of you, Stetten. Very decent. *Au revoir*."

"Good night, Dahnwitz," Baron Stetten said, putting his coat on. He had stopped himself in time from calling, "Heil Hitler." "Too bad it had to come like that. But then—we don't know what's in store for the rest of us."

"Quite," said the general; they both saluted somewhat stiffly. He went politely to the door with his visitor and held it open until Stetten's trim figure had disappeared around the bend of the corridor. Then he closed it carefully and took off his monocle. He took out his eyeglasses and, automatically, glanced first at the maps on the wall and then at his calendar. At ten in the morning he had a date with the dentist. What a joke on Fischer! He unbuttoned his tunic and went over to his night-stand. As usual, his orderly had put his old Luger in the little drawer there. He took it out, carried it over to the table, and put it in front of him. He sat down, took off his eyeglasses and, dropping his head, tried to line up his thoughts in battle formation.

It was twelve minutes past midnight, and the hotel was beginning to put itself to bed. Schmidt had soaked his tired feet in a pail of cold water in the locker room and gone home to catch a few hours' sleep before his medical examination. Another Gestapo agent had relieved Heinrich and taken his post next to the revolving door. Yawning policemen, plain-clothes agents, and SS guards were watching exits, stairs, and corridors. A few perfunctory arrests had been made; the waiter Gaston, the wine steward Philippe, two members of the czardas band, a Danish chambermaid on the fifth floor, and two travelling salesmen in Number 78 had been taken to police headquarters on Alexanderplatz as suspects. The telegraph woman had shuffled in and put down a batch of telegrams and dropped a few rumours. "The Brunner factory in Tegel is on fire. They found a war widow with her two children drowned in the Landwehr Canal. Something funny going on in Italy. They haven't got Richter yet," she reported and shuffled out again, a Cassandra in a crumpled uniform. Under the thick blanket of the blacked-out night new scrawls began to blossom on the walls of Berlin. "You can kill Richter—but you can't kill his spirit." The hotel doctor, who had gone up to the desk and riffled through the telegrams, returned to the table in the smoking room where Johannes Koenig and Geoffrey Nichols were finishing their game of chess.

"They haven't got Richter," he remarked, dropping into his chair. He was responsible to the authorities for the English prisoner's health and kept a steady eye on his frail charge. Also, he had come to like Nichols during the four years of his enforced stay in the hotel.

"Who's Richter?" Nichols asked indifferently.

"Richter's one of those immortal, quixotic fools who doesn't acknowledge the fact that a bullet in one's belly is a stronger argument than the most beautiful revolutionary slogan," Koenig said. He was old and very effective with his blue eyes, the powerful chin and the flame of white hair over his wide brow. On closer inspection, though, he looked like a Goethe monument of imitation marble. His eyes were watery and red-rimmed and alcohol had made deep inroads into his mind. He had been a great writer in his youth and was still a writer. In fact, he was *the* writer of the Third Reich, the only writer of European standing who had stayed on when the others went into voluntary or enforced exile. He produced, to order, sonorous, resounding, swollen odes and battle hymns for official consumption. Otherwise the queer little fact remained that Germany's Great Writer had not written a line since 1933. His impotent efforts to finish the fragmentary manuscript of a play, *The Purple Hour*, felt like a chronic itch, a boil, a sore on his literary conscience.

"Good reason for us to be jealous of him, what, Koenig?" Nichols said. Most of their conversations were fencing duels with swift lunges and smart counterthrusts, and Geoffrey Nichols, a sick man and, since 1939, a war prisoner, always looked forward to the few weeks his German fellow writer spent in Berlin as to a rare holiday and a feast of shop talk. Koenig pretended not to have heard the barbed remark. "It is said that this boy, Richter, is hiding from the Gestapo here, in this very hotel," he said musingly. "There you have a good starting point for a drama that would quite naturally lead to a catharsis. The psychological problem: How would I or you or anyone else react if we stumbled accidentally upon the fugitive? Help him or give him up?"

"In theory every one of us would act like a veritable hero, I'm sure; in practice there's no doubt that the Gestapo has an edge on us," Nichols said.

"I like this hotel; there's always something going on. Lots of material for short stories."

"Why don't you write them, Koenig?"

"Don't you like this hotel, Nichols? I like it very much."

"The difference between us is that you're a transient, while my status as a permanent guest is rather bothersome at times."

"That's only for the duration, Nichols, only for the duration."

"I have a good idea that this time the duration will last longer than the war."

Johannes Koenig savoured the little crack. "Not bad," he said, "not bad. Why don't you save it for your next broadcast? I'm sure your countrymen will appreciate it." At which Nichols fell into a glum silence.

"Aren't we all prisoners, Nichols?" Johannes Koenig said rhetorically. "Let's drink to our comfortable prison. Each man his own prisoner, eh?" He was only a little drunk, and he could never go to sleep until he was very drunk. Nichols, too, suffered from insomnia; he was afraid of his room and his bed. It was terrible to sit propped up in that bed hour after hour, all alone, with one's heart beating like a temple gong and the fear strangling one's throat. His fear of dying all alone in his room some night had become an obsession. He had implored the authorities to let him have a night nurse. But while the authorities generally treated him with kid gloves because he was such a useful prop of propaganda, they had politely regretted that during the war there were no private nurses to spare for coddling a prisoner.

"I haven't told you yet how much I admired your last broadcast," Koenig said. "It was a masterpiece. If I try to imagine myself in your place—no, I should be completely incapable of telling my own country twice a week how wonderfully everything is going with their enemies. And you, my dear fellow, do it so smoothly, with so much finesse and humour—and with such a marvellous pretence of conviction. The effect must be devastating."

"But my dear fellow, I don't pretend, I'm indeed convinced that it is better for England to know how matters stand. It can't be good for her to harbour the dangerous delusion that the strength and morale of Germany is dropping. I believe I am doing my own country a service by telling her the truth—that is, the truth as I see it," Nichols said and tried pathetically to make himself believe it.

"The truth about Germany! Congratulations if you have been smart enough to find out the truth about Germany. For five hundred years the best brains of Germany have tried to find out the truth about her and failed. She is a very complicated lady, is Germany, and each trait of her character contradicts some other one. But I'm glad you have such noble reasons for doing these broadcasts—and such sensible ones, too. Shame on you, Doctor. You see, our medicus here seems to think that your broadcasts are the price you pay for your room, board, and medical attention in this high-class hotel. Look here, Nichols, just between us, wouldn't it be more honest to say that you gave in because you were afraid of being sent to a prison camp? Remember Ibsen, *Peer Gynt?* What Ibsen calls 'the great crooked one'? Go round about, the great crooked one says. Go round about. Compromise."

"Don't we all compromise, Koenig? Or do you claim to be an exception? I mean—I really hadn't much choice. I'm a prisoner and sick and I'm not much of a hero. When the authorities put before me the subtle choice of either dying miserably without medicine or bartering my broadcast against the necessary doses of Coramin, of course I gave in. But you, my dear chap, you whose writings are of the heroic type, you're here of your own free will, aren't you? You don't seem to like it here. You grumble and growl so much that every night I think you'll grab your suitcase and be off for Switzerland the next morning, *sans adieu.* And then you amaze me by producing another eulogy or another ode to Fortress Europe. If I were a free man like you——"

"But I am not a free man, damn you," Koenig shouted and banged his fist on the table so that the chessmen jumped from the board. "I am a man without a passport, and what's more, I am a German. German is the only language in which I can express myself. This is my country, mine. Whatever this unhappy, sick schizophrenic country of mine may be doing, it is my country. Listen," he said with great urgency, while his speech and his vision began to get a little blurred and the first drunken heaviness pressed down on his eyelids. "Let's take the case of a man who loves his wife; he has taken her for better, for worse. It's his wife; his. If his wife should get sick—if she has cancer—if she should go insane—if she should commit a crime—could he cast her off? Could he leave her in her misery and say: I am a free man? I am going away—to Switzerland, to Sweden, to the United States?"

"A very effective simile—but not quite fitting," Nichols said agitatedly, and the doctor gave him a professionally worried glance. He might as well gulp down a bottle of poison every night before going to bed as have these disputes, he thought. "The others went away," Nichols went on. "They had no passports either. But they had courage. They gave up everything and went away—while you stood by when their books were burned and cashed in on their exodus. Wait a moment for what I have to say. Goethe was a German writer too. Remember what Goethe said? He called the Germans an accursed people; he said that their only salvation would be to be scattered over the earth like the Jews. Goethe said——"

"Goethe was a snob. Goethe didn't understand Germany. He, with his yearning for the harmonious, the measured, the poised, the balanced; Helena—Rome—Italy—and his whole damned *bellezza*——" Koenig shouted, quite drunk now. "He disliked Beethoven. He snubbed Kleist. He was repulsed by the great masters of the Gothic. But the German soul is Gothic. It's an abstruse soul, full of darkness and with the face of a gargoyle, and it's twisted and tortured and it loves pain. Only the Russians understand something about the boundless German capacity and eagerness to accept suffering. It loves to inflict pain and to suffer pain. You don't understand Germany, none of you. Regimentation, you say; militarism, discipline, the Prussian law of command and blind obedience. You don't understand that Germans are forever yearning for the chain and the whip, because they are afraid of their own fathomless emotional furore and depth. The German doesn't want freedom, because to him it would mean self-destruction. That's what you Anglo-Saxons will never understand, you with your shallow humanitarian ideals and your kindergarten optimism; you don't know what it is to live with the demon in you. Go ahead, tell that to your countrymen in your broadcast !"

"I think I will repair to my room now—I don't feel quite up to a discussion tonight," Nichols whispered; there was a bluish tinge to his lips which the doctor did not like. "I think I should try to get some sleep—oh, Doctor, would you mind hauling me upstairs ? Their bloody elevator is out of order again."

As the doctor piloted the sick man toward the stairs, there was a clanking of spurs; from the bar came the Rumanian Military Mission, loud and slightly drunk, marching out into the night in quest of more amusement. A moment later Tilli and Kauders emerged from the bar, carried on a gust of strident laughter. Then the doors of the bars were shut and the tired barman hung the "Closed" sign out for the night.

"Just a second, Schnucki," Tilli said to the flier and, leaning him against the fountain as though he were a wooden figure unable to stand on his own feet, she hastily crossed the lobby and caught up with Nichols and the doctor before they had reached the foot of the stairs.

"Good evening, Mr. Nichols," she said; suddenly her face was transformed, less harsh, almost tranquil.

"Good evening, Tilli," Nichols said, detached.

"Aren't you feeling well tonight?"

"On the contrary. Excellent."

"Didn't the alarm hurt you? I mean—a shock is bad for your heart, isn't it?" she asked fumblingly.

"I wasn't shocked," said Nichols. Tilli gave the doctor a vaguely imploring glance. Go away and leave me alone with him, this glance meant to say. But the doctor clung to his patient.

"Well—good night, Tilli," Nichols said and walked on.

"Tomorrow is Monday," said Tilli.

"Indeed. So it is," Nichols answered; he turned around to face the girl once more.

"I mean—d'you want me to visit you after your broadcast, as usual?" she asked him with a timidity that seemed like an incongruous mask on her hard, shopworn face.

"If these be your orders, I can't prevent you," Nichols said, and, turning his back, he was on his way again. Tilli grabbed his shoulder and stared into his eyes. "Sometimes

I'd like to slap your face," she said under her breath. Nichols shook off her hand. "Thank you. Likewise," he answered. He went toward the stairs, and Tilli returned to her drunk little hero. Kauders, with a silly, vacuous smile, was holding onto the rim of the fountain.

"What are you waiting for? Let's go to my room," Tilli snapped at him and dragged him off. Nichols, in the meantime, laboured his way up to the fourth floor, step by step, his heart pumping hard and his breath loud and short.

"I didn't know you could be brutal," the doctor said as they paused at the second landing. Nichols shrugged his bony shoulders.

"It's very thoughtful of the propaganda ministry to take care of me in regard to what is known as the biological urge. Except that I can't feel passionate over a bitchy little Gestapo informer who is paid for giving me candy every other Monday after I have been a good boy and delivered my broadcast."

"But, Nichols, Tilli is harmless. She is a poor little fish in a high sea."

"Well then, let's say that some animals lose the biological urge when in captivity," Nichols closed the discussion. "Shall we try another flight of stairs?"

Behind them, clutching another bottle of Burgundy to his side, Koenig came up, grumbing and complaining, but at last he let himself be pulled along, too.

It took the doctor quite some time to get them both to bed, the drunk one and the sick one. There he was now, left alone in the middle of the night, with nothing to do, while the front-line hospitals were short of doctors. He had a brief, lovely vision of abdominal wounds and smashed legs. A ditch full of sleeves and bloody trouser legs, cut off the injured soldiers. "If I don't get a telegram soon the war will be over before they call me," he muttered to himself as he went down the corridor along the row of doors toward his own inhospitable, incurably empty room. A gramophone was playing hoarsely in the monkey cage where Tilli was now entertaining the young flier with his first-degree burns.

Otto Kauders was lying on the lumpy studio couch that served her as a bed. He had taken off his blouse, and his shirt was open at the neck. On the wall across from the couch a series of photos was pinned up in a row, for an artistic effect. They all showed an almost nude girl in different poses. "Whose photos are those?" Otto asked after staring at them with half-closed eyes, his mouth slackly open.

"Don't ask silly questions, Schnucki. Whose act would I hang up in my room?"

"Yours?"

"Naturally mine, stupid."

"Pretty," he said. "When were they taken?"

"What do you mean, when were they taken? When were they taken! Six weeks ago, that's when they were taken."

Otto thought that the photos didn't look like Tilli now; maybe she had looked like that a few years back. He dropped the subject and leaped to another theme.

"That actress," he said; "that star I met in the lobby —that Lisa Dorn——"

"Yes. What about her?"

"She's damned pretty."

"I know lots of girls who are prettier and don't make the money she makes. Did you see her dress? I wonder who paid for it."

"Young, too," said Otto, pursuing his own trend of thought. "She looks even younger in life than on the screen."

"Come off her; listen—would you like me to play some forbidden records for you?"

"Why not?" Otto said. . . . She made eyes at me, that actress, he thought. I bet she is not a saint. They all go for us fliers like mad. You have to brush off girls all the time. Trouble is you can't go after a classy woman like that actress within three days. It takes more time, lots of fuss, I'll bet, lots of chichi. Tilli is a good sort. No chichi about Tilli. If you have only three days you've got to take what you can get and not lose time chasing butterflies.

"Listen to that," said Tilli, who had fiddled around with her records. A husky voice filled the small room with a heavy, knowing sensuality that made fun of itself:

> "*Falling in love again,*
> *What am I to do——*"

"Say, what's that?" Otto asked, with prickling nerves.
"That's Marlene."

"That's not 'Marlene,'" said Otto. He whistled a few bars of the soldier song that swept the country:

> *In front of the barracks, in front of the gate,*
> *Under the lantern we once had a date.*
> *When the war is over we'll meet again,*
> *Make love again and kiss again,*
> *Under the lantern, Lilli Marlene.*

"Not that Marlene. This here is Marlene Dietrich, stupid. It's a forbidden record. I've had it for a long time—it's a bit scratchy, but nice. Like it?"

"Who's Marlene Dietrich?" he asked.

"Don't tell me you never heard of her?"

"Not that I remember," he said. Tilli stopped the gramophone abruptly and stood there for a moment, her back turned to the boy, her shoulders hunched up. They were all so much younger than she, all these boys who blew into town and grabbed a bit of fun and landed on her studio couch half drunk and went off again. Like this one—he hadn't even heard of Marlene Dietrich. It made him a whole generation younger than herself. Sim had given her that record in the old times. He had played it for her the evening they had first come together. It was old and scratchy now, but it still went down sweet and thick and sticky like too big a spoonful of honey. Sim Baruch. The first one in her life. Poor Sim. There came a wild bumping from the ceiling, and a roaring voice demanded, "Silence, or I'll call the police." "There's that uncle again. He's from Muenster. He says he couldn't sleep for a week because of the air raids," she said.

"Well—we didn't sleep much either out there," replied Otto. "I'd like to put him to bed, that slacker, but real good."

She put the record away and went over to the boy. She was wearing a Japanese kimono, real silk, and her bedroom slippers with the marabou trim, and she felt rather seductive.

"What's that noise in the wall?" Kauders asked as she bent over him.

"That's the W.C. It's right next door. Very handy when you want to go and make peepee in the middle of the night."

"Don't be so damned unromantic," he said.

"Oh, come on. I'm just joking. Here I am breaking my

neck being romantic for you, and the Herr Oberleutnant still complains."

He stretched out his arms and said lazily: "Come here. Let's have a kiss. Really, I like you, Tilli. Do you like me?"

"Why should I take you to my room if I didn't like you, Schnucki?"

"No. I want you to say it. Come on, say it."

"All right—do you want it in writing too? I like you. Is that better?"

"No," said the boy. He wanted something, he did not know what. He stayed restless and dissatisfied under her kiss.

"Say, 'I love you,'" he demanded as she left his lips and straightened her hair. "Come on! Say, 'I love you.' Why don't you say it?"

"People don't say such things. It sounds silly. I couldn't say it to save my life." Her face had become stubborn and sullen. He pulled her to his side and took her in his left arm. The right one with the bandaged hand hung over the edge of the couch. "Shall I make you a baby?" he whispered in her ear. She shook her head. "If you loved me you would want a child by me," he said. "I'd like to make you one. See —I like you enough to want you to have a child by me. Would be fun to come on leave and have a little boy at home. Our major told us that every soldier who goes on leave and doesn't leave a pregnant woman behind has failed in his duty. I'm just in the mood to be a good soldier. You'd get part of my pay, too."

"That's not a proposal, is it?" Tilli said, nuzzling up to him. For a second she had been touched by the boy's clumsy groping for something to hold on to. They all wanted children. . . . It's because they want to live, Tilli thought. They don't know it, but they want something to be left after they're gone. They all carry death in their packs, and that's why they always yammer for babies. . . . When she held one of those strong young bodies in her arms, she could never help thinking that he was marked to die. But the boys never thought of it. It was never tomorrow with them, always Now. Well, good for them.

Otto closed his eyes for a moment, and immediately he cut through the threadwork of the tracers and there was the jolt, and the blue flames and the air draught blew them into the pit and it got hot in the crate and there was that awful moment when his foot got stuck and he was done for and then he began falling. . . .

"Don't go to sleep on me, Schnucki," he heard Tilli say and was relieved that she had got him out of it. It repeated itself again and again; the tracers, the burst, the jolt, the blue flames, and his foot getting stuck; it was like a film that rolled off incessantly the moment he let himself go, and he couldn't stop it. The effect of the Pervitine, too, had begun to wear off and he could feel the blue jitters coming on.

"Come, have a drink," Tilli said, expert as a nurse. "It's my own special. Strictly dynamite." He drank the powerful, nasty-tasting synthetic stuff and felt better.

"Maybe it isn't so terrible that I lost her," he said, deep in thought. "I felt terrible about it when it happened. I could have cried, honestly. But maybe they'll give me one of their new ME-109s, that would be something ! Millner took one up the other day and he was simply crazy about her. And that's not all. A fellow who came over from Linz the other day told us that they are preparing for a big surprise. But a *real* surprise—I can't talk about it, but I have a good idea what it will be."

Speculations about secret weapons, new super methods and miracle planes were the daily bread of all air bases. Like children they waited for the great magician who had pulled so many rabbits from his hat to pull out a few more and win the war by some spectacular, entirely unexpected trick. They saw the might of the Allied air raids increasing, the strain on themselves getting harder and harder; flying a plane now was not the hilarious fun it had been for those early heroes who had gone over to London once or twice a week and had been cuddled and pampered like precious racehorses in the comfortable, long periods of rest in between. Now they had to go up every night, stay up for hours, fight never-ending waves of bombers. Invariably there were not quite enough of themselves and too many of the others, and the Tommies and Yankees always got through. But while this made the boys feel depressed and overworked at times, they never doubted for a moment that they were winning the war and that their difficulties were only temporary. Things might not be so good in their own sector at the moment, but look at the brilliant victories we're having elsewhere ! The Fuehrer knows

what he's doing. He has something big up his sleeve again
—and that's why he keeps us short of planes just now. . . .

"How long do you think this war is going to last?" Tilli
asked, interrupting his fantasies.

"That's all you civilians ask! How long is it going to
last?" he said, disturbed. "It'll last until we have beaten
the others to a pulp, that's how long it will last. If you ask
me, I hope it won't be over too soon. I like war," Otto said
with innocent conviction. "I don't even want to think of the
end of the war. War is good. It's a man's life; I like it. Peace
is like stagnant water. It stinks, it's rotten. Peace——" he
said, and suddenly his voice began to waver. "I can't see
what a fellow like me will do after the war. Go back to
school? That's a bad joke! Well, what? Become a taxicab
driver? That's what flying in peacetime amounts to. No,
thanks, not for me."

"That's true. You boys are getting the best of everything,"
Tilli said. She had been trying all the time to find an opening
for what she wanted to ask him. "Nice uniforms, good food.
Plenty of meat and butter, and coffee and everything. Is it
true that they give you real coffee?"

"Yes, and we need it, too. You have no idea what a cup
of real coffee and a cigarette will do when you come down—
like I came down, for instance."

"Could you get some for me?"

"Get what? Coffee? You must be crazy. I'll give you
fifty marks. How's that?"

"I need coffee," Tilli said, stubbornly steering her course.
"Listen, Schnucki," she said and turned the sex tap full on,
"I will tell you how it is. I need shoes and I can't get shoes,
not for fifty marks and not for a thousand. I don't want
money from you. I like you, I'm crazy about you, Schnucki;
keep your money. I wouldn't take money from a sweet boy
like you. But I think I could get shoes for half a pound of
coffee. Adolf says his father knows a party who might barter
a pair of shoes for coffee. Adolf is one of the little pageboys
downstairs and his father has a small shoe repair shop; he
had to close up on account of the Total Mobilization, and now
little Adolf has to support the whole family. And Adolf
says if I'd give him ten marks and get some real coffee for that
party, there is a good chance of me getting the shoes. Look
here, Schnucki, you told me yourself that you shot down eleven

planes and that you might get the Knight's Cross. Well, if
they can give you the Knight's Cross, why couldn't they give
you half a pound of coffee ? Maybe the doctor could prescribe
it for you, since you got these burns."

Otto had hardly listened; his thoughts had taken a hazy
promenade.

"I'll bet you if I made a play for that Lisa Dorn she wouldn't
hold out long," he said, his nude, bare eyes dreamily fastened
on Tilli's act photos on the wall.

"Yes, and if I wasn't a fool I would have spent the evening
with a good friend of mine—a very high man in the party—
a Gauleiter—and he would have got me a pair of new shoes
like that !" Tilli shouted, getting very sore. The flier laughed.
He wanted her now; she was angry and he liked her angry.
He wanted to pin her arms down and wrestle with her and
feel very strong and masterful and do with her anything he
wanted. "Come, come," he said. "I was only joking. I like
you—sure, I'll get you coffee. I'll get you shoes—anything
you want. Don't let's talk so much—turn down the light—
take off that silly kimono—why are we wasting so much time ?"
He opened his arms, closed his eyes and moved over on the
narrow couch to make space for her. Dammit, and there it
was again. The tracers, the burst, the jolt, the blue flames;
he was burning, he wanted to jump and couldn't. Suddenly
his nerves went all to pieces. It was an awful feeling. He felt
like crying and he didn't want to cry. He felt like trembling
and he didn't want to tremble. He felt like dying and he
didn't want to die. He heard Tilli rustle in the corner, and
then the gramophone began once more to play the old forbidden
record. But neither Pervitin nor the coarse temptations of
sex could overcome the deadly exhaustion any longer. He
bailed out and began to fall and to fall and to fall. . . .

Look at our hero, Tilli thought grimly, as she scrutinized
the scarred, slackening face of the young flier. Passed out
before making love. His mouth hung open and he breathed
stertorously. She picked up her kimono, wrapped herself in
it and, lying down at the exhausted boy's side, switched off
the light.

Number 69, too, harboured an exhausted sleeper. Martin Richter had talked to Lisa until he had been overcome by a sleep as deep and dark as a well; sleeping, he had slipped down a bit in the easy chair near the window, his long legs sprawling, his hands limp but restless as the paws of a dreaming dog. There was now a fresh bandage on his shoulder, and as he shivered from time to time Lisa had thrown a rug over him. But he had fought with it and torn it away in his sleep, because, dreaming, he was caught in coils of barbed wire and had to get away and save Annemarie.

Lisa pulled up another chair, and with her elbows between her knees, her chin resting on her knuckles, she watched over his sleep while she was thinking. As it was the first time in her life that she thought independently and for herself, it was hard work. Her untrained mind had trouble sorting out the lies from the truth, the right from the wrong. Hardly five hours had passed since this rebellious, burning, demanding stranger had broken into her room, but it seemed like a lifetime, and yesterday had been a thousand years ago.

It was ten minutes to two when she heard familiar steps coming down the corridor and stopping in front of the door. All her senses were sharpened, so that she even heard the general's heavy breathing as he inserted the key in the keyhole. The bolt was locked. There was nothing now between Martin and his discovery but this little bolt.

The danger woke up every instinct in Lisa and made her alert as a hunted animal. She pressed her hand tight over Martin's mouth before he could make a sound. With a start he woke up at the click of the key, and his eyes, his crouch, his fist were those of a killer. They had stopped breathing, both of them. Then the key retreated and there came a gentle, polite knock at the door. "Who is it? Is it you, Arnim?" Lisa asked, as if anyone but the general had a key to her room.

"May I come in for a moment?" the Victor of Kharkov whispered outside. It sounded so meek that Lisa regained her balance.

"It's very late, dear—and I'm so tired," she said in her sweetest voice to the door. A throat was cleared out there, and there was some more heavy breathing.

"Please open the door. I must talk to you. Now," said the general. It was not a lover's plea but a military command, and Lisa obeyed automatically. Martin had vanished without a sound; she did not know where to. She steadied her breath, went over and opened a small slit of the door, but the general pushed it open and entered.

"You weren't asleep? I saw light under your door," he said.

Lisa's first reaction was not fear but anger. Suddenly she found it preposterous that the general had a key to her room and could enter whenever it pleased him, day or night. . . . As if I were something stored away in an old trunk, for him to take out and put back at will. Does he think I belong to him? I belong to no one but myself, she thought. . . . It was one of the many amazing new-born thoughts of this amazing night.

"I was working on my part. Portia," she said pointing her chin at the book as at an alibi. The general did not seem to listen. He dropped down in the chair where Martin had just now been asleep, and took out a cigar. "Do you mind?" he asked perfunctorily, and lit it. This, again, appeared preposterously possessive to her. Yes, I mind, she thought in full rebellion. She did not know that the general was holding on to this cigar as to a lifebelt in great distress. In a cold panic Lisa realized that the general would proceed to make love to her as soon as he was through with his cigar—and with Martin as a secret witness. Suddenly this seemed the worst danger of them all, worse than anything that might happen. She wondered where Martin was hiding, while her heart grew hard and small, like a clenched fist. A little disc of light flitted over the ceiling. It was, she perceived with her sharpened sensibility, the lamp reflected in the mirrored bathroom door, which moved ever so slightly. She went over, closed that door and leaned her back against it.

"I really didn't expect you so late," she said. "I was just about to go to bed. I'm tired."

"I'm sorry. I had to see you now. Had to."

"Why now? It's a funny hour to make a visit."

"I tried to phone you, but there was no answer. It's very urgent, very urgent, or I wouldn't break in on you like this, child."

Lisa threw a quick glance at the unplugged telephone. So did the general. She gave a little laugh. "It's a habit—

when I memorize," she said. "What happened? Do you have to go back to the front at once?" she added. The general took a long pull at his cigar and watched the ashes turn white at the tip of it; he was trying to gain time—and time had now become so short and precious.

"No. I don't go back to the front. In fact, I'm not wanted at the front," he said at last.

"I don't understand——"

"I'm out. I'm *persona non grata.*"

"Oh, my dear heaven!" Lisa said, sincerely startled. "Why? What happened?"

"There are certain questions of a military nature on which I don't agree with the commander-in-chief."

"Oh," said Lisa. It was the small staccato cry of a frightened bird. Her image of the world had changed very much during this night. But the Fuehrer was still untouchable to her. To disagree with the Fuehrer was blasphemous.

"But you said he was a genius. You said he was charming," she said, groping through the fog.

"I don't wish to discuss with you now what I really think of this corporal Schickelgruber. There is not enough time. We are flying to Sweden tonight. You must get dressed."

"Flying to Sweden? But Arnim——"

"Yes. Tonight. Now," the general said. The ashes from his cigar dropped on his lap, but he didn't notice it.

"But Arnim, what is all this? How can I fly to Sweden with you? I have a rehearsal at ten in the morning and a performance tomorrow night."

"Don't be so childish, Lisa," he said with a smile that was much too small for his face. "Have you no sense of proportion? Someone else will play your part tomorrow. It's entirely unimportant."

It was a remark that set Lisa Dorn ablaze. "Unimportant? And what would my audience say if someone else were to play Portia?"

"I don't know and I don't care. Get dressed now, get dressed! I'll arrange to get some sort of a car to take us to the Tempelhofer airport. I phoned my pilot to have the plane ready." He saw the expression on her face and tried to be persuasive. "If everything goes well we can have breakfast in Stockholm. You'll like Sweden. It's a beautiful country, beautiful."

Lisa kept on shaking her head; she had almost forgotten the boy hidden in the bathroom. "You sound as if you were drunk, Arnim. You don't want me to break my contract just so you can have breakfast with me in Stockholm? Or is it all a bad joke? Don't you know what discipline is? Do you think only generals have discipline? We of the stage have our discipline too. Unimportant! Portia, unimportant! Why, it's one of the most important parts there is; it's not something any little understudy can play. I'm sorry, Arnim, but you'll have to go now. I must have my rest or I'll make a mess of the part tomorrow."

During the two hours since Von Stetten had left him, the general had made a complete departure from every law and tradition a long chain of ancestors had bred into him. Honest, proud, stiff-necked, one-track-minded men, every one of them, without any imagination but the peculiar one that thinks up battles. Until tonight Arnim von Dahnwitz had been such an honest, proud, stiff-necked, one-track-minded man himself. Toe the line. Abide by the laws of the caste. Live and die according to the hidebound rules of Prussian nobility, that sparse, hardy product of the sandy fields, the sour meadows, the harsh north-eastern winds, the grey cloudy skies, the underprivileged landscape, the meagre soil from which they sprang. Only under the impact of the final and irrevocable decision of this night had the general rebelled. . . . Goddamit, I'm no goddam bloody Japanese and I don't have to commit this goddamned hara-kiri. Kill myself—why? To please the pack? To make way for Hitler's smart boys? Honour? What has my honour to do with these criminals? I don't want to kill myself, I want to live. Disgraceful, ignominious, dishonourable? No—only rational. Simple common sense. I want to live and see the day when that whole baggage of Piefkes will be done away with and I'll be vindicated.

Steaming with sweat, swearing, suffering, fighting himself into retreat inch by inch, the general had reached his extraordinary decision. It had catapulted him into Lisa's room, for if they wanted to flee to Sweden there was no time to lose. But not for a second in all this mortal struggle had it occurred to the general that Lisa could make difficulties. It left him helpless, and the cold sweat began to pour out of his pores again. He got up and moved toward the bathroom door.

"What do you want?" Lisa asked, pressing herself against

the door; she was suddenly made of steel and iron, hard to the core, not even frightened any longer.

"A glass of water. I don't feel quite well. This dentist and his goddamned novocaine," the general said with laborious composure.

"Wait—I'll get it for you," she said; she went into the bathroom, closing the door behind her and struggling for breath. It was dark in there and she couldn't see Martin, but she felt in every vibrating nerve that he was there. If the general came after her now, everything was lost. She groped for the tap and let the cool water run over her wrists. Then, in the deep, thick darkness a hand came and pressed down on hers, reassuring, calming, deeply dear and familiar. She stood for a second motionless, in the centre of a rainbow; then the bathroom door opened and a trickle of light filtered in. "What are you doing in there so long?" the general asked.

"I'm getting the water really cold," she said calmly; with the glass in her hand she pressed against him, pushing him gently back into the room.

"Thanks," he said, after he had emptied the glass. She sat down quickly because now her legs seemed to be without bones.

"Look here, child," the general said—and he heard the clock tick and felt the time running away like sand and he tried to be patient. "I don't seem to have expressed myself clearly. I don't want to sound melodramatic, but the climate here isn't healthy for me. The Gestapo are an impatient crowd, a most impatient crowd, and they have very few inhibitions. As matters stand there's no other way open but to fly to Sweden tonight. I have good friends in Sweden. We could live on some charming country estate and bide our time. There are nice lakes for swimming and fishing, and I could teach you horseback riding—good shooting, too——"

"You sound like a travel advertisement for Sweden," Lisa said dryly. "But I don't see what I've got to do with it. If you feel like taking a vacation from the war and leaving your post in the midst of the fray, that's your business. I can't understand it, but it's your business. As for me, I couldn't dream of going with you. I'm not your private property," she said, getting more and more agitated. "I'm not a parcel you can ship around at your pleasure, I have my own life. I'm an actress, I want to act. I want to be on the stage and play my parts. That's where I belong. Why should I go to Sweden? I couldn't understand a word of their language. I would be nobody. I know how it would be. I would sit with your fish-eyed Swedish friends and let them snub me while you go hunting. I see no reason in the world why I should go into exile with you."

Because I need you; because you can't leave me when I'm down. Because I love you, was what the general felt; but being entirely incapable of expressing such things, he drew himself up and said rather stiffly: "You misunderstand me completely, Lisa. I don't ask you to run away with me like a gypsy. I don't invite you to go on a week-end trip with me. I'm asking you to be my wife."

After putting down this trump, the general stood straight and erect, his hands at the crimson stripes of his trousers. Lisa did not know whether to laugh or to cry. It was so hopelessly outmoded, a bad scene from a very old, very poor play. . . . Poor Arnim, stupid Victor of Kharkov, haven't you noticed that times have changed?

"Thank you, Arnim. That's very sweet of you—and—and I appreciate it. Believe me, I do. But I don't want to get married," she said with as much politeness as she could muster. She saw herself walking down an avenue with Dahnwitz, and he was old and rheumatic, a retired general hobbling on a cane, and she wasn't a day older than she was now, but dressed in a horrid black alpaca dress and wearing a nightmare of a hat—the dress and the hat the general's dead wife wore in that photo he always carried around with him—and the path was covered with yellow autumn leaves and lost in fog. "No—I don't want to get married," she repeated gently. "I'm too young—and too greedy."

Suddenly the general had enough of this, and his Mongolian temper broke over the dams of his Prussian self-control. "You'll go with me," he said under his breath. "You'll go with me whether you like it or not. You'll do what I tell you. You're a child and you don't understand what is at stake. If you don't go with me, I can't go either. It makes it impossible. I can't leave you behind. Impossible." He took her shoulders in his hands and began to shake her. "Don't make me angry. Don't make me impatient," he said, still holding on to himself. "I've made my decision, and, by God, it wasn't

an easy decision to make, not easy. I'm ready to give up
everything, but I won't give you up. I want to live and I
want to live with you, do you hear me?" He let go of her
shoulders and squeezed her between his arms, but it was not
an embrace. He linked his right hand around his left wrist
behind her back and pressed her to him in a cold fury, increasing the pressure until he hurt her, until his wrist turned white,
until his muscles began to tremble with the strain and Lisa
felt as if she were caught in the coils of a python. "I can't
go away and leave you here," he began between his clenched
teeth, but before he knew it he had thrown off the bridle and
was shouting and screaming. "You don't know what will
happen to you. You don't know what is in store for Germany.
The war is lost. It's going to end more horribly than anything
in all history. It will make the blood bath of the French
Revolution look like a puny drizzle. Everyone against everyone. The party against the people, the army against the SS,
the Gestapo against the army, the workers against the soldiers,
the South against the North; oh my God, brother against
brother, and the whole world against Germany! Rivers of
blood, rivers! Barricades in the streets—they will build their
barricades from the bodies of killed people. You don't know
slaughter—but I do, I've seen its face, I know what's coming.
Not a stone left of the cities—not a safe corner for you to
hide. You do what I tell you! You go away with me tonight.
I can't go without you. If I go and leave you behind they'll
take it out on you. Don't you understand? Are you too stupid
to see what's at stake for me? And for you too, yes, for you
too. Do I have to beat you up to make you understand?"

He let go of her abruptly, his chest working like a black-
smith's bellows, sweat streaming down his temples. He
paced up and down the room twice and then came back
to her and began pounding her shoulders with both his fists.

Lisa was impressed. She was also somewhat disgusted.
He had frightened her and hurt her physically, and a hysterical
general was a disappointing sight. And that boy behind the
door heard every word of this, she thought fleetingly. She was
ashamed for the general in some queer way; she had lost
all respect for him during his outburst; nothing was left but
some faint pity.

"I think you have a bit of a fever—that's what's the matter
with you," she said; it sounded flat and much too sober after

the apocalyptic storm of Dahnwitz's prophecies. "You can't go around making defeatist speeches like that. Maybe you're a bit overworked. And that whole idea of going to Sweden sounds insane. Why don't you take a leave and go to Elgede and rest for a few weeks? Let the High Command take care of your war for a change."

The general tried hard to regain his countenance after the outbreak. Such rages always left him limp, with a bad taste and a feeling of having been beaten. "Come, sit down with me, child," he said civilly. "Let's talk sensibly. It's getting late." He threw an anxious glance through his monocle at his relentlessly ticking wristwatch, lifted Lisa up and placed her on his lap as if she were really only a child. She struggled, but he was too strong and she gave in. "You remember who York was ? York von Wartenberg ? He was a Prussian officer as I am—in fact our families are related to each other. Some day I'm going to show you a golden travel necessaire of his which we still have in Elgede. [No, there won't be such a thing as some day, he knew sadly.] Well, York was one man who didn't toe the line. Didn't toe the line, no. When the King of Prussia and all the little potentates of Germany had their armies fighting on Napoleon's side, York was the only one who foresaw what was coming and acted accordingly. He went over to the Russians and fought Napoleon before anyone else in Germany did. You see, child, York made his decision. Yes, he too made his decision," Dahnwitz said. "For a while he was looked upon as a scoundrel, a deserter, a traitor. But when the war of liberation came and all of Germany rose against Napoleon, York returned as a great hero. Yes. He returned with honours. Do you see what I want to tell you ? I want to serve my country the way York did. I refuse to go on covering the bloody, costly blunders this crazy corporal is making, this gambler, this Piefke and his men, this adventurer, this cursed dilettante! I have had enough of it, enough, enough. I have it up to here. I'm a soldier, I'm not a butcher's apprentice. I'm in disgrace now. But there will be a time when they'll need men like me, as truly as my name is Dahnwitz. That's why I want to go to Sweden. I have friends through whom I can keep a hand in the game, and prepare for the day when the country will call me back. It will take an iron hand to prevent chaos and revolution, an iron hand; reorganize the army, drive out these punch-drunk Partei-Bonzen; get the

country back to our old ideals of discipline and obedience.
That's when Germany will have a place for me again."

He thought that he had said everything that was to be said;
Lisa remained silent and the minutes ticked swiftly, irretrievably by. Lisa was fighting her way through a tangle of bewilder-
ing thoughts. Her world had come crashing down on her, and
she was trying to make order out of the debris. The strange
thing about it was that Martin Richter and General von
Dahnwitz both seemed to have no doubt that the war was lost,
that the State was rotten, and that Germany was going down;
both wanted to be there to help the country. Both were
persecuted because they had given up their allegiance to the
Fuehrer and his men. The difference was that Martin Richter
and his friends were only a few, and what they wanted was
freedom. But the general and his caste hoped to sweep the
whole army with them when it came to the final showdown,
and the only solution they knew was the old one: Power.
Iron discipline. Blind obedience. Keep the army intact for
the next war and the next one. . . .

"Don't you ever get tired of war?" Lisa asked when she
came to the end of her thoughts. It was an unexpected
question, and the general groped for an answer.

"Very tired. Unspeakably tired sometimes, child. But man
is a fighting animal. There will be wars as long as there will
be men. All we can do, then, is to breed and train the best
soldiers in the world, keep a strong army, and believe in God."

Lisa struggled faintly in his arms: the smell of cigars on
his breath irritated her. Up to now she had thought it a
manly smell. She was only beginning to grow up and become
a woman.

"I've said all I have to say; what is your answer now that
you know everything?" Dahnwitz asked, almost humbly.

"You know it even before asking. You can't run away.
You wouldn't be the man you are if you did. You aren't
meant to have breakfast in Sweden while Germany is at war.
We need you here; it's your war. The Fuehrer won't drop a
man like you because of a disagreement. You'll be back at the
front in a week."

"What a bright little girl you are!" he said grimly. "You
think it's like your theatre. First there is—how do you call
it?—a row and a stink and after a little while you shake
hands and everything is forgotten."

"Generals have been dismissed and called back again, you know."

"I didn't think you noticed," Dahnwitz said. He had lost, and this was his last battle. He was stone sober now, very tired, very sad, but calm and at ease. . . . No breakfast in Stockholm for Arnim von Dahnwitz. No, it doesn't do for a Prussian officer to use common sense. We aren't made for it. We've got to leave that to the Jews, and the Americans, he thought.

"You must go now," Lisa said. "I can't keep my eyes open much longer." She was still on his lap, her warmth still seeping through his tunic into his chest.

"Can't I stay with you a little while?" he whispered into her ear. He was a humble old man again. One more time, something demanded in him. One last time.

"No. No," she answered in a panic. "Not now. Not tonight. I'm tired. And your toothache—we're not in a romantic mood, are we?"

"As you command," he said with great correctness. He put his arms around her small weightless person and pressed the air from her lungs in a desperate hard embrace before he let go of her.

"Good night, my love. Sleep well."

He put her down on the floor and straightened his tunic. She looked at him faintly worried.

"You won't do anything silly, Arnim?"

"No; I'm an old hand at this game. Don't worry about me."

"And what have you decided? You won't go to Sweden?"

"No, I don't think so. You've changed my mind for me. It wouldn't make sense to go there without you. Please, do me the favour and forget it. It was just a mood. Maybe I had a little too much champagne on top of the novocaine. Good night. Good night, my dear."

He marched to the door so rigidly that Lisa felt sorry for him. "Do you want to take me out for lunch tomorrow?" she asked, to make up for having treated him badly.

"Tomorrow? For lunch?"

"Around one o'clock. After my rehearsal."

"Yes. Of course. That would be charming."

"Good night, my little toy soldier," said Lisa; it was a name she had given him in the beginning of their affair, and forgotten. She was so happy to get rid of him at last that she could afford to be generous. When the general reached the door something strange took place. He took the monocle from his eye. Lisa had never seen him without it. It made him much older and took all his arrogance away. He had taken it off because it had been blurred by something, and now he wiped it thoroughly with his handkerchief before he clamped it into his eyesocket again. Lisa did not know that she had seen the Victor of Kharkov cry.

"*Au revoir*," he said and marched back to the Luger that was waiting for him on the table in his room.

Lisa looked after him until he had disappeared down the stairway. The guard was still there, a young fellow who seemed to have started a little flirtation with the sleepy chambermaid at the night desk near the stairs. Lisa closed the door softly and locked it with the bolt. Martin had come out from the bathroom and pulled back the black-out curtains. The first glimmer of dawn came up over the city. Beyond the bombed houses on the other side of the street, the sky began to dilute in a thin lemon-coloured gleam. Martin stepped out on the little balcony warily, like an animal stepping out into a clearing in the woods at dawn, and studied the situation. When he turned his face toward her, she could see from his expression that the Gestapo had its men down at the main entrance too.

"I am lots of trouble to you," he said.

"I know," said Lisa.

"You could have given me away. But you didn't."

"No. I didn't."

She was still standing at the door, and he was standing over there, at the opposite wall, near the window. She had known him a hundred years. She had never known anyone but him.

He lifted his arms and she rushed toward him, as if the room were on fire.

SHE was braiding her hair before the mirror on her dressing-table, at the same time examining her face with a curious, close scrutiny. She studied her eyes, her mouth, she lifted her arms and looked at them, she even turned and tried to examine her own shoulder from the back. No. Nothing had changed, and yet everything was different.

"As if I were still the same person," she said accusingly to the mirror. Martin was standing at the window, protected from sight by the folds of the curtains. Lisa couldn't cease to wonder at his sure movements, each of them designed to give him cover and yet leave to him the freedom of choice of defence or attack. Outside there was a cold, bright morning with streams of yellow sunlight.

"As I thought," he muttered, stepping back. "They're all over the place."

"I wish I could say abracadabra swish swish swish and make you invisible."

"Gaston will spirit me away somehow; trust the old man."

Lisa went to the alcove, plugged in the telephone and picked up the receiver. "Room service? Please, will you tell Gaston to bring up my breakfast? . . . Oh. Oh—I see. . . . No—thanks; in that case I'd rather go downstairs to the breakfast room. Thanks."

She was a little pale as she put down the receiver and mechanically unplugged the telephone again.

"Gaston has been arrested," Martin said behind her, and it was not a question.

"They say he won't be here today. They're short of waiters, they say."

"I was afraid of it. Poor Gaston. Poor old fellow. They'll try to make him talk."

"Don't worry. We'll find something. I'll get you out of here somehow. Please, please don't worry."

"I'm not worrying," Martin said. "I'm not worrying a bit about myself, and you mustn't either. This is nothing. It's fun. I've been in other spots. Lord, you don't know what spots I've been in and got out of alive. I'm worrying about Gaston—and about the others. They still had three of us to execute. And Father Antonius in prison—he was the one who sent me to Gaston and Philippe; and the guard on the truck— I couldn't have got off if he hadn't looked the other way. They'll all suffer hell on account of me; instead of helping the others, I make it worse for them." He bit his lip, thinking hard. "And you," he added. "I've got you into this, and, by God, it's no game for a helpless little fool like you."

"I'm not helpless. That's just a pose," she said absent-mindedly. She felt storms of strength surging inside of her. She bent down, plugged the phone in once more and called Number 86 on the fifth floor. "Johannes Koenig. He'll help us. He'll know what to do," she said gaily over her shoulder. "He always has ideas. He's a great big bag full of imagination. Good morning, Your Majesty," she called into the telephone. . . . "Yes, I know, it's wretched to wake you up so early, but I've got to see you. Put on your least disreputable gown and be ready to receive me. Yes, yes, it's very important. It's about your play. Wait here," she said eagerly to Martin. "Lock the bolt, and not a sound out of you while I'm gone. I'll get an army to break the siege. This is no Stalingrad. Quiet now."

Johannes Koenig was no morning beauty; he had thrown a soiled, tattered mandarin coat over his old-fashioned night-shirt, and his eyes were glued like a new-born kitten's. The black-out curtains were still pulled down, it was dark in his room and the fumes of wine and sleep hung around him. A half-empty bottle stood on the table.

"'Air for the wretched one,'" Lisa quoted *Faust* as she pulled curtains and windows open.

"I don't like hurricanes to get into my hair at the dawn of morn," Johannes grumbled. She pushed him on to a chair, sat down opposite him, took his hands in hers and began to talk at once.

"Listen to me—this is important. It is about your play. It's time you finished it, and last night I got an idea for your third act. Listen well. At the end of the second act a company of Napoleon's soldiers have been billeted in Schloss Adlersruh. Irene has gone to her room. Now then: the third act doesn't play in the village inn as you planned it, it plays in her room. She finds a stranger hiding there, a young man, dishevelled, wounded, desperate. At first she is mortified; then he begins to talk and she realizes that he, too, is German. One of the few and young conspirators who are preparing the future uprising against Napoleon. He is a fugitive, and there is a high price on his head. Irene has always been a pampered, spoiled, thoughtless creature, blinded by Napoleon's glory and pleased to flirt with his smart officers. Now, for the first time, her eyes are opened. For the first time she learns the truth, she hears about the gallant young men who are willing to give their

lives to fight the usurper. You're a poet, Johannes, you'll
be able to explain what happens to her soul—much better than
I can. It is something like a rebirth; she helps the fugitive,
hides him during the night—and when the morning comes she
knows that she, too, is ready to die, if she can help him in
the liberation of the country——"

"She has fallen in love with him," Koenig broke in; he
had listened with faint interest at first, then with growing
attention, and at last fascinatedly. His faded blue eyes came
creeping out of their nests of bushy white brows. "Yes; she
falls in love with him. It may be melodramatic, but it's inevitable."

"Do you think that's what happened to her, Johannes?"
Lisa said, and there was a strange humility in her voice. For
a little while she sat deep in thought and then she took the
hurdle bravely. "Yes. You're right. I believe she couldn't
help falling in love with him. Can you picture that night?
There is death waiting behind every door. Downstairs the
Napoleonic officers are drinking—one of them even tries to
break into her room——"

"I can see it. I can see it. Love and death, the eternal
brothers. All they have is this bitter, sweet, dangerous,
one and only night. They know there is no tomorrow for
them. The proximity of death makes their love flare sky-high
—the curtain comes down on their first embrace," Koenig
recited enthusiastically. Suddenly he sobered up and threw a
shrewd glance at Lisa. "Not bad," he said. "Melodramatic,
but not really bad. And where do we go from here? We've
got your young man trapped and your heroine madly in love.
The curtain goes up—and what happens then?"

"We have to get him out of Schloss Adlersruh and into the
fight for the liberation of Germany."

"Ah! Indeed? And how are we going to do that?"

"I don't know. I don't know, Johannes. That's what I
came to you for. You're a great writer—you must find a
way. All exits are watched—Napoleon still has all the power.
It takes a better brain than mine to find the twist that will
get him past the guards."

"Wait a moment—couldn't we use the old shepherd we
had in the first act? He has been Irene's friend since her
childhood. He is an old man. Life has almost run out for
him. 'I'm only holding on to the shirt-tail of life; take the

tattered bit and use it to save this fiery youth,' he says to her."

"Yes, Johannes. I was sure he would say that. He is the only real friend she ever had. He must help her," Lisa said, summoning every shred of intensity as in a climax scene on the stage. Koenig gazed at her through a long, undulating silence. Suddenly he took his hands out of hers and pulled back his chair. His coat and the wine-stained nightshirt stood open, and with a small shudder of disgust she saw the shaggy white hair on his old man's chest. He walked up and down the cramped room twice and stopped in front of her, once more fixing his watery, red-rimmed eyes upon her in a mute question. Lisa answered with a nod and a guilty smile. Slowly the smile faded while the roots of her hair began to tingle with shame and anger. She saw Koenig's face clear and unmasked as never before, with its lines of slackness and stagnation and decay. Even before he opened his mouth she knew the answer.

"Don't let's misunderstand each other, my dear," he said. "We are discussing my play. We're talking about the third act of *The Purple Hour* and of nothing else. Of nothing else ! I want you to realize this quite definitely. I don't want to hear anything else. I don't want to know anything else. I refuse—do you hear me ?—I refuse to be told anything else. On second thought I don't like your idea anyway. Melo-dramatic. Cheap drama. Very old-fashioned, too. If—if Irene follows a little whim and amuses herself for one night with some sort of young firebrand—*bon!* Such things happen and are soon forgotten. If she has any sense she'll wash her hands of the whole affair the next morning. Let him see for himself how to get out of the trap, the young fool. Yes, Lisel. That's the only thing I have to say. I don't want to hear any more of it, and I don't want—Irene to have any further traffic with her idiotic *Freiheitskaempfer.*"

"Is that your last word ? Really ?"

"Yes. My first and my last word," Koenig said. Lisa dropped her hands in her lap in a gesture of despair. "So that's that," she said, crushed. "And I counted on you."

Suddenly a slack, resigned, tired variety of agitation over-took the writer. "How could you count on me, of all people ? What have I ever done to justify your childish faith in my vulnerable person ? What could you expect from a punctured old windbag like me ? All the beautiful words I have written ?

All the golden sounds and clarion calls that come out of my pen? Don't you know the difference between writing and doing? I'm a writer and nothing else. I'm not a hero and not a fighter and not a doer; maybe I'm not even a man. My business is piecing beautiful words together so that they make music. I can write you a battle hymn that will drive cohorts of young men into the fray and make them win or die. But I can't shoot a gun myself. I can tell you in emerald language all about freedom and human dignity and the beauty of self-sacrifice. Having done so, I've exhausted myself and there's just enough energy left to order a bottle of Burgundy. Heavens, Lisel, if I were constituted differently, do you think I should still be here, in this hotel, in this town where the ground under our feet is rotten and the roof will cave in any moment? Wait—there's something else I have to say. Things are never simple, they always have three dimensions—and sometimes more. I didn't string along with the Nazis because it was the easiest thing to do. I believed in them. I believed in the Fuehrer, for a long time. I believed in him. I believed that here was the saviour of this unhappy, tragic country of ours. I was made drunk, we all were. Then, when I sobered up and the most horrible hang-over on a nation-wide scale began to set in, it was too late to extricate myself. Now the substance of myself is gone. I'm a writer who doesn't even write. I'm a coward. I'm an impotent eunuch, and I forbid you to come here and disturb me and blow trumpets into my ears. Go to the devil, you and your third act and your young man. Go, leave me alone. Out with you. I'll have to get very drunk very quickly and forget what you've told me. There must still be some wine left from last night. . . ."

Lisa went heavily up the stairs to the fourth floor and past the SS man who was trying to look as though he were not posted there but were a casual and accidental visitor to the hotel. She did not dare to knock at her own door but signalled her presence with a little cough. When nothing happened inside she pressed the handle down and found the bolt unlocked. For a moment she could not find Martin, and then there was some rustling and he stepped out of the big wardrobe; he was grinning widely as if he were enjoying himself.

"You see? I said abracadabra swish swish swish and became invisible," he announced cheerfully. "Well?" he asked as he noticed the drawn paleness of her face.

"I brought you some cigarettes and a shirt," she said. "It will be too large, but it's better than nothing."

"I see. Is that all?"

"Yes, that's all."

"I didn't think the old man would function," he said. For a few minutes they smoked silently. "What are we to do now?" Lisa asked at last.

"Now you're going to your rehearsal as if nothing had happened and let me look after myself."

"I won't leave you now; I'd rather die."

"What is this? Big drama?" he said. "We can't afford to be noble now. We must be practical. If you miss your rehearsal there will be endless fuss and I'll be caught. With you out of here and everything normal, I'll have a good chance. If you don't want me to be caught, you must take orders from me."

"Yes, I see. At your command, Corporal Richter."

"First you must put a little pink on your cheeks. You look like apple sauce with spittle. Then you go downstairs and have a good, big breakfast and you go to your rehearsal and see that you don't fumble your lines. Afterwards, if I am not wrong, you have a luncheon date with the Victor of Kharkov and you will be very charming with the old devil, and tonight you'll give a beautiful performance. Afterwards you will be dead tired because you didn't get much rest last night and you'll sleep very well. Tomorrow—but tomorrow will take care of itself. It always does."

"And where will you be while I do all these charming things? What will happen to you? If they get you— Martin, don't you see it's impossible, I can't do what you want."

"What a confounded theatrical little fool you are," he said, and he was very sorry for her. "But that's the only way to be brave. That's the only way to help me."

"Yes. All right. I will try. When am I going to see you again?"

Martin's smile deepened; there were two clefts in his cheeks when he smiled. "Fool!" he said; "you silly, dumb little fool!"

Never again? Lisa thought, but she did not say it. Never again? the man asked in his heart. "Soon," he said. "If things don't work out well, it's quite possible that you'll find me still hiding in your wardrobe when you get back."

"But if things do work out well—where can I find you? Can you give me some address? You said you had friends who would help you on from there——"

Rittergasse 39. Ask for Walter, he thought. "Sorry— I can't tell you anything," he said curtly.

"Can't you?"

"No. They have rather unfriendly methods for making you tell what you know. It is better for you to know nothing."

Lisa's lips went stiff and cold. "Makes me feel awfully important," she said, trying to smile with these stiff, cold lips.

"You must go now and have breakfast," he said strictly.

"Yes, I'm getting ready."

The grey suit, the hemstitched blouse, the impertinent little Parisian hat, the bag, the gloves. "Now," she said, without breath. "Now."

"You were very good to me. I won't forget it. And you must not forget what I told you last night," Martin said, standing over there, at the other end of the room. Lisa went over to him and looked up to him, seriously and steadily like a child. "Tell it to me once more—please," she said. "You know; what you told me last night. How it will be."

"It will be like being healthy again after a long, bad sickness," he said, almost soundless, reaching out for her hands and slowly pulling them up to his chest until they came to rest over his heart. "There will be a day when all this will seem like a bad dream and a fever, all of it. There will be peace, and the prisons will be opened, and we shall all go back to the sweet, simple business of living. The farmers in the fields and the workers in the factories and the students in the universities and the scientists in their laboratories and the women and children and the old men; they will all do nothing but live. Nobody will be afraid and nobody will have to be killed and nobody will have to be ashamed. I don't speak about the fight that will go before. It will be a cruel fight, but hopeful. I speak of the days afterwards, when everything will be good again."

"You must be very careful, promise me. I want you to be still there when your time comes. Promise me you will be there."

"I'll try very hard. I'm a great hand at surviving. You'll see."

"And until then—what am I going to do?"

"What you've done up to now. Be the best actress in the country. Some day I might sneak into the theatre and watch you and applaud you."

"Will I know when you are in the audience?"

"I don't think so. It's more like a lottery. Just suppose every time you act that I am there to watch you."

"Yes. That's good. Thank you. It's very nice of you to come and watch me playing."

Martin pushed her hand away from his heart. "Good-bye. You must go now," he said; his voice was rough with excitement and bitter grief.

"Good-bye," she said. She did not cry. She picked up the small paper-bound volume of Shakespeare and went to the door. When she looked back at him once more he was lighting a cigarette as concentratedly as if nothing else existed. His chest was still bare, the gothic framework of his ribs finely sculptured under the young skin, his shoulder bandaged, his arms boyish yet but strong, the thick unruly ringlets of hair falling dark over his forehead. . . . That's how I must remember you if I am never to see you again, she thought. . . . She closed the door behind her without a sound and fought down the sob that wanted to break her apart. As she went down the corridor she saw no guards, but that might only mean a better trap. Suddenly there were the lines of her part, taking her mind off herself, cooling, soothing, consoling—and now they had assumed a new sense and a fuller meaning:

> One half of me is yours, the other half yours—
> Mine own, I would say; but if mine, then yours,
> And so all yours. O! these naughty times
> Put bars between the owners and their rights;
> And so, though yours, not yours.

At ten o'clock, and with the usual fuss and flurry, Herr Wiedemann of the Deutschlandsender appeared in Geoffrey Nichols' room and handed him the manuscript for the broadcast of the evening. Fairly refreshed after a night without too much heart trouble, Nichols took the three pages and scanned through them.

"Once again I am speaking to you, an Englishman to Englishmen, to warn you against the propaganda lies your press and your government are spreading. Germany is as strong as ever, even stronger in its unbending determination to fight this war to a final and complete victory. You have tried in the past week to soften this will to victory through several air raids on defenceless cities, and you have paid with extremely heavy losses in planes and lives. Far from lowering the German morale, these air raids have only served to incense the inherent fighting spirit of the German people, and I feel bound to warn you that this *furor teutonicus* will take its ample revenge. My heart is bleeding, not only for the lives of the women and children who have been ruthlessly killed in these air raids, while the damage done to military objects was negligible. Nay, even more do I grieve for the English people who will have to pay tenfold and a hundredfold for the brutal and unwarranted attacks on civilians. . . ."

Nichols dropped the manuscript and began to haggle with Wiedemann. "Really, my dear fellow, I'd like to fluff it up a bit. This is not in character at all. If you will permit me to make it sound a trifle more natural. If you people insist on employing all these blockbusting sentences, none of my friends over there will believe that it is I who's talking."

"Sorry, Nichols. This is the manuscript that passed the control desk, and nothing can be altered in it."

"But, my good man, I don't question the content. I am talking about the style of the thing. After all, I am a writer of a certain reputation, and it seems utterly silly for me to hold forth like that."

"I don't see that anything is wrong with the style of the script," Wiedemann said stiffly. "It was written by one of our best men."

"Exactly. It's too dashed obvious that it wasn't written by myself. 'This *furor teutonicus* will take its ample revenge.' What an abominable mixed metaphor ! And 'my heart is bleeding.' Really, my dear Herr Wiedemann, you must know that an Englishman would rather swallow his tongue than broadcast to the world at large that his heart is bleeding. If you'd only permit me to make a few little changes. . . ."

It was the same quibble every Wednesday and Saturday ; Wiedemann was stubborn and dense as only an employee

D

afraid of losing his job can be, while Nichols, ironically enough, was agonized by the idea of lending his name to these badly written manifestos. During his imprisonment he had lost touch with reality to such an extent that he was afraid his style would be criticized in London's literary circles, but did not seem to realize that these broadcasts had made him a contemptuous outcast and that nobody gave a hoot for his style any longer. As usual, his heart began to get tight with the excitement of the dispute; his upper lip moist with perspiration, his breath pumping laboriously, he gave in, as usual. Wiedemann left, flushed and breathless himself. The spineless scoundrel! he cursed as he walked down the corridor. The piece of slime! Nobody could have a deeper contempt for the Englishman than the Germans who used him as a requisite of their propaganda.

Left alone, Nichols waited until his heart found its beat again. He took twelve drops of the medicine the hotel doctor had prescribed for such minor disturbances and let the bitter taste come to rest on his tongue. His room had no window toward the street but gave on the square courtyard framing the glass roof of the lobby away down below. On the little loggia that jutted out from his room like a bird's bath from a cage, he had a deck chair and what he called his garden: two pots of ferns, two pelargoniums, and one rather measly fuchsia with a tendency to drop its buds before they had time to open up. These five flower-pots represented all the company and joy permitted to him outside of Tilli's regular visits, which rather disgusted and tortured him.

Nichols went out on his loggia and watered the five pots with all the loving care of a frustrated, garden-hungry Englishman. He picked a few wilted leaves off the pelargoniums and fed the tired fuchsia a shot of vitamins. A slight mist had come up, and the bit of sky he could see above the yard began to cloud over. He entertained himself for a little while by thinking of various places where he would like to be just now. In a punt, near Islip, for instance. Or sitting on the rocks at Santa Margherita and looking down into the green surge of water dotted with swimming youngsters. Or simply in his little house near Hampstead Heath. The Lady Hamilton roses should be in full bloom by now. If the house hadn't been bombed into shambles, that is. . . .

He called his thoughts back from whatever unpleasant

turns they were about to take and settled himself in his deck chair. Like most ailing people, Nichols had a deep attachment to the chair in which he spent so many hours of his empty and fragile existence. In optimistic moments he could almost convince himself that this really was not very different from the sanatoriums in which he had been compelled to spend the greater part of his life. He pushed the pillow behind his head into the right position, pulled a thin rug over his thin knees, and began to study the confounded manuscript. So concentrated was he on this despicable rubbish that he noticed nothing until a shadow fell across the pages, and as he looked up, there was a man standing in his loggia whose coming he had neither heard nor seen.

"Who are you? What do you want?" Nichols asked with a start. The man gave no answer but darted past him into the room. "Don't talk," he breathed, swishing by. Nichols' heart began to pound, very hard and badly out of rhythm. He dropped the manuscript, left the chair and followed the man inside.

"You're an Englishman, aren't you? You're Geoffrey Nichols. You must help me," Martin panted.

"And who are you?" Nichols asked again. "How the deuce did you get in here?"

"From there," Martin said, pointing vaguely to the courtyard where Nichols could see nothing but walls, straight up and down.

"I've read some of your books; I liked *Sunset* best," Martin whispered, out of breath. Strangely enough, it was this casual compliment that prevented Nichols calling for help. He scrutinized his visitor, taking in the heaving chest, the large shirt, torn and soiled from the precarious trip across the wall, the shiny black trousers, the unruly hair, the tense face, and the blue light in the depths of the eyes. For a moment he had the fantastic idea that this was a man of the British Secret Service who had got into trouble and had come to him for assistance. A spark of pride and satisfaction flared up and went out like a wet match. "What do you want? What can I do for you?" he asked in English, forgetting his heart trouble for the time being. Martin, bringing up his best school English, which wasn't very good, answered: "I do not know whether you heard of me. My name is Martin Richter. They are after me. You must help me."

Nichols gave him a dry smile. "Yes, I've heard of you, accidentally. Really, my dear boy, your confidence is very flattering. But you couldn't have picked out a worse man. I'm entirely without resources, I'm sick, and I'm a prisoner."

"That's why nobody will suspect you. Besides—I had not much choice. Neither have you now."

"I suppose I haven't," Nichols said. He felt happy and elated and strong; that a persecuted man should come to him for protection gave him back some of his self-respect and his lost integrity. The first thing he did was to turn on the radio in order to cover their voices. As he did so, he was surprised by his own presence of mind.

"Sit down; make yourself comfortable," he said. "Tell me your story and we'll see what can be done. You can talk freely. There is no telephone in this room and no one listens in. Wait—are you hungry?"

"Yes; but it is not important."

"Wait," Nichols said again. He rummaged happily in a chest of drawers and at last produced a few dry biscuits and one small, shrivelled apple.

"My sister sent it to me; through the Red Cross, you know. I saved it for a holiday. This is a holiday," he said, talking with elation. "Eat it. It's an English apple. It's from the tree in my sister's garden. It doesn't look very impressive, but it's a good apple."

The friendliness of this gesture came down on Martin like an unexpected blow; it was like breaking through ice, and he found it hard not to cry. He sat down, bit into the apple, swallowed its musty sweetness down through his tightened throat. When he had himself under control again he began to talk. For the first time in these four long years Geoffrey Nichols received a true report about the things that had happened and kept on happening in that wide free world outside this hotel that was his prison.

PAGEBOY Number 6, whom his mother, in her mistaken enthusiasm for the Nazi movement, had named Adolf, was a thin, gangling, unlovely boy of fifteen. He had the grey

anaemic face of all the undernourished adolescents
growing up in the over-crowded workers' quarters of North
Berlin. There were angry red pimples and acne scars on his
grey skin, he had a snub nose, and Schmidt had a hard time
teaching him to keep his nails clean. However, even this
proletarian urchin's face had its good points. Adolf had nice,
alert eyes and a rather intelligent brow. On closer inspection
one might have discovered that his ears would have been fine
and well set had the left one not been deformed.

If Schmidt had not been absent this morning on account
of his medical examination, he would certainly have noticed
that Number 6 was restless and negligent in the pur-
suit of his duties. However, neither Ahlsen nor Kliebert was
acquainted with the psychology and the personalities of the
pageboys, and, besides, they were too busy themselves keeping
things going without the help of the all-efficient Schmidt.
And so Number 6, left more or less to himself, loitered here and
there, observed this and that, and finally switched up to the
fourth floor; in front of Number 67, where Geoffrey Nichols
lived, he took off his cap, slicked back his hair, knocked, and
entered without waiting for an invitation. It was one of the
humiliating rules in Nichols' life that his door was to remain
unlocked, day and night. However, nobody ever came to
disturb his privacy, and at times this unlocked door even gave
him the sensation of not really being a prisoner.

"Heil Hitler, Mr. Nichols," Adolf said. "How are you
this morning?" he added in the rocky bit of English he had
learned from Nichols.

"Good morning," Nichols said weakly. The radio was
going full blast, and there was Martin Richter, big as life.
There was no explanation for the presence of a visitor; Number
6 held his bright blue eyes firmly and inquisitively fixed on
Martin Richter. For a desperate second Nichols considered
bribing the boy into secrecy, but dropped the idea as being
dangerous. He had always had an inkling that Number 6
was a Gestapo agent, especially entrusted with spying on him.

"Yes, Adolf?" he said.

"I brought you the morning papers, Mr. Nichols."

"Thanks. How's the news?"

"Fine," said Adolf as if the question weren't worth an
answer. Nichols essayed an explanation of Martin's inex-
plicable presence.

"The doctor sent me a gardener to look after my flower-pots," he said weakly.

"Hmm," said Adolf.

Nichols opened the papers from which the censor had cut several items that were believed unhealthy for an English prisoner. It was a rather ridiculous measure, considering that in any case the papers were not allowed to print anything without government order. Adolf was still staring at Martin; for a brief moment Martin considered knocking the boy out and depositing him in the men's toilet, but he rejected the idea.

"Here. Give my regards to your sweetheart," said Nichols and put some money into Adolf's clammy hand. "Run along now, Adolf."

His heart was very bad now. There were express trains racing through tunnels, and hammers pounded entirely without rhythm on huge anvils, and Tibetan temple gongs were being beaten until they almost burst. . . . I hope I won't make a spectacle of myself and have my heart failure just now, he thought; it helped him somewhat.

"You didn't have to crawl out of the window when I came into the men's room; it was stupid. You might have broken your neck," Adolf said to Martin. "You're Martin Richter, ain't you?" he went on before Martin had caught his breath. "Here I've been chasing after you all morning, and just when I find that you locked yourself in the toilet you crawl out of the window! What do you think we're playing? Hide and seek? Gaston gave me something for you before they took him away. Here."

He lifted the lining of his cap and produced a thin white roll, a leaf of cigarette paper. Martin took it hesitatingly, unfolded it and read. "Trust Number 6. He knows where to take you. Don't contact Walter. Adieu."

He tore it up, went into the bathroom and flushed it down. "Pretty silly to carry that around in your cap, my boy," he said. He was thinking hard and fast. This might be nothing but a trap; again, it might be everything it pretended to be and poor Gaston had sent him a saviour in the unassuming person of Number 6.

"I know what you're thinking. Forget it, Richter," Adolf said with keen perception. "I'm all for you. I know what it's all about. I've been in Sonnenburg myself. Fourteen months, see? Want to see my badge?"

He flicked his head around and exhibited a cauliflower ear that sat incongruously on his small boy's skull. He pulled up his upper lip where the gum had healed unevenly over a fracture and one tooth was missing.

"Did you get that in Sonnenburg?" Martin asked, still not trusting.

"Yeah. They kicked me in the face. Blew my eardrum out too. I can't hear very well on this side."

"I thought Sonnenburg was a good prison," Martin said.

"Yeah. Sonnenburg isn't so bad. The bulls there treated me fine. I got this before they took me to Sonnenburg. When they beat me and grilled me. I guess I was lucky to be taken to Sonnenburg. On account I'm under age. How was it in Ploetzensee?"

"They're an impatient lot in Ploetzensee. They don't make much of a fuss. Either you talk or they take you out in the yard," Martin said and let his hand drop like a guillotine. Nichols listened with shuddering respect to the discourse of the two experts. He deduced that Dachau was "good," but Sachsenhausen was "bad," and Adolf could tell about a friend who had been in Esterwege, which had been "very bad." Martin had meanwhile decided that he could trust Number 6, but was still groping his way.

"Why did they take you to Sonnenburg?"

"That? Oh, they took a lot of us on March 21st, 1941; haven't you heard of us? We were the boys of the Neue Heimat Youth movement. You must have heard of us."

"No. I was at the front then. Tell me about it."

"Oh, what is there to tell? We had all been Hitler Jungen and for a while we liked it fine, but after a while we got our noses full of it. Drill every day and marching until your feet were just one stinking mess of raw flesh and having these bulls tell us what to do every minute and night manœuvres and sleeping out in the cold and if you couldn't keep up with the others you got the stripes. That's what we called it when we got flogged in front of the group. I don't know. We just got tired, I guess. We didn't have much to eat, anyway, and we got tired. I don't know how to say it. We wanted to do what *we* wanted to do. Take a hike when *we* wanted. Or go swimming out Wannsee. Or just sit around for an afternoon and do nothing. First we just stayed away once in a while;

like playing truant at school. Then we met other boys the
same age and we got together and went out hiking and swimming and having fun. Then we had fights with the good little
boys who were still sticking it out with the Hitler Youth. We
ganged up and they ganged up, and we had some super fights.
Then we found out that we in our neighbourhood weren't the
only ones. We met other boys from other parts of town and
then we heard that boys in other towns had got just as tired
of the whole damned Hitler Youth and split up. There were a
few older boys and a few of our teachers took the thing in
hand and sort of organized us. That's what you call a movement. In a way it wasn't so much different from the Hitler Youth,
only that it was ours. We weren't commanded and bullied and
barked at and beaten up all the time; we had meetings and
talked over what we wanted to do and then we went ahead
and did it. We didn't do anything wrong. We weren't sissies
either. We just wanted to do things our own way, that's all.
At the spring solstice we had a meeting of all the Neue Heimat
groups from Berlin and surroundings, out in Werder. The
cherries were in bloom and we had a fine day. March 21st,
1941. That's when they clamped down on us and arrested
us all. Well, I don't complain, Richter. I learned a lot of
useful things and I won't forget it. So now let's see how I'll
get you out of here. This place is lousy with Gestapo. There's
something in the air. They must have blown Bremen to
kingdom come last night, and everybody's having the willies.
Something stinks something awful."

And Number 6, having delivered his individual sympto-
matic if inelegant version of the urge for freedom that is
universal, puckered his brow, began to chew his nails, and
went into a deep meditation.

"Can you trust him?" he asked after a while, pointing
his chin at Nichols, as if being an Englishman had also rendered
Nichols deaf and dumb.

"I hope so," Martin answered, with a quick smile. "To
some degree, at least."

"Of course you can, old boy," Nichols said, astonished.
Not for the fraction of a second had it occurred to him that
he could do anything else but help Martin. . . . Help him, at
the risk of your life? he asked himself. Don't be silly. Of
course; at *any* risk, and no reason to get melodramatic about
it, he answered himself without hesitation.

Adolf brought up a small pearl of enlightenment from the deep sea of his ponderings.

"Can you play the fiddle ?"

"No—why ?"

"If you could play the fiddle I might get you out with the czardas band. They're good boys. For a thousand marks Sandor might let you have his costume and help me smuggle you out."

"Well, I can't play the fiddle and I don't have a thousand marks. I don't look like a Hungarian either."

"Hmm," said Adolf. "The furnace room is out. Wine cellar is out. Laundry is out. Hermine's been arrested. Electricians all over the basement."

"Maybe I could get out as an electrician."

"No. I bet you half of the lot work for the Gestapo. There's not a mousehole that's not watched. Maybe you'll have to shoot your way out of it."

"I wouldn't get very far, would I ? And I have no gun."

"Yeah. Well, let me think," Adolf said, chewing his nails. "I'll find something." He was not in the least discouraged. The bright, keen little boy's joy at playing cops and robbers shone in his eyes.

"How long can you keep him here, mister ?" he asked Nichols.

"Not very long, I'm afraid. It's the day of my broadcast. The radio people will be running in and out all afternoon."

"Hmm. How good are you at getting over roofs, Richter ?"

"Fairly good. I had some fairly good training in Stalingrad," Martin said. "It's coming down from the roof when they mostly get a pot shot at you."

"That's true," Adolf conceded out of respect for Richter's experience. For the moment he had run out of ideas.

"Supposing you tell me where to go if I get out of here and let me worry for myself," Martin suggested. "I can see it's great fun for you, but it's my neck that's at stake."

"You'll stay with my father overnight. Reinickendorferstrasse 84, third court, basement. You take the underground train Seestrasse. If you get there before I'm home you tell the old man I sent you. Tell him you're a friend of Gaston's. He'll know what it's all about. He'll know what to do. He's a bright bird, my old man."

"Does your father know the risk he takes if he shields me?"

"Oh, sure. He's so mad he'd do anything to gyp the police. Since they closed his shop and put me in prison and my brother was killed in Africa he's through with the Nazis, only they don't know it. He's an old red front fighter, then he joined the party and now he's back with the underground. You wouldn't believe it when you see him. Party badge, SA uniform, Heil Hitler, and everything. He's keen as a razor blade, is my old man."

"If I hide there, what about the house warden?"

"*He* is the house warden. It's a good house, you'll see. All sorts of people; Italians and Dutch and what not; they brought them in to work in the ALMO factory. Once you get to the house you're safe."

"Good. Where do we go from there?"

"Tomorrow the professor can take you over. He'll take care of you. He's taken care of many."

"Who's that—the professor?"

"I don't know. We don't ask questions in this game, do we? We call him the professor on account he looks like one. Frau Blanke says she seen a poster for a concert with his picture on it, playing the piano or something. What's it to you? You'll meet him."

"Yes. If I get out of here I'll meet the professor. It's all beautifully arranged except for that. How the hell will I get out of here?"

Nichols had taken pains to follow their swift, vernacular dialogue that was, moreover, covered by the radio. Someone was giving an inspired lecture on the vitamin content of sauerkraut, which seemed to indicate that after weeks of sauerkraut famine a few truckloads had arrived in town. The two conspirators appeared to have forgotten his very existence in their eagerness to find an avenue of escape. "May I say something?" he asked timidly. "Of course, I'm not an expert by any means; I'm only a writer. But I should approach the problem quite differently."

"How, f'r instance?" Adolf asked, unwilling to let the Englishman join the game.

"Use a bit of psychology. Some wit. Some imagination."

"Aw, *you* can talk. If you're that bright, how come you're still here?" Adolf said rudely.

"That's another question. Let's suppose that I like it here. But if I were to make plans for an escape, I'd get myself some protective colouring," said Nichols, who had spent many hollow, idle hours planning it all.

"How's that ?" Martin asked with a flicker of interest.

"Protective colouring, my boy. Be a brown rabbit in a brown burrow. Be a green grasshopper in a green meadow. A polar bear in the arctic. You see what I mean ?"

"Not quite."

"It's perfectly simple. If you don't want to be noticed in this hotel you must wear a uniform."

"Unfortunately they took mine away from me in Ploetzensee," Martin said with great bitterness.

"Ah yes, but that wasn't the kind of a uniform I'm talking about. I'm certain your uniform was faded and patched and worn. You see, your uniform had been in the war. That's not the kind of uniform one meets in the lobby of this hotel. What I mean is an officer's uniform, a dress uniform, all slicked up and spit-polished."

"He's got something there, Richter ; holy mattress, wouldn't it be a joke if you were to march straight across that lobby in a general's get-up ?" Adolf said, warming up to the subject.

"You'll never get away looking as you do: every inch a fugitive. No, my dear fellow, that won't do at all. You must make use of your opponent's weakest point—didn't you learn that at the front ? Well, the German idolatry and worship of the uniform is a very weak point. Remember the immortal Hauptmann von Koepenick ? He had wit, that fellow. Slip on a uniform, be a strutting, heel-clicking, arrogant ass of an officer and I'll wager my life you'll bluff your way past the Gestapo."

Adolf's face was one gape of intense listening; his eyes, his mouth, even his twitching nostrils seemed to suck up the Englishman's suggestion; but Martin remained cool and clouded. "Is that what's known as the British sense of humour ?" he asked with a little sharpness. He was a rebel, but he was also a German, and respect for the officer's uniform was bred into him through many generations; he was born with it and brought up with it. With a stab of pain he remembered their Lieutenant Granne, who had fought with them to the last in that cellar in Stalingrad ; fought like a good man and died like a good man. . . . It's no joke to be a German officer, he thought bitterly—and a chasm opened between him and Nichols, the eternal chasm separating the Anglo-Saxon from his Teutonic cousin.

"Probably," Nichols said. "A sense of humour is a good thing to have when you're in a jam. If I had anything to say after this war I'd suggest teaching a sense of humour in every school in the world. It might go a long way toward keeping us out of a cosmic mess like the one we're in now."

"I'm not in much of a mood to discuss theories," Martin said, more brusquely than was his intention. "The fact is that I have no uniform. Your idea is probably humorous and subtle and superb and everything—but I have no uniform and that's that."

"I can get you a uniform," Number 6 said in great commotion. "I can get you one like that! Schmidt isn't here today, that's lucky. I can take his master key from the desk and break into any room and steal you any uniform you want. I'll get you a general's uniform that will make you dizzy. I'll promote you so quick that you won't know yourself when you look in the mirror. I'll——"

"Nothing higher than a captain, Adolf. Even Nazi generals aren't as young as all that," Nichols warned the hopping, dancing, finger-snapping young devil.

"And where do I keep myself until you get me that uniform? Do I flush myself down the toilet to be out of sight?" Martin asked. His nerves were raw, his shoulder hurt and he didn't believe at all in Nichols' scheme.

"I'll take care of you. I told you I'd take care of you, didn't I?" Adolf said pompously. "I have a place for you. It may not be very comfortable, but it's safe anyway. And it won't be for long."

"I've hidden in a sewer pipe before, and I didn't like it, if that is what you have in mind."

"Not half as bad, Richter. I'll give you the key to the door of the service elevator on this floor. It's out of order, see? You can hide in the shaft for a little while. You swing yourself over the cable to the traverse, and there you can sit quite comfortably. I've tried it just for the fun of it. Not a living soul ever looks into that shaft. Meanwhile I'll get you the uniform, and when I whistle for you, out you come. Do you think that you could put it on in the room of Fraulein—I

mean in the room where you spent the night—in 69, I mean ?"
Adolf said, putting on the brakes just before Lisa Dorn's name
slipped out. It was an unexpected demonstration of tact and
chivalry, and Martin, suddenly burning like Moses' bush, was
grateful for it.

"You know a lot, don't you ?" he said, patting the boy's
slicked-back hair. "I could really have stayed there if a brigade
of cleaning women and chambermaids had not chased me
into the men's room."

"That's just it. You stay in the elevator shaft until the
coast is clear and I'll whistle for you. You have good arm
muscles, haven't you ? You can chin yourself and swing
over on that cable ?" Number 6 asked with faint apprehension.
Martin flexed his aching shoulder. "I guess so—if I have to,"
he said.

"I'll take you to the elevator now. I'll go ahead and re-
connoitre. When you hear me whistle, you come after me.
Agreed ?"

"Agreed."

Adolf raised his right arm. "*Heil und Sieg !*" he said.
Martin, too, raised his arm. "Thank you, comrade," he
answered. Adolf turned smartly on his heels, saluted, and
marched off. Nichols watched the little ceremony with astonish-
ment. . . . No, they will never be like the rest of us, he thought
with a discouraged sigh. He turned off the radio to listen for
Adolf's whistled signal.

"Everything's going to turn out all right, Richter," he said,
noticing the strained tension in the boy's face. Martin pulled
himself together.

"Thanks. You've been very, very decent to me," he said.
"I want to tell you how much I appreciate what you've done
for me." He cleared his throat to add solemnly: "I always
admired the English very much. We all do."

It was so absurd in its beastly German seriousness that
Nichols was put to it not to laugh. "I thank you sincerely
in the name of my country," he said, just as solemn. But
Martin was not in the mood for irony. There was too much at
stake for him just now.

"You've risked a lot; don't think that I don't know that. I'm
sorry I had to trouble you," he said. He opened the door without a sound and stood there, crouched as though for a leap.

"Don't mention it," Nichols said. The whistled signal

came, the door hardly moved, and where Martin Richter
had just been crouching there was nothing. Geoffrey Nichols
waited a few seconds, listening into a silence that roared in
his ears. When no crash, no shot, no scuffle, no sound
occurred in the corridor, he tiptoed to the door and closed
it quietly and carefully. He felt very weak after he had done it,
and his heart was an African Kraal beating on five hundred
drums. He dropped into his chair and had not enough strength
left to pull up the rug. No excitement, the doctors told him.
Not the least bit of excitement, the hotel doctor repeated every
day. Nichols grinned. . . . This was bad for me, he thought.
This was, no doubt, exceedingly bad for me. But I did not die.
No, I didn't even have a heart attack. I'm feeling very well
indeed. I believe I am happy. However—if I had a telephone
I might call for the doctor now. . . .

THE telegraph woman shuffled into the lobby and up to
the desk in her old man's shoes. "Telegrams," she said,
holding her pad up for Kliebert to sign. In broad daylight
she looked as if she had spent the night in a coffin and had,
moreover, got under an express train on her way.

"What news ?" Kliebert asked.

"They say that Bremen took such a bombing last night
that there's hardly a house left. Sixty thousand are dead.
Trains are jammed with wounded. The Pope has been taken
prisoner. The Yankees have taken Rome. Our soldiers are
laying down their arms in Russia and want to be commu-
nists, but Stalin has had them all shot."

"Is that all ?"

"They haven't got Richter yet," the old woman said in
her gravedigger's voice, and shuffled off.

"What did she tell ?" asked Ahlsen, returning to the desk
in a sweat. What with Schmidt absent and the elevator out
of order, he had reluctantly lowered himself to the menial
task of carrying suitcases for the guests.

"She isn't quite right in the attic," Kliebert said, making
a circle in front of his forehead. But he knew, and Ahlsen
knew it also, that while the rumours which came out of that
woman, lifeless, as from an old broken gramophone record, were

exaggerated and absurd, their gist and substance and essence were usually correct. In other words, yesterday things had looked well. Today they looked bad. Things looked very bad on this bright, sunny morning. In the hotel bedlam was loose and hell to pay. It was as though all the guests were pushing around the desk at the same time, driven by the same impulse: to get away. To get away by hook or crook from this imperilled city, this doomed country. Asking for trains, planes, timetables, connections, schedules, flooding the two helpless old men with questions, trampling over them with their demands for changed departures, cancelled reservations, wires for long-distance calls, telegrams to Stockholm, Zurich, Amsterdam, Ankara, Bucharest. The hotel doctor, sitting in his corner, diagnosed the symptoms and summed them up. The terminal euphory is over; now comes the end, he thought. He left his table and stalked up to the desk.

"Telegram for me?"

"No. I *told* you I'd call you when it comes," Ahlsen shouted rudely. The doctor analysed the condition of his nerves.

"Having the jitters?" he asked, not unfriendly.

"No!" Ahlsen shouted. "But I can't do everything alone in this damned pub. What's the matter with the pageboys today?"

"Calm down, man," the doctor said. "Relax. This isn't the first panic in this war, and it won't be the last."

"I don't know what you're talking about. There is no panic. And why should there be one?" Ahlsen said, snapping back to party discipline.

"I could mention one or two reasons," the doctor said, faintly cheered by the general pessimism that had hit the lobby like a hailstorm. . . . I think we'll get a few nervous breakdowns today, he told himself as he wandered back to his table. It was a faintly pleasant prospect.

Schmidt appeared at ten-thirty in a sulphur yellow, vitriolic mood. He slammed his cap on his head with a hollow bang, grabbed his keys, his pencil, his list, and dived into the confusion around the desk with venomous fury.

"Did they take you?" Ahlsen asked, inflated by the national, peculiarly German brand of joy aroused by a neighbour's misfortune.

"Yes, they did. And they'll take you too, and soon, party

badge and all, let me tell you. They'll soon be sweeping up every bit of scrap and spit and dirt in the Fatherland, every cross-eyed, decrepit old cripple, just as they did in 1918, and shipping them to the front in a hurry. They don't even give a fellow time to take care of his family. This is my last day in the hotel.   Tomorrow I'll be a soldier, and you can take your grin you know where. You'll be a soldier too."

"I'd be proud if they took me in spite of my age and my rheumatism," Ahlsen said pompously.

"Rheumatism. They'll show you what rheumatism is," Schmidt said in a rage. He felt so miserable he would have liked to throw himself over the desk and cry. Suddenly he began to shout at the pageboys; it gave him some faint relief. "What's going on here ? Where are those rascals ? The moment I'm not around they just loaf. Report for inspection!   Attention ! Where's Number 4 ? Where's Number 6 ?" One of his arms shot forward like an uncoiling snake and caught Adolf. "Where do you keep yourself all the time, you snot-nose ? Comb your hair. Number 63 wants his mail brought up, and 47 is asking for the valet. As if we still had a valet. Ach! Monsieur Rougier is in the smoking-room and wants to be paged when Herr Gauleiter Plottke asks for him. Go on ! Get going ! Do something or I'll teach you your manners !"

Pageboy Number 6 flitted off, and Schmidt dried the perspiration from his face and strung a polite smile over it like a tight mask.

"Heil Hitler, Herr Baron. Nice morning, isn't it ? What can I do for the Herr Baron ?"

"When Herr Commissar Helm asks for me, I'm in the conference room with Herr Dahlin. Elevator still out of order ? Well, never mind," Von Stetten said and went up to the mezzanine.

No one had more reason to be near a nervous breakdown that morning than Baron von Stetten, and no one gave a better show of being in a fine mood, completely unconcerned and perfectly sure of the outcome of it all. On days like this, when the final smash-up of the whole structure seemed inevitable, and everybody got hysterical, when all the Plottkes lost their heads, and when whispered reports had it that even the Fuehrer had suffered one of his fits of manic depression, Baron von Stetten was grateful to his ancestors for having handed down to him a sturdy nervous system and to his upbringing as an officer for having taught him to keep a stiff upper lip. Like General von Dahnwitz and Herr Schmidt and millions of other Germans, the baron had served under three different German flags: the black, white, and red of the Kaiser Reich, the black, red, and gold of the short-lived Republic, and the swastika of the Third Reich. He had sworn allegiance to all three of them and believed in none. If, underneath his smooth cynicism, he believed in anything, it was in his country, which was permanent, while her political form was changeable, fluid, and passing. He had done his best in every job entrusted to him, and yet he had always remained a spectator rather than a partisan. He was not conscious of having been without character in this. He had clean hands and a good conscience. He had always done his duty and would go on doing his duty for Germany under whatever government she might emerge after the war. He never doubted that any future government could and would use him, and therefore he remained detached and went about his business as usual.

At seven o'clock in the morning he had found on his desk in the Foreign Office a summary of all the radio reports, regular and illegal ones, which the monitors had digested for the benefit of those high officials who had not the time to listen in methodically themselves. By synchronizing them with the news which the office had received directly during the night, he got a fairly complete picture of things as they were. What had looked last night like a successfully averted air raid on Berlin turned out to have been a devastating bombing of Bremen. Details were still drifting in, but what was known so far was bad enough. The same story as in Hamburg and Cologne. Factories destroyed or laid waste. The population fleeing in panic, hospitals overcrowded, trains, railways, roads clogged with evacuees, the Danish workers escaping to their home country in droves to spread the ill news there, and the entire organization of food distribution, industrial output, transport, shipping, and housing disrupted. This was the worst, because the machinery of the Third Reich was not constituted for improvisations. This was chaos, and, to the German mind, chaos is unbearable. They had started out to bring order into Europe, and what they had achieved was chaos and again more chaos. Von Stetten was glad that it was not up to his office to stem the tragic breakdown in the North-west. Let the boys in the War Department worry about the bogging down of the offensive in Russia. Let the Gestapo take care of the growing unrest in the big cities, and the old party horses be concerned about the health of Hitler, Goebbels, and Goering, not forgetting their own delicate condition. His most pressing problem, and the problem of the entire Foreign Office, was the storm signals that came from Italy. As an ally Italy was through and done for and of no more use to them than a carcass. An emergency meeting had been called for this afternoon. But between this nasty morning and this stormy afternoon, Von Stetten had sandwiched in several most unpleasant conferences with some members of the Central European Trade Commissions. Toasts and banquets were one thing, but Von Stetten was a realist and knew that talking business with the hard-headed men from Turkey and Sweden, Rumania and Holland was something entirely different. Yet as he entered the conference room where he had kept Dahlin waiting for ten well-intended minutes, no one could have read anything in his face but jovial self-confidence and cheerful optimism.

"Good morning, Dahlin, good morning, gentlemen," he said briskly, taking stock of the men around the oval table. "Sorry to be a few minutes late. I haggled with my chief at the last moment to get a few more advantages for you, Dahlin," he said, giving the Swede a confidential wink. Dahlin was a tall, powerful man in his fifties, baldheaded except for a bit of blond fuzz, with cold, ice-grey eyes in a stubborn long-chinned face. He had brought with him a secretary, one Swedish and one German lawyer. Stetten had no other support than an interpreter, in case Dahlin's otherwise perfect German should be stumped by the intricacies of legal language, and a clerk to keep the minutes of the session. Dr. Kremer, one of the top men of Duisberg Steel, had let him down—simply excused himself in a telegram and stayed away from the meeting. It was a bad sign. The Fuehrer's picture looked down haughtily from the wall.

"I'm going *in medias res*," Stetten said breezily. "There has been a regrettable stoppage in the consignments of ore coming from your mines to our factories, and I'm here to find out what we can do to remove whatever is blocking the free flow of goods from Sweden to Germany. We're old friends, Dahlin, and I'm speaking off the record when I tell you how badly we need your ore. I'm not making any bones about it, we need it badly. Maybe it isn't very clever of me to talk as straight as that, but Dahlin, old Swede, you're not a newborn lamb and I know it's no use lying to you. So here is the situation. We need your ore and I want you to tell me what we can do to get it, as we did regularly until—let's see—April 17th of this year."

"My good friend," Dahlin answered, "you know the facts as well as I do. Our deal is a simple barter. Let's cut out for the moment the detours our two governments make in clearing our goods through the banks. That's only a formality. We give you ore, you give us coal. You need ore, we need coal. Good. Simple. You send us trains of coal, we send your trains back loaded with ore. Now you're having trouble with your transportation system. I have here the number of locomotives you have lost during the last six months—it's rather frightful—well, never mind. We are your friends. We understand. We load our ore on ships and send it via Rotterdam and you send the ships back with a cargo of coal. But boom !—Rotterdam harbour is bombed off the map; good, we are patient. We wait. Our government waits, our banks wait, our mines wait. We load our ore on ships and ship it to you via Emden. Emden harbour is ruined by bombs. The waterways of the Ruhr are ruined, the Ruhr is one big ruin. Hamburg is bombed—Bremen is bombed—we're sorry for the hard luck you people are suffering. But, man, this is no way to do business. We are patient people and we give you ore even when you send us less than half the coal that is due to us. We give you credit till our backs break. Now our backs are broken and our banks will give you no more credit. We have the ore ready for you and will be happy to let you have it, all the ore you want, the day we receive the coal you owe us. We Swedes are simple people and react in a simple way. No coal, no ore."

"But, my dear Dahlin, this clearly is a vicious circle. We can't send you coal because, as you observed quite correctly, we have suffered some losses in our rolling stock, as is inevitable in a war. We need ore to build new locomotives. If you don't send us ore we can't build the locomotives to send you coal. It's up to you to take the next step."

"It's you who wants something, not we," Dahlin muttered. He had an infuriating habit of glancing just past one's temples and playing the yokel, although he was known as one of the shrewdest and most ruthless men in his business. Stetten

gave him his most charming smile. "Cigarette ?" he said
amiably, snapping his smart, flat case open and holding it out
to Dahlin.

"Thanks. I'll smoke a cigar," Dahlin said, took out one of
his own cigars, bit off the tip, and allowed his lawyer to light it
for him. To Stetten this seemed like the seal on the refusal of
the deal. He swallowed hard as he looked into the disillusioned,
stony faces of Dahlin and his Swedish lawyer. Only two or three
years ago these people had been fawning, begging to be let
in on the big fat deals with the Reich. They had traded with
Germany out of fear and necessity, as long as Germany held
all the trumps. Now he could read in their features that they
were getting ready for the big sell-out. They thought that
Germany had already lost the war. Wherever you turned
there were the same symptoms. Even German capital and
industry were giving up National Socialism as a lost cause.
They had put Hitler upon his spurious throne, and now they
were getting ready to tear him down again, throw him to the
wolves, him and his men and his ideology. Stetten knew that
German industry was putting out feelers toward its former
friends and partners in the United Nations. Dr. Kremer had sent
a telegram and regretted being unable to attend the meeting.
Everyone was trying to scramble over to the other side in a
hurry. An illegal, grand-scale flight of German capital into
the international banks of neutral countries was under way.
All signs pointed the same way. The war was lost. Who, then,
still believed that the war could be won ? Who kept the soldiers
fighting like lions on all fronts ? Stetten thought. The people,
he answered himself. The simple people on the streets, the
masses, the mob, the crowd. Kept ignorant, poor, dumb,
dominated, oppressed, but loyal; the people still believed, and
the people were Germany. Stetten straightened up.

"I'm convinced it is not your intention, nor the intention
of your government, to make a momentary difficulty permanent.
I must warn you that my government would necessarily look
upon such an attitude as malicious, not reconcilable with the
friendship that exists between our countries. It would be
most regrettable if my government should feel compelled to
undertake measures to secure an undisturbed delivery of
Swedish ore."

Dahlin began to laugh; he laughed a loud, resounding,
good-natured laugh, put down his cigar, took out a handker-

chief, wiped his eyes, stuck the cigar in his mouth again, and grew serious. "I've just remembered an old proverb of ours," he said. "If you want to beat the dog, you must have the stick. Or, as the Chinese say: He who wants to ride the tiger must first saddle him. Measures! Measures, my friend? What measures did your government take when Rumania jacked up the price of crude oil by fifty per cent? What measures does it take to make Turkey export her chrome as before? You speak for your government, and I'm only a simple, private business man, a miner. But if your government takes measures, so can mine."

Stetten swallowed the bitter pill and kept on smiling. "Don't let's quibble, Dahlin, old boy," he said. "Don't let's deviate from our subject. You mentioned the rise in price of the Rumanian oil. Confidentially, I believe we could come to an agreement on some similar basis. We're willing to pay you twenty per cent more for your ore in money than we paid in coal. It would tide us over this transitory period until those little repairs in the Dutch harbours are finished and we can take up the old shipping routes again."

"Pay in money, eh?" said Dahlin.

"Yes. I understand the main difficulty at this point is that your banks refuse to extend credit to us any longer. But if we raise the price and pay on delivery——"

"In what money? German money?" Dahlin said. It sounded as though he had said: German money stinks. Stetten decided not to take notice of it.

"I am not at liberty at this moment to make you a concrete proposition. But I believe that we are about to find a way to satisfy even your overcautious financiers," he said. "In fact, I have a conference at half-past eleven which will clarify matters considerably. For the time being, here is what we have to propose. . . ."

At the same hour that Stetten was doing what he had done all his life—pulling chestnuts from the fire for his office—Gestapo Commissar Helm was involved in a similar task. Except that Helm derived a certain pleasure from his part in the complicated Swedish deal. He was sitting under another one of the Fuehrer's pictures, in the small office the Gestapo maintained on the uppermost floor of the hotel. There was a desk, filing cabinets, a washbasin and a couch. It looked almost like a dubious doctor's surgery, and under certain circumstances that couch could assume a strangely sinister appearance. On the chair opposite Helm sat Gauleiter Plottke, and his face was so yellow that his freckles looked like a crust of rust on an old pot. Helm watched pleasurably how the sweat broke from Plottke's pores, formed glistening little rivulets, and ran down into his wilting collar.

". . . if I didn't mean well by you, I wouldn't give you this warning," Helm was saying. He held a ruler in his hand and accented every word by beating it sharply against the edge of the desk. "Our Fuehrer is outraged and rightly so; he would like to see you shot without any ceremony. I am risking my own neck by suggesting a way out to you. You're at liberty to refuse it. But you know what will happen to you. You wouldn't be the first or the only one to die in an accident."

"But what have I done? What have I done?" Plottke moaned. "I haven't done anything the others didn't do. I could name you dozens who have much more money in foreign banks than I have."

"Right. I can name you hundreds. We know every one of them. And they're all in the same boat with you."

"In the beginning, the Fuehrer encouraged us to fill our pockets. 'I want my old comrades who fought along with me through all these bitter years to get their full reward'— these were his own words. He can't turn against us now."

"He turned against Roehm—and Roehm was an old comrade and fighter too. Here I have your dossier, Plottke, and here are the facts. Shall I read them to you?"

"Don't make a mistake, Helm; I happen to have your dossier, too. You're not as pure as an angel yourself. If I go to the Fuehrer and show him the bribe you took from Mercereau, I wonder who'll have an accident, you or me!" Plottke screamed. Whenever he was cornered he trumpeted like a persecuted elephant, and his rust-coloured small eyes and his rust-coloured hair and the rust-coloured freckles on his face and hands stood out violently against the yellow paleness of his skin.

"If you know so much you know also that I wasn't alone in accepting money from Mercereau; I did it with the full knowledge and participation of my chief, so don't worry about my neck. Worry about yours. Here are the unsavoury facts. In May 1942 you acquired from the Jewish banker

Jacques Brancourt a big parcel of shares of the Société Anonyme Chimique de Lyonnaise; in return for it you had this banker furnished with a travel permit and visa to go to Lisbon. After paying certain commissions to the people who helped you in this shady deal, you deposited the shares in a safe of the Bank for International Settlements in Basel. By all standards the shares represent a value of at least two million dollars. I speak in dollars because since last March you have been trying through some middlemen to turn these shares into money and you've tried every forbidden trick to come into possession of United States dollars. You're not only a cheat and a thief but a traitor. You act as if you hadn't heard that we are at war with the U.S.A. If I didn't hate to get this office messed up I would take my gun and shoot you right here and now."

"I have a gun too," Plottke muttered. "And you don't have to play a big scene for me. If you want to blackmail me, you'd better come right out with it. How many of the shares will make you shut up?"

"Plottke, Plottke, what a poor psychologist you are. How little you know me! I am your friend, I'm here to help you! I want to show you a way to atone for your criminal—yes, criminal—behaviour. You want to sell these shares. All right. You can sell them to our own government and help our Reich at the same time. And I will take it upon myself to whitewash you with the Fuehrer."

"Ach, does *he* want the shares for himself? Our darling little Adolf? Why didn't he tell me?" Plottke asked with the coarse and complete cynicism of an old party hack who knows all the tricks. He suddenly saw daylight, and he dried his face, opened his collar, dried his neck, and stopped sweating. Helm didn't deem it necessary to refute the crude attack. He, too, had come up in the ranks of the party.

"Wrong again. The ministry of economics needs foreign currency to pay for Swedish ore. There's some trouble with the Swedish banks, and the boys in the WM are raking in all the foreign currency and securities they can, to get that Swedish trouble cleared up. They'll talk to you and tell you how many marks you'll get for your French shares. I have nothing to do with that part of it. I have only to see that you do your duty to the Reich and, if necessary, force you into doing it. Do we understand each other?"

"Yes. We understand each other perfectly, Helm. You blackmail me into selling my good, solid foreign shares for German money, and at an arbitrary price at that. Ach, what a stinking deal I get!"

"You should be grateful to me for helping you to be noble."

"A nice turn things are taking. Now that we have no more Jews to squeeze for money, the Party is bleeding its own men. It's a bad sign, Helm, a bad sign."

"If I were you I wouldn't holler so much about giving the State a loan; that's what it is. Just a loan. After the war is won you'll get your shares back, with accrued interest and dividends."

"After the war's won," Plottke murmured bitterly as he left the office, a broken man. "After the war's won. There goes the bit of security I've saved up for my old age. After the war is won." He was numb and hollow, too numb to feel the full impact of the blow that had come down on him; what he feared most at the moment was the necessity of telling his wife that he had lost two million dollars at one fell stroke. He still had something like three hundred thousand dollars worth in assorted securities and currency in various foreign banks, but that seemed a measly, insufficient amount compared with his loss.

Commissar Helm, meanwhile, added Plottke's name to a list of several others and drew a careful little circle around it, a sign that the conversation had been successfully terminated.

As soon as the numbness left Gauleiter Plottke, panic set in and he reeled off with great velocity as though falling faster and faster, pulled down by a special and disastrous law of gravity. He grabbed the arm of little Monsieur Rougier, who had waited for him all the morning in the lobby, and whisked him into the conservatory behind the empty yellow pavilion where no one could overhear their conversation. Under the neglected and hungry palm trees and dried-out ferns of this quiet island, he gave Rougier the order to proceed at once with the purchase of a certain little chalet on the west shore of the Vierwaldstaettersee in Switzerland. Its price was eighty thousand Swiss francs, and after penetrating the twisted, tangled and complicated financial transactions—every one of them illegal—that were necessary to realize this acquisition of a bit of property in some safe neutral country, Plottke felt

as though he had cut through a maze of barbed wire and left
pieces of flesh hanging in it. "You're bleeding me white,
Rougier, you're bleeding me white," he moaned, but Rougier
remained slickly adamant. The Gauleiter had no power over
this dark-haired bounder. He could not put him into a prison
camp or threaten him with arrest and grilling, and he felt
impotent and at a loss. In whatever dark Balkan corner
Monsieur Rougier's cradle might have stood, he was now a
Swiss citizen, a neutral, a free man. Desolately Plottke
stared at Rougier's bluish cheeks. "How often do you have
to shave?" he asked him. It was only remotely what he wanted
to know. What he meant was: You're dark and hairy and alien
and I don't trust you. Maybe you are even a Jew; you're too
damned clever with money.

"Twice a day, Herr Gauleiter. Why do you ask?" Rougier
answered, astonished.

"I'm trusting you an awful lot," Plottke said.

"And I am taking a very great risk for you," Rougier
answered pointedly.

The next action in Plottke's busy day of disaster was to
get reservations for his wife and his two children on the
first train or plane that would take them to Switzerland. The
necessary documents, passports, travel permits had been
ready for quite some time, for such trips had become almost
a pattern. You presented a doctor's testimony that your
family needed a rest or a cure, you sent them off to a neutral
country and anchored them there securely by acquiring some
property: a home, a house, a little chalet on the shore of
some pleasant lake. Then, if things went wrong at home, you
simply went to visit your family—and there you were, far from
the native explosions and in safety.

But when the Gauleiter went to the desk and asked for
a timetable he discovered that many people seemed to have
been gripped by the same urge for the faraway. Trains and
planes were booked to capacity, and even Herr Schmidt
seemed to be leaning over like the tower of Pisa in the storm
of requests that surged and pushed and yelled around him.
Plottke could push as hard as the best of them, but it was a
new experience to him that he had to push at all. He was used
to having a respectful lane opened up for him wherever he
went, in deference to his title and power, and he had almost
forgotten the pushing period of his life. However, stepping

on a few toes and digging his elbow into several ribs, he told Schmidt to cancel somebody else's reservations and hold three seats for him on the morning train for Zurich.

"Going away, Herr Gauleiter?" Mazhar Cevdet Onar asked, popping up at his side. The old Turkish economist had a way of flicking his white moustache when he smiled, which kept you wondering if he was only making fun of you.

"It's for my family. The girls had their tonsils taken out, and the doctor tells me they need mountain air more than anything else."

"Of course. You're very right, Herr Gauleiter. Everybody should evacuate his children from towns that are on the bombing schedule of your barbarian enemies," Onar said with impenetrable politeness, made a little bow and stepped back. Plottke muttered a curse at his retiring back. On his way to the telephone booth Plottke ran into Stetten, who was coming from the conference room with Vanderstraaten. Stetten was a bit wilted after hours of difficult haggling, and Vanderstraaten's sandy face looked desolate as the Gobi Desert.

"Good that I meet you here, Plottke," Stetten said. "My chief is expecting you at four o'clock in the AA to discuss a few details with you. You know, it has to do with the matter Helm took up with you this morning. We'll have the necessary documents ready."

"I wanted to drive to my country place after lunch," Plottke stammered. "My family is leaving for Switzerland tomorrow —lots of things to attend to at the last moment."

"Ah—to Switzerland? So suddenly?"

"No, not suddenly at all. The doctor told us weeks ago to take the children there, but my wife never wants to leave our place—she's so attached to Karinsee."

"Well, at four o'clock then," Stetten said with finality. It was as good as an order.

"Vanderstraaten—telegram for Mynheer Vanderstraaten," called one of the pageboys, sailing a zigzag course through the crowded lobby. It was almost lunchtime, and the élite who could afford to pay for the non-rationed delicacies of the hotel began to file in, stand around for a few minutes, sip a drink at one of the small marble tables, gossip, do business, pursue a career, a love affair, or a combination of both, and drift toward the dining-room. "Mynheer Vanderstraaten—telegram for Vanderstraaten."

"Here," said the banker and lifted two fingers. The page-boy handed him the telegram, waited for his signature, waited for a tip, and left.

"Excuse me," said Vanderstraaten to Stetten; he took out his pince-nez, tore the envelope open and proceeded to read. He read it twice, and then he looked around for some place to sit down; he put the telegram on the marble top of the table in front of him, straightened it out carefully and read it once more. Suddenly he looked very old and very white.

Vanderstraaten was a man of great fears. Out of many fears he had handed himself and his bank over to the Nazis immediately after the destruction of Rotterdam in the spring of 1940. Fear for his family, fear for his life, fear of losing his money, his business, his position, his home. Fear of being put in prison, of being beaten, fear of a radical change in his way of living, which is the most common fear among those who have never encountered hardship and who therefore overrate its impact and underrate their own endurance. For a while he was convinced that he had chosen the right side. Like all the Quislings and collaborators and appeasers, he had made himself believe that what he was doing was good for his country; he belonged to the tribe whose battle-cry through the ages has been: Better slave than dead. But for many months now this man of great fears had been threatened by the invisible people who were Holland. "The day of the axe is coming" was scribbled on the pages of the newspaper which he unfolded over the breakfast table. "The day of the axe is coming" he read on the blotting paper spread on his office desk. "The day of the axe is coming" was whispered behind him as he left the streetcar. It was written on the collars which came back from the laundry and on the flower-pot he bought in the market. "The day of the axe is coming" spoke the telephone that rang in the middle of the night. He saw it in the closed faces of his employees, he heard it in the voices of his children. His former friends cut him dead on the street, his wife hardly spoke to him any more, his dog pulled in his tail when he called him, because even the dog could scent the smell of fear. The day of the axe is coming . . .

"Unpleasant news, Vanderstraaten?" Von Stetten asked indifferently. Vanderstraaten's chin quivered, and he had to start twice before he could answer.

"Yes," he said. "It's from our contact man in Antwerp;

we have some sort of a code. It says that there are rumours
of an attempt on Laval's life. That's the end. First Mussolini
—now Laval. One after the other, Herr von Stetten——"

"Oh, that!" Von Stetten said evenly. "But there's nothing
to it, Vanderstraaten. It's last week's rumour. And anyway,
the end of Mussolini means no more nor less than the end of
Mussolini personally. The same for Laval. I shouldn't let
it frighten me if I were you. Will you excuse me now? I
have to see a friend."

"Fraulein Tilli! Paging Fraulein Tilli Weiler! Paging
Fraulein Tilli!" called pageboy Number 6; he meandered
through the lobby, poked his head into the bar, and came
back to the desk. "Sorry, I can't find her," he reported. A
little old lady was standing there, waiting for the result of his
search. She had white hair and big blue eyes in a wrinkled,
bloodless face. Her skin looked like crumpled white tissue
paper, and she was dressed in a black suit and a black hat, both
rather outmoded and worn. She wore very clean white cotton
gloves, like a badge of gentility. She looked like thousands of
other old ladies who had seen better days.

"I regret, lady," the harassed Herr Schmidt told her, "we
can't find Fraulein Tilli."

"Oh, can't you ?" said the old lady. There was a nervous
twitch in her left cheek, and her voice was cracked. "But you
don't think she has gone out ?"

"Her key is here," Schmidt said impatiently. If the old
lady hadn't been so obviously a fine old lady he wouldn't
have troubled about her any longer. The old lady stood there
looking very downhearted. She clasped her gloved hands as if
to hold on to one with the other. Her face was twitching, and
she had no control over it. No one could have understood
what it had cost her to come to the hotel on this errand.
Pageboy Number 6 observed her with keen, calculating eyes.
She didn't look rich; on the other hand, people who weren't
rich usually gave bigger tips. She looked like the kind of old
lady who might give a very big tip.

"Want me to phone her room once more ?" he offered.

"Yes. If you would be so kind."

"Who shall I say wants to talk to her ?"

"Frau Mueller. Yes, Frau Mueller. She might not remember my name, but we are old friends. No—better say Sim's
mother."

"Frau Mueller. Sim's mother," Adolf repeated and took the receiver from one of the house telephones. "No answer," he reported. "Maybe she's asleep. . . ." She'll have a hangover the size of an elephant, he thought, but tactfully kept it to himself.

"Number 6, take this parcel up to 88," Herr Kliebert ordered with some sharpness. "Yeah," said Adolf, waiting for his tip. The old lady realized it, and her twitching cheek began to burn under a hot, shameful blush. . . . I have not a single groschen, she thought desperately. . . . She had planned and outlined every move and word of her perilous expedition, but she had forgotten that pageboys in the hotel expected tips.

"I thank you; I thank you so much," she said with too much emotion.

A bit plemplem, thought Pageboy 6 as he took the parcel and went towards the stairs with it. Herr Kliebert, feeling some affinity with the old lady who had seen better days, went out of his way to be agreeable.

"Any message for Fraulein Tilli?" he asked and took the pencil from behind his ear to make a note.

"No. No, I don't think so. No. I will come back later. Thank you."

General von Dahnwitz, who came to the desk at that moment, stepped politely aside to let the old lady pass. She accepted his courtesy with just as polite a nod. Her left hand with the white glove was buried in the pocket of her jacket, crumpling the yellow star which she had taken off and hidden during her expedition into these select realms forbidden to Jews.

"Fraulein Dorn returned from the theatre?" asked the general.

"Not yet, your excellency."

"Good day, Dahnwitz," Von Stetten said, arriving at the desk.

"Good day, Stetten. Nice day today."

"Very nice. A bit too warm, but nice anyhow."

There was a pause in which Stetten did not ask what he wanted to ask, and Dahnwitz forgot that Stetten was there.

"I'm having lunch with Lisa," he said when he remembered his former comrade again. "Any objections?" he added with a Prussian sharpness in his voice.

"But, my dear Dahnwitz——"

"Pleasure before duty, what? After lunch I'll attend to my affairs."

He saluted and marched stiffly toward the dining-room. Stetten gave a sigh and went into the men's room to wash his hands, which felt extremely unclean. The old lady with the yellow star in her pocket walked shakily past Gestapo man Heinrich, out through the revolving door and past the two SS men posted there. . . . I must see Tilli, she told herself as she stood in the relentless sunlight of the street. I *must* see her today. I have no choice. I must see her.

Tilli, who had slept long and was still wrestling with her usual morning-after headache, was at this moment standing in the open door of Number 69.

"I tell you, Fraulein Tilli, you've never seen anything like it," said the chambermaid Katrine. "Not two or three new dresses but a dozen of them. And what dresses! Like a princess. I didn't know the French still had all that stuff. It makes your mouth water."

"New shoes too?" Tilli asked. Hers was a one-track mind.

"I should say there are new shoes. Even silver ones. To go with that silver evening dress, I figure."

"I'd like to have a peek at it too," Tilli said, overcome by the irresistible hunger of a female left too long without something to wear.

"Well," said Katrine hesitatingly. She had a broom in her hand and a pail placed on the threshold. She sent a furtive glance up and down the corridor. The floor inspectress was nowhere in sight. "It's against the rules, but I guess there's no harm in letting you look at the fashion show," she said, pointing over her shoulder at the big wardrobe. Tilli sniffed, analysing the air of the room while she looked around curiously. Perfume, good soap, cigarettes, wilted roses —and what else? She made a grimace at the general's photo. "Is he the one who's paying for it?" she asked.

"I'd say it takes a shareholder's corporation to buy all those Parisian dresses," Katrine remarked. She took up the blue chiffon nightgown from the bed and held it out to Tilli. "Take a look at this," she said. "It's indecent, that's what it is."

Tilli took it and held it up to herself in front of the bathroom mirror. "What does she wear? Size twelve?" she asked with the angry admiration of an ample sixteen. Katrine slid back the doors of the wardrobe. "There's the whole caboodle," she said. "And see you don't leave fingerprints on them."

Gingerly Tilli took out one dress after another, fingered the material and held them up to herself. Instead of amusing her, the sight of all this luxury made her feel bad. It was like a flat, stale taste which she couldn't get rid of. Katrine stood by, critical. "Not your colours," she said expertly. "It takes a different skin to wear these. You are the flashy type, Fraulein Tilli. You look your best in black satin."

She picked up the pail and disappeared into the bathroom. "What a pigsty!" Tilli heard her grumbling from there. She hung the dresses back in the wardrobe and nervously examined the rows of shoes which were lined up on a rack. Rows of shoes. That's what some women had. Rows of shoes.

"I can always tell when a lady has had a gentleman visitor," Katrine remarked, sticking her head through the bathroom door. "The gentlemen splash so much more. They have the fun and I have the work. That's life for you."

She disappeared once more and Tilli pulled a pair of high-heeled patent leather shoes from the rack; her hands shook and her knees felt funny as she examined them. They were dream shoes. They were exactly the sort of shoes for whose possession she would gladly give her eternal soul. She sat down quickly on a chair, with her back turned to the bathroom, kicked off the old mules she was wearing and tried to get into the patent leather.

"What are you doing there?" Katrine asked from the bathroom. She was scrubbing the tile floor now and trying to look through the door slit at the same time.

"Just playing around," Tilli said with a strangled voice. She squeezed and pushed and tried to get into the shoes by hook or crook. And then a grey wave of disappointment swept over her and she had to give up. Too small. . . . Well, what of it? she told herself. They're hers, not mine. I wouldn't have stolen them if they had been right, would I? But she knew that she would have. She got up, feeling empty and very depressed after the brief uplifting excitement, and carried the glossy things back to the rack. Listlessly she played with the street outfits hanging in the same compartment; jacket and skirt and another jacket and skirt and another one; far too many for one single girl. Suddenly something caught her attention. It was a black garment, apparently a very strictly tailored suit; there was an expression of stupid surprise on her face when she discovered that it was a man's tailcoat. . . . The funny things an actress has to wear in some roles! she thought at first, but then she noticed that this coat was much too large for our Lisel. As if a knob had been turned, Tilli's mind began to work furiously and intelligently. . . . I wonder how much this will be worth to Commissar Helm, she thought. Maybe not much. Again, maybe a lot. Maybe I'll get my pair of new shoes after all. . . . She never knew beforehand how the commissar would receive the ragged odds and ends of information she retrieved for him. Beyond paying for her room, his appreciation ranged from five marks to as much as a hundred. . . . Looks as if our Lisel were cheating the general with a civilian, she thought. A tailcoat. Who would wear a tailcoat now but perhaps the ambassador of some neutral country? And if our Lisel was secretly receiving foreign ambassadors, that should be interesting news for the Gestapo.

Tilli tenderly flicked a bit of fuzz from the lapel of her discovery and hung it carefully back in the wardrobe. "Thanks, Katrine," she called through the bathroom door. "I think I must be going along."

Katrine mumbled something unintelligible, and Tilli was on her way to Gestapo Commissar Helm's office.

Aт five o'clock in the morning General Arnim von Dahnwitz had awakened as usual. As usual he was completely clear-headed and alert the moment he opened his eyes, and his first action was to reach for the monocle on the night table. The pulled-down black-out blinds kept a thick darkness in the room, but he knew at once where he was. Berlin, the hotel. Last night he had had a little quarrel with Lisa but had made it up with her in the end. Groping back through the past evening, he came to his conversation with Stetten. In the soberness of the early morning it all seemed somewhat fantastic. That conversation, then his mute dialogue with his pistol, the plan to escape with Lisa which, on this sober early morning, appeared absolutely crazy. . . . Probably the Gestapo would have arrested me in Tempelhof, and Lisa too. I would have embroiled Lisa, it would have been a colossal mess, he thought, and folding his hands, he said aloud: "Thank you, God, for preventing it."

Like most members of his caste, the general was religious in an unquestioning and stiff-necked way. He knew that God could not win battles for an army if that army did not have a sound strategic plan, good officers and soldiers, courage, discipline, fighting spirit, perfect equipment, and, if possible, a fair numerical superiority. On the other hand, the general was unshakably convinced that none of these could win the battle if God wasn't on your side. In times of stress he kept in steady communication with God, and he believed in the power of prayer. Therefore he had never been reconciled to the paganism of the Nazis, and in moments when his sober, sparse Prussian mysticism got the better of him, he was convinced that the Fuehrer's blunders were not alone responsible for the Russian disaster of the last winter, but also God's disinclination to associate Himself with a commander-in-chief who did not believe in Him.

After his usual ten minutes of meditation and clarification in bed, the general got up, pulled up the blinds, and stretched his solid, muscular body in front of the open windows. The first grey of dawn was coming up over the quiet city, and from the suburbs the steam whistles of one factory after another called the workers to the morning shift. Besides the dominating discomfort of knowing that he had promised to shoot himself today, he became aware of a secondary unpleasantness. It was the sore place where Fischer had opened the abscess. The general probed it with his tongue until the tiny wad of cotton came loose, and then he proceeded briskly to brush his teeth, pain or no pain. After this he went through a whole set of rather old-fashioned exercises with an old pair of dumb-bells that accompanied him through life. He had never allowed his iron thigh muscles of an old cavalry officer to get flabby, and he was proud of them. Horses and women like a firm knee grip, was one of his maxims. By the time he had had his cold shower, had massaged himself with eau de cologne and rubbed his shaved head dry, it was six o'clock and the orderly appeared with his second uniform brushed to perfection and his second pair of boots polished like a mirror. The boy began to brew some real coffee on the general's old little

E

alcohol burner, and the bitter fragrance was the first comfort the general had on this cheerless day. He had felt like that as a cadet, and later in the military academy on the mornings of exams, and as a young officer before inspection, and at manœuvres before the cavalry attack and in the World War before his first battle. Every time there had been the same cold leaden hollowness in his belly and the same question: Would he succeed? Would he prove himself a good soldier? If it was true that a real man showed his worth by the way he faced death—then no man could be sure of himself as long as he was alive. Today he would have to face the last and most severe test and examination. He was not afraid of dying; he was only afraid of not dying as well as a general and a Dahnwitz should. There had been moments of a great weakness last night which had shocked him very much. Army lingo had a name for it, and a thorough understanding of it. *Der Schweinehund im Mann.* The son of a bitch in every man. To live down this inner son of a bitch was the main goal of all the Prussian drill and discipline that had been inflicted on him and that he had inflicted on others.

While the orderly silently straightened the room and the morning came creeping over the roofs and over the skeletons of bombed houses, the general drank the strong hot coffee and began to feel better. He began to feel that he would be able to face the necessary like a man. In theory this was simple. In practice he balked at it: he didn't go over the hurdles, but around them.

At half-past seven, as ordered, the hotel barber appeared, an old Italian who had been a fencing master in his youth and always attended to the general on his visits to Berlin. Dahnwitz yielded his head to old Giannini's pleasant ministrations; he closed his eyes, heard the razor swish on the strop, the lather being clapped on, and at last the scraping noise of the blade on his shaved head. The many fastidious and methodical stations of his morning toilette were an indispensable stimulant for the general. Step by step they built him up, from a tired middle-aged civilian in a crumpled nightshirt to the shining, exemplary, strong, masculine, domineering idol of the German nation: the officer.

As Berlin was still wrapped in its civilian slumber, the general took out his eyeglasses and began to read. He had planned to go over a certain part of Schlieffen's *Battle of Cannae* last night, but unexpected events had prevented his doing so. Now he took the book from a small stack and tried to concentrate on it. But there was a flat taste to it this morning, and the general pushed away the book which could not hold his attention, and reached for another. This was an old ragged Lutheran Bible, printed on the very thinnest paper. It fell open by itself, and the general adjusted his eyeglasses and began to suck up some calm and composure from its worn pages.

> *I have seen the wicked in great power, and spreading himself like a green bay tree.*
> *Yet he passed away, and, lo, he was not; Yea, I sought him, but he could not be found.*
> *Mark the perfect man, and behold the upright: for the end of that man is peace.*

His eyes ran down the familiar lines and came to rest on the one that said:

> *O spare me, that I may recover strength, before I go hence, and be no more.*

He read the Psalms of David, and as he did so he was not in an impersonal hotel room in Berlin, a room which had been destined to assume such tragic importance in his life, but he was back in the ugly, cosy small church of the village of Elgede, and he was a stiff, dignified little cadet who had come home for the funeral services of his grandfather, General Joachim von Dahnwitz. It smelled of autumn, of the smoky mist over the burned-off potato fields, of wet sheep dung on the pastures, of the grease on the farmers' boots, of laurel wreaths and flowers and wax candles. The funeral of the retired general had brought a resplendent crowd to the small church; sabres and spurs and medalled chests, catching here and there a spark from the candles. Over the coffin a flag was spread, and on it were placed his late grandfather's helmet and sword and a red velvet cushion with all his decorations. Six uhlans were posted as a guard of honour at the sides of the coffin, and the organ played, and the six uhlans, their simple country-yokel faces bulging with the effort of doing it right, lifted up the coffin and carried it outside, where the mourners were lining up to follow the hearse on foot through the village and out the other end of it toward the old cemetery and the vault of the Dahnwitz family. Arnim walked between his parents and a fragile venerable old relic, the field marshal under whom his grandfather had fought in 1870–71. But between them and the hearse, in step with the sour trumpets of the funeral march, walked Odin, his grandfather's favourite horse, covered with a dragging black blanket and led by his grandfather's old stable-boy, Anton. And this had seemed so sad and heartbreaking to little cadet Arnim that suddenly a big sob burst like a bubble in his throat and he tried to sniff up the grief of an eleven-year-old into his nose, mortified at making an undignified spectacle of himself in the presence of the field marshal. At which his late father, Oberstleutnant von Dahnwitz, had looked down at him with the cold, critical glance of a dissatisfied superior officer, and commanded under his breath: "Control yourself, Cadet. *Haltung!*" But his mother had squeezed his gloved hand, and that had almost broken down the last bulwark of his manly countenance.

The general closed the Bible and took off his eyeglasses. He had come to a decision. There were only two ways for a Dahnwitz to die: in combat or in Elgede.

At nine o'clock sharp he telephoned Von Stetten in his office.

"Morning, Stetten. Am I disturbing you?"

"Not at all. How are you?"

"Thanks, fine."

"How's your toothache today?"

"Much better. Thanks. Listen, Stetten—I've thought about our conversation of last night."

"Yes?"

"I think you will agree that it is better if I go home, to Elgede, today and—er—take care of matters there. Better taste, I mean, much better taste. Not as vulgar and indiscreet as this caravanserai."

"Well—in a way——"

"If I understood you correctly, the Gestapo will be pleased to avoid notoriety; I mean—where would they hide the body, what? In Elgede there are lakes, there is my shooting box— I could go hunting. Are you listening, Stetten?"

"Yes, of course I'm listening."

"Also there are very many things I've got to get in order in Elgede, many things. What with both boys dead and my nephew too, no male descendant I know of, no next of kin, the question of proper succession of heritage is complicated. I'll have to consult our family lawyer. Old Dr. Bricker in Hanover."

"Yes. I see."

"Legacies and stuff, too. There are the old servants, and my foresters, my horses, my dogs. I can't leave a pigsty behind. It's funny, but I never made a will, never did. It didn't occur to me. No."

"Quite," said Stetten, and then there was a silence in the telephone, while a busy and ingenious little device took down the conversation twice. Once in the switchboard room of the hotel and once in the Foreign Office. "I beg you most obediently to let me talk the matter over with—another office. It doesn't come under my authority——"

"I didn't ask your permission. I told you that I'm flying to Elgede this afternoon, so you shouldn't worry about my whereabouts."

"Well—no—I'm afraid the situation isn't quite as simple as all that; I advise you most obediently not to undertake anything until I call you back."

"If I want to fly, I must give orders to my pilot."

"To be sure, Dahnwitz. I'll call you back presently."

The general felt his temper rise as he slammed down the receiver, but took a firm grip on himself. To calm down he went over to the wall with the maps, put on his eyeglasses, and two minutes later he was immersed in the finely-drawn contour lines of that sector west of Kiev. The phone called into his gloomy speculations, and there was Von Stetten once more.

"I'm sorry, Dahnwitz. Your trip to Elgede does not seem to be feasible. In fact, it is not desirable that you leave the hotel at all."

"*Himmelherrgottkreuzdonnerwetter*—does that mean that I am a prisoner? I won't accept it. I won't. I demand a court of honour. I want to be court-martialled and convicted by my fellow officers! I refuse to take orders from these SS bastards," the general broke out in a rage that had been a long time overdue. The telephone remained coolly polite and unimpressed.

"My dear Dahnwitz! Be sensible. You acted irresponsibly last night. Our talk was a matter of mutual trust. But you telephoned your pilot at two-ten a.m. to get the plane ready and keep it warmed up for an emergency flight. Naturally, a certain office took this as a signal that you were trying to bolt. You must understand that they are suspicious now and are tightening their belts."

"But I didn't fly last night. I didn't."

"No. Possibly you realized that you were too closely guarded."

"I wanted to fly back to the front," the general said morosely. He did not like to be forced into lying. "I wished to make use of an officer's privilege to fall in combat."

"And take Lisel with you? You were heard quarrelling with her about it. My *dear* Arnim!"

"I hope you don't believe that Fraulein Dorn is in any way involved in anything I may have planned or done?" the general shouted, and for the first time he was really and deadly frightened. "I give you my word of honour that she is completely unaware of this whole mess I got myself into, my word of honour. Moreover, if one of those Gestapo men should dare to molest her, I'll shoot him down like a mad dog, so help me God!"

"Calm down, calm down, my friend. That won't be necessary. I have it on well-informed authority that there is not a breath of suspicion against our Lisel. Not to forget that she is *persona grata* with our Fuehrer. No reason for you to get excited or worry about her. And—Dahnwitz—you must understand that I am only a mouthpiece. I receive orders and obey orders. My personal feelings are not allowed to enter into this."

"I understand perfectly; perfectly," answered the general, who had given and received orders all his life with complete disregard for personal feelings and who had coldly commanded operations which had of necessity cost hundreds of thousands of lives. Even if he had gone over to the Piefkes, Stetten belonged to the same caste and had been an officer. Most probably Stetten realized very well that the conspiracy of the generals, if successful, would have saved the country: it was quite possible that he was completely on their side and not very happy that the plan had gone sour. But personal feelings didn't enter into the situation.

"If you really want a lawyer, I could send you Justizrat Doehneke," Stetten said, conciliatory. "I am certain he would advise you well, help you draw up a will, and take care of everything that's necessary."

"That would be very kind. Thanks most obediently," said the general. "Not later than ten, though. I have a lunch date with Fraulein Dorn."

"You lucky fellow!" Stetten said over there in his office. He knew that parting with a masculine joke would make it easier for Dahnwitz than any word of sympathy.

"What can I do until that lawyer comes?" the general asked himself, pacing up and down the room. It did not enter his mind to make an end right now. Last night, immediately after Stetten had left him, there had been a moment when he could have done it easily and spontaneously and without a struggle. But the farther away he moved from that moment, the harder it seemed to do it. For the time being, the general stalled and built up alibis and valid reasons for stalling. He had dished out death in superhuman portions, but it was different when it came to dying himself. And so it seemed very necessary to him first to call up his dentist and cancel the appointment. And then write some letters and pay a few bills, and burn the two epistles Lisa had sent him to headquarters during the last months; not because they contained anything compromising, but because he did not want to leave anything personal behind. By that time the desk announced Justizrat Doehneke, a civilian of military bearing who also wore a monocle, and whose every word and every movement betrayed the former officer. Together they worked for almost three hours sketching a will, and then Doehneke left with the promise that he would have it drawn up the same afternoon and bring it for the general's signature the following morning.

The general stared with his unmonocled eye at the blurred figure of the lawyer. "I would prefer to sign it today. It is possible that I shall be called away before tomorrow," he said.

"I shall try, I shall try, your excellency. Shall we say this afternoon at four? If I can't come myself I'll send it by one of our clerks."

"At four. Good," said the general. He took a breath after the lawyer had left and looked at himself in the mirror. Until four, then. It was not quite one o'clock yet. More than three hours' postponement. It seemed like a very long span of time as he looked down its stretch. Sometimes a battle was decided in less than three hours. He intended to spend every minute of it with Lisa. He picked up the telephone and asked the desk: "Fraulein Dorn returned from the theatre?"

"Not yet, Herr General," the desk informed him.

"Will you be kind enough to ring me up the moment she comes?" he said and hung up, but his impatience mounted from minute to minute. Three hours with Lisa, that was all that was left to him, and here he was waiting for her and the time passed and could not be stopped and passed and passed. At last he could not bear it any longer and went down to the lobby to intercept her there. He could not see any guards watching him, but he knew they were there. A man in a tight blue suit, who had been reading a paper nearby, dropped it, took out a huge white handkerchief, and blew his nose. Two guards in SS uniform suddenly became visible out of nowhere; one took his place next to the door, the other went outside on the street. It was at that moment that the general was hit by the full impact of the realization that he was a prisoner and a man sentenced to death. Suddenly he felt strangled, suffocated. There was not enough air coming into this gloomy lobby with its boarded-up windows and blacked-out glass roof. He sat down again, and only the crimson collar of his tunic and the monocle held him up like crutches in a sudden weakness. . . . As if the sawdust were running out of me, he thought unexpectedly. He left a message for Lisa and went into the dining-room.

Time passed. Twenty-four minutes past one. Time chewed big hunks out of the bit of life that was still left. Gauleiter Plottke walked past, saw the general and stopped.

"'l Hitler, general. How's your toothache today?"

The pox on you, thought the general. "Thanks. Much better."

"Did you hear anything about it?" Plottke said confidentially.

"Hear what, Herr Gauleiter?"

"You know. The developments in Bulgaria," Plottke whispered.

"I didn't know there were any."

"I understand our Fuehrer is very much concerned."

The pox on our Fuehrer; the pox and the cancer and the bubonic plague on all of you, the general thought in a sudden fit of rabid rage. "You must excuse me," he said, and got up. "Here's Fraulein Dorn. I'm having lunch with her."

Never had Lisa gone through a torture like this lunch. Never had the general known that being with the woman one loved could be such a hollow, aching pain. They went bravely through all the motions, smiling with the skin of their lips only, walking, choosing the dishes, selecting the wine, lifting their glasses and clinking them together and looking into each other's eyes as if they meant it and falling into sudden holes of silence and crawling out again with some bright remark between their teeth. And while they did all this, they were as lonely as oysters in their shells, each one locked tightly into an impenetrable casing of anxiety and despair. All through the meal Lisa waited, tense as a bowstring, hoping that perhaps one of the waiters would give her some sign or slip her some message about Martin's whereabouts. But Gaston and Philippe were absent in a sinister way, poor brave old fighters, and none of the others seemed to belong to their secret brotherhood. At last the head waiter brought the bill and reminded them softly that, according to the new war law, the dining-room had to be closed at two.

The elevator was still out of order. As the general walked up the stairs behind Lisa's lithe figure he was suddenly overcome by a furious, brutal storm of desire such as only a soldier knows coming out of battle or going into it. It is the desire that comes out of the deepest depth of the race; the urge to beget, to propagate, to pass on life before having to die. To the general it seemed at that curious moment that taking Lisa in his arms now, passing with her from kisses into union, from embrace into sleep, from sleep into death, would mean to end in a fireworks of glory, a last fulfilment and then a soft blotting out as easy and natural as the soaring end of insects or their wedding flight. He took the key of her room from his pocket; Lisa, walking down the corridor in front of him, heard the faint sound and turned around.

"May I come in with you for a little while?" he asked, his voice thick with excitement.

"Not now, dear. The chambermaid is cleaning my room," Lisa said as a desperate excuse.

"Then let's go to my room. I haven't been alone with you for months. I need you. You have no idea how much I need you. What has happened to you? You're holding me off at arm's length. Don't you care for me?"

Lisa didn't know what to answer. "Of course I care for you. Don't be so possessive; and in the middle of the day at that," she said; she was trying to sound whimsical, like the girl she had been yesterday. The general put his arms around her and pressed her to his hard solid body, the body of an old cavalryman. In a wave of revulsion she felt muscles and buttons and a whole hardware store of decorations crushed against her breasts. It was not like him to make love in a hotel corridor. Not when he was sober, in any case. Before she knew what she was doing she had pushed him away. He stared at her with an expression that frightened her. She laughed a little.

"You are not going to rape me, or beat me up," she said, so afraid of him that it made her impertinent. "Not here. This isn't Kharkov, you know. You have to act civilized."

The general stepped back, struggling hard for countenance. "Forgive me," he said; "forgive. I might not see you again."

"Forgive me, too. You must know that I am of no earthly use before a performance. I'm sorry, Arnim. Do you want to come to the theatre with me tonight?"

"Tonight?"

"Yes. Tonight. *Merchant of Venice*. It's a good performance. I must leave here at six, if you want to take me there."

"I'm afraid I have another appointment," the general said. "But maybe I could arrange it."

"Yes, do, please," said Lisa, who couldn't wait for the moment to break away from him and search for Martin. "*Auf Wiedersehen*, then."

The general saluted, and she went into her room. He stood there another moment, stiff as a log, and then he turned hard on his heels and marched down the corridor, down the stairs to the second floor and into his room.

"Heil Hitler," somebody said as he opened the door. The general adjusted his monocle that the excitement of the scene in the corridor had dislodged and examined the unexpected intruder.

"Ah, it's you, Helm," he said, speaking down to commissar from a high tower of arrogance. "How did you get in? With your jemmy?"

Helm decided to ignore the insult. "I thought you would like to know a few things," he said, stretching his long legs and leaning back in the leather chair. The general remained standing.

"For instance?"

"For instance, that you can save yourself the trouble of telephoning Tempelhofer airport. We arrested your pilot. And don't bother about your orderly either. He was sent back to his regiment."

"Anything else?"

"Yes. Something else," Helm said, and now he got up and stood close in front of Dahnwitz. "I don't like your attitude. We've treated you with velvet gloves. We've been more than lenient; we've given you every chance to die like a gentleman and an officer. But if you prefer to be treated like the criminal you are, you can have that too."

Dahnwitz's face took on a bluish shade under the reddish tan; the veins stuck out on his shaved skull. "You know that I might shoot you?" he said hoarsely.

"I don't happen to be afraid of you, your excellency," Helm said coldly. "We have no cowards in the SS. It seems they're all on the general staff." For the moment the general felt as if he would have a stroke right then and there and not have to kill himself; but the feeling passed and left him spent and shaky.

"I am talking as a psychologist," Helm said evenly. "For a man who plans to make an end of himself you're too damned cheerful. Why the hell should you take all sorts of cosmetic treatments in the morning when you know you'll be dead in the evening? It's very suspicious. You don't act like a potential suicide, you act like a bridegroom. I watched you in the dining-room just now, Dahnwitz. You seemed to be having an excellent time with your—er—lady love. In fact, you give the impression of a man who has some good tricks hidden up his sleeve. I don't trust you."

Strangely enough, the general derived a queer satisfaction out of this. Toe the line. Keep a good front. Don't let anyone suspect the cold, quivering fear underneath. Fear? Yes, nude, simple, overpowering fear.

"Why shouldn't I enjoy myself, when the food is bearable, the wine excellent, and the company very charming?" he heard himself say. "You seem to have funny ideas about the attitude of a man of my kind. Do you expect me to tremble and be sorry for myself? I don't know how the well-publicized heroism of the SS stands up under a real test. But I assure you that my kind knows how to die almost from the day we are born."

"Listen well, Dahnwitz," Helm said softly. "We have been extremely pleasant so far. But we can be extremely unpleasant. Extremely unpleasant, Dahnwitz. Also, our patience is about exhausted. If you are such a virtuoso at dying, then, damn you, go ahead and die, and die soon. My chief expects from me the report that your case is closed."

"You can report to your chief, on my word of honour, that the case will be closed before midnight."

"That's fine. But I'm here to make sure that you keep your word of honour."

"I suppose you and your chief do not know what a word of honour means."

"My chief and I don't believe in the word or the honour of a traitor."

Here were more than two men and two enemies lashing out at each other. Here were the latent distrust and contempt and hatred of one military body for the other, of the army which belonged to the country against the SS which was the personal tool and prætorian guard of the Fuehrer. Here were the two rivals for power which would tumble Germany into civil war if the war were lost. Here was what always waits at the bottom of the German character: the seed of fratricide, the raging darkness, the tragic urge to beat and strangle and kill one's own kin.

"I shall be generous," Helm said. "You expect to sign your will at four o'clock. At four-thirty I shall be back. That gives you two more hours. You know what you have to do if you don't want to be arrested. Heil Hitler."

General Arnim von Dahnwitz, strangely enough, spent the last two hours of his life trying to write a love letter. He took off his coat and in his shirt sleeves went to work. He laboured over it as he had laboured as a little cadet over difficult equations; he sighed and moaned, he peered through his eyeglasses at the words he had written and tore up sheet after sheet, threw them in the wastepaper basket, paced up and down the room, kicked the furniture, sloshed cold water over his shaved head, drank the last bit of cognac left in the bottle and settled down at the desk once more.

In this hour it seemed all important for many things to be brought to Lisa's attention. That he loved her; how much he loved her. That he loved her not the way an officer and noble-man usually loved a pretty actress. That he loved her more than he had ever loved his wife, or any other woman. Also, it was necessary to explain to her that his suicide was not committed cowardly but for honourable and compelling reasons. And that, whatever she might be told about him, he died with the knowledge of having served his country well and conscientiously. But all these were intangible things, hard to catch in the right words, especially hard for a man whose mind had been schooled on the iron prose of Schlieffen and Clausewitz, and whose pen had never ventured beyond making notes for strategic plans, memoranda, and com-muniqués.

"My love, when you receive this letter I shall not be among the living." No, that was the way a lovesick governess might announce her end. "Dear child, conditions over which I have no command compel me——" This sounded dry as sand.

"Dear Lisa, the hour has arrived when I must part from thee." No, this wouldn't do either. He threw a furtive glance at his wristwatch. Three twenty-one. Time was running out. He tore another sheet from the pad of writing paper and wrote hastily:

This is to say good-bye and thanks for everything and God bless you. Forgive me for leaving you to join my sons who went ahead of me.

ARNIM VON DAHNWITZ.

As he put the note in an envelope without reading it over, the telephone rang and announced a gentleman from Doehneke's office. He had him sent up, and there appeared a grey mouse of a man with shaky fingers, a rusty voice, and a nervous drive to talk incessantly. "It's beginning to rain," he said, clearing his throat and peering out the window. "Thank God, it's raining. If it would only rain real hard, I mean all night long! If we could get a real, good, hard, long rain, if your excellency will kindly sign here—that's correct—and here—right—and initial every page—thanks most obediently, your excellency. I understand it is your excellency's wish that we keep the document in our safe awaiting further developments—my deepest respect, your excellency. Yes, if it would keep on raining tonight, that would be a godsend. . . ."

It was four-twenty as the clerk left. Now everything was in order. The general looked around and was pleased with the flawless condition in which he left the room. He wrote Lisa's name on the envelope and then took off his eyeglasses and dropped them in the wastepaper basket with the crumpled sheets. Now I don't need them any more, he thought.

There was a queer small relief in that thought, and from the eyeglasses that relief spread out and took in more and more territory. No more eyeglasses and no more need for self-discipline and no more humiliating dealings with the Piefkes. From now on the Piefkes would have to carry the responsibility for the mess on the eastern front. Let them try to organize the retreat. Let them decide whether to throw in the last reserves on a gamble or whether to admit defeat and pull the troops back all the way. Let them go begging for an armistice when everything was lost. And when the civil war comes, let them fight it out among themselves. He, General Arnim von Dahnwitz, was well out of it. All his life he had accepted grave responsibilities as the natural lot of his class; now he could at last throw off the load and take a rest. By shooting himself, he gave up a few meagre joys. Elgede, the hunt, riding across the stubbled fields of a morning. Holding Lisa in his arms. But by the same token he saved himself untold ugly, nasty, disgusting difficulties. . . . It's really a bargain, he thought almost gaily, as he got up and took the receiver off the hook.

"The desk, please. Yes, will you send me a pageboy, immediately. He must be here in a minute. Thanks. And connect me with Baron von Stetten, at the Foreign Office."

"Sorry to disturb you again, Stetten," he said. "Oh, you're in a conference? Would you do me one more favour? Yes, one more favour. I can't take Lisa to the theatre tonight—for obvious reasons. Will you substitute for me? You understand—take her to the theatre. Get her out of the hotel. Get her out of the way in case there should be a certain excitement. You have known some young actresses in your time too, haven't you? Never excite them before a perform-ance. . . . Oh yes. Quite well, thanks. I rely on you—you will take care of Lisa as well as I would myself. Yes? Thanks. Good-bye."

He put down the receiver, looked at the clock. Six more minutes—and there was the pageboy knocking at the door.

"Here are thirty marks," the general said. "You take this letter, order one dozen red roses from the florist, and put both in Fraulein Dorn's room. But don't put it there until she has left for the theatre. You understand? Under no circumstances do I want her to get them before she returns from the theatre tonight. Repeat these orders."

Number 6 murmured that he understood perfectly. "One dozen red roses and this letter to be taken to Number 69 after Fraulein Dorn has left for the theatre. Very well, your excellency."

"You can keep the rest of the money for yourself. *Abtreten*," said the general, and Number 6 turned smartly on his heels and marched off. Five more minutes.

There was nothing left to do now, no more delay, excuse, or postponement. The general slipped on the tunic of his dress uniform and stretched himself on his bed, as if he were lying in state already. He closed his eyes and put the muzzle of the Luger to his right temple. Then it was as if time lost its validity and the next minutes stretched as long as a life and an eternity. There was first a raging hatred for those who forced him to die this way; and then an unspeakable nostalgia for the rapture of battle. Oh, to die in the heat of it, oh, to die in the frenzy of the attack, in the burst of shells, to die like a Dahnwitz! Then there came a great blunt animal fear, the fear and horror of the body, and during that minute the general was nude before himself and sorry for himself and ashamed of himself and entirely without power over himself; sweat poured out of every pore; he trembled and cried out for his mother and for God. And then came the worst of these minutes, when God did not answer and the general rode over a battlefield after the day's horrid fighting was over and there was that stench that goes with war and there were corpses of men and horses, millions of men, millions and millions of men, dead, killed, bloated, torn open, smashed by the imper-sonal death of war, and he was responsible for every one of

them. And then, with his finger on the trigger he was not
dying one time but a million times and a million times, dying
into a sucking, unbearable emptiness; then the last minute
was gone on his wristwatch.

The two SS guards in front of Number 26 heard the muffled
shot and turned their eyes toward each other. One of them,
a very young boy, looked a bit frightened, but the other one
gave him a shrug and a reassuring grin. They remained standing
on guard before the door, as were their orders. In the room
the general had stretched a bit more and seemed a bit taller
than a few minutes ago. He lay there, very correct and
arrogant, the two highest decorations the country had to offer
glittering from the crimson collar of his dress tunic, and he
waited.

It was four-thirty. But Commissar Helm did not come.

Lısa opened the door to her room and closed it quickly
behind her, and then she stood staring at the mirage or whatever it was she saw before her eyes. There was Martin and he
was alive and he was real and he seemed gay and he was just
buttoning the coat of a somewhat fantastic blue uniform.
In front of him stood pageboy Number 6, polishing a black
leather belt with his sleeve. "At last!" Martin said. "I
thought you would never come home."

"What's this?" Lisa asked, very weak all of a sudden.

"This is Adolf. He's a friend. He fed me his own sandwich
and got me this uniform. Nichols thinks I might be able to
get away in a uniform, and he's right."

"Who thinks what?"

"Nichols. Geoffrey Nichols, the English writer. He's
another friend."

"The hotel seems to be full of friends all of a sudden," Lisa
said, overcome by amazement and a queer little stab of jealousy.

"Yeah. And full of Gestapo too," Adolf said. He looked
somewhat guilty as Martin took the belt from him, put it
around his middle, examined the effect in the mirror, shook
his head and took the belt off again.

"I can't help it," Adolf said. "It's the best I could get.
Herr Schmidt is in a fierce mood today." He wandered

around Martin critically and pulled the uniform straight on him, but the effect was still dubious.

"How does it look to you?" Martin asked Lisa.

"You remind me of Captain Donescu, that Rumanian military attaché we had here last year. And that's not much of a compliment."

"It's the best I could get," Adolf said again. "It's lucky I found this one in the locker room. It's your size too, isn't it, Richter?"

"It fits fine," Martin said, patting the boy's head. He felt good and strong, his mind functioned with great accuracy, and since he had eaten there was a wish in him to laugh and joke and be gay. "It was the doorman's uniform, when the hotel still had a doorman," he told Lisa.

"Exactly. I used to tell Donescu all the time that he and our doorman were doubles. George was his name. I remember him well. He joined the army and got——"

"What?"

"Nothing," Lisa said, clouding over. "Come, take it off. We must be serious. You didn't really think that you could walk out of the hotel in this masquerade?"

"I've seen worse uniforms walk in and out of that lobby," Adolf said pompously. "And no one paid any attention."

"I'll have to take the chance," Martin said. "I can't hide here much longer. I must get away, and this is as good as anything I can think of."

"But in this uniform! It's a farce!"

"I know. But Nichols is right. This is no time to be timid. Only the most outrageous audacity will get me out of this trap. You know, like a fox, biting his own leg off to get away."

His merriment made Lisa gloomy. "I don't think I can stand much more of this," she said plaintively. "All during rehearsal this morning I did nothing but think of you. What had happened to you—would you still be here when I came back—and if not, would I ever see you again? And if I didn't see you again, how would I know that you were still alive? And when I came home and couldn't find you—and that awful lunch with the general—where were you hiding all this time?"

"In various places—none of them very comfortable," Martin said; he was still stiff and sore from crouching precariously on one of the steel beams in the elevator shaft, with the darkness falling away under him without end. His eyes were still not used to the daylight after more than two hours in that shaft.

"And now that you are here and everything could be good for a few hours, you want to experiment with this awful costume. Don't you know it's dangerous?"

Martin's smile deepened as he said: "Don't you know that everything is a little dangerous from now on? I might stay here for another night and there might be an air raid and a bomb might hit us both. Or you might just go on living like a blind mouse as you did before, and when the day of revenge comes you'd be thrown in with your friends of the party, and that would be much more dangerous than letting me walk out in a doorman's uniform. I warned you that it will be dangerous to associate with me, for a little while yet, at least, and you said you didn't care."

"I'm not afraid for myself," Lisa said.

"Well then, will you be a good soldier and let me try to bluff my way out?"

Lisa contemplated him thoughtfully and yet absent-mindedly. "You look impossible," she said. "You look exactly like the students who are sometimes allowed to work as extras in mass scenes. You need a lot of coaching. All right! All right—I will coach you. I'll give you a lesson in dramatic art and deportment. I'll show you how Captain Donescu walked and talked and bowed and scraped, everything. Wait," she said, beginning to be carried away, "didn't you say you were in some Rumanian hospital? Do you know a few words of Rumanian?"

"*Buna seara, sunteti bine?*" said Martin. "*Sunt incântat ca v'am intâlnit.*"

"Good, good!" she cried enthusiastically, while Adolf broke into one of his devil's dances with delight. "Maybe it will work out. You must have some talent, I'm sure. You must be able to act for five minutes as all these idiots on the stage act all their lives. Let's practise for half an hour and I'll turn you into a perfect captain of the Rumanian Guard."

"That's it, that's it. Listen to her, she knows the tricks," Adolf said, chewing his nails with excitement.

"And then," Lisa said, husbanding her breath as she did on the stage when it came to the most important passage of her part, "and then we'll simply go downstairs and walk through the lobby and past every goddamned spy and guard and Gestapo man and out through the revolving door ! And not a soul will think anything else but that I'm having a flirtation with one of those slick, smooth Balkanese."

Adolf stopped chewing and began to comb his hair wildly with his fingers; the muscles in Martin's face worked, and the two clefts appeared in his cheeks.

"That's nonsense. You know I wouldn't let you take that risk," he said curtly. "Walk out with me ! Be seen with me ! What a fool you are. You must be crazy. This is not a comedy. We are not acting for fun."

"You mustn't be rude to me, Martin. You mustn't hurt me, because I'm going downstairs with you whatever you may say. I'm very stubborn and you won't shake me off. If you try to walk out by yourself, the way you look, you have a very poor chance. But if I'm with you you're well covered. I'm your camouflage, don't you see ? And I can prompt you when you get stuck. I'm good at ad-libbing, too. I'm a very good liar. If you want to get out in this uniform, an actress is a much better protection to you than a gun would be. Listen to me, Martin," she said urgently as she saw his face tight and hard as a stone. "You didn't worry about my safety when you came into my room last night and almost forced me to help you. Now your cause has become my cause —you've become my—— Oh, I don't know how to say it. Just that I should die if I let you go away all by yourself and they should catch you. You are mean to me," she said, and the tears sprang into her eyes. "You let everyone help you but me. Father Antonius, Gaston, Philippe—that English prisoner—even him; and this little pageboy. Why ? Are they better than I am ? Yes, yes, I know I wasn't very good until yesterday. But that was yesterday, Martin; I didn't know any better. Don't you see that you must help me to make up for a lot ? Is your skull so hard and thick that you don't understand at all what's the matter with me ? Don't you know why I must stand by your side when things are getting dangerous?"

Martin stared at her, blinking, as if what he saw were a white-hot flow of glowing steel. "Oh, you——" he said under his breath—"you blind mouse—you little fool—you crazy one—you——"

Adolf, whom they had both forgotten completely, had

another of his occasional attacks of tact. "Well, I must shove off now," he muttered, "or Herr Schmidt will get me by the shirt-tail."

Martin took his eyes off Lisa with an effort and turned to his young friend. "Yes, Adolf," he said gently. "There are a few things I want to say to you before we part. Listen to me and remember every word," he said, very serious and with great intensity. "You are a bit young for the game you're in; that's why you're still playing cops and robbers. But there is more to it than just the fun of cheating police bulls and playing tricks on the Gestapo. You know that, don't you? But have you ever thought why people risk their lives just to listen to a radio or to hand out pamphlets or to fight for the right to read the books they want to read? Did Gaston ever talk seriously to you about it? Whatever happens, you must promise me to start thinking and reading and asking questions. Now listen to me, Adolf. At the front, when you're in an advanced position and the commander falls, the next in rank takes over. When we were dug in in a cellar in Stalingrad our lieutenant fell and the sergeant took over. The sergeant fell and the older of the two corporals took over. When he fell, I took over ; I was the younger of the two corporals, and there was only one private left with me when I got wounded. It's the same here. We're the last ones left of my group. If I fall you'll have to take over. This, what I say to you now, is as solemn as though I were pinning a stripe on you. If I fall, you must take over and carry on and do everything I would have done. I guess the man you call the professor will know how to teach you and where to use you and how to put you in touch with our comrades. And listen, Adolf: If I should have bad luck, don't let it frighten you and don't give up the fight. The statistics are in our favour. For every one of us who is lost there are a few hundreds who remain. Now give me your hand and promise me this. Say: I promise to carry on and not get frightened if anything happens to Martin Richter and to fight for everything he would have fought for. Say it."

Adolf swallowed hard and then he repeated it. Martin held his hand for another moment, and then he pressed it once and let go of it. He gave the boy a pat on the head and said: "That's it, comrade. And now run along or Herr Schmidt will give you hell."

He turned to Lisa after the boy had gone and said lightly:
"He's only a kid. They like it to be solemn. I had to give
him a speech he'll remember."

"Yes. I can see that. Please, give me a speech, too; I need
it," Lisa said. He came quickly over to her, and suddenly he
found her small person in his arms; it made him feel as nothing
had ever made him feel in all his life. He cupped his hand
around her head and pressed it to his sound shoulder.

"What do you want me to say to you?"

"I don't know. That everything will come out well."

"Of course everything will come out well. When you are
with me everything must come out well."

"Tell me more."

He dropped his head until his forehead touched her hair—
warm, lively, sunbleached meadow; fragrant; restful. "That
I care for you?" he asked soundlessly. She nodded, pressing
herself harder to him.

"I care for you, very much. I never cared for any girl
before. I didn't know it could be like this."

"Tell me more."

"What else can I tell you? I care for you. I love you. I
want you, I want you very much, for myself and forever."

"Tell me that we will be together when everything goes
well."

"Everything will go well and we will be together. If you
want us to be together we will be together. I know a village
in the Harz where we could go in summer; there is an old inn
you will like. Or what would you like to do? I can take you
to Vorarlberg ski-ing, at Christmas——"

"Yes. Please, take me ski-ing, please——"

"Or if you like we can take my little folding boat and paddle
through all the lakes around Berlin and into the Spreewald;
I did it once with Annemarie."

"Yes, let's do that. I know I shall be very stupid with a
folding boat, but you could teach me. And the next summer we
could go to Austria and I could show you my country—do
you know how to find mushrooms? I know places that are full
of them; you must look for them in the deep moss; I shall
teach you——"

"And I shall be in the theatre every time you play. But I
shall be very jealous when the other actors are kissing you on
the stage."

"Nonsense. They all smell of onions and are sweaty under the grease paint. And after the performance we shall go home and I'll cook for you. You don't believe me, but I can cook very well. What would you like me to cook for you?"

"Sauerbraten with dumplings. The way my mother made it. With red wine and a green bay leaf and thyme and sour cream."

"Yes, I shall cook Sauerbraten for you, with sour cream. If we can get sour cream, that is."

He let go of her and began pacing the small space between the window and the table. There were too many mirrors in the room, and he could see himself three times, front and back, looking ludicrous and impossible in that stolen uniform. . . . I shall never get through, he thought; and he also thought— but vaguely and incapable of putting it into words—that he was only a link in a chain, an incident, a receptacle, passive as the carrier of some bacillus is passive, except that he carried the dangerous, contagious bacillus of freedom and rebellion, and now this girl had caught it from him and would go on spreading it even if he himself were to go down.

He felt immeasurably old and wise, a veteran saturated with experiences and kaleidoscopic memories of disaster, broken ends and bits of the miseries he had lived through. He knew that it was of no importance whether he came through alive or not, because he had grown up in a world where human lives were cheap as brambleberries and the individual had no rights or value. But there he was, in spite of it all: the individual, Martin Richter, he himself; a boy of twenty-four who had fallen in love for the first time and who wanted to study medicine and to be happy.

He had never thought much about happiness, and he was amazed at the rich number of inventions for happiness that he could think up all of a sudden. To lie on a beach, let the sand run through his fingers, have the deep rolling sound of the surf in his ears and Lisa at his side; she wore a blue bathing suit and he had covered her arms with sand. The next moment he was still lying at her side, but in a bed now, with clean white sheets, so fresh that he could see the sharply ironed creases in them; the Venetian blinds were down, and the sun made a zebra pattern of dark and bright on Lisa's nude body. Then again she was dressed in a white dress and a red apron and she held a glass of milk out to him; and she was reading under a lamp,

with the light soft on her hair, and they were walking through
a forest together, with the dappled play of sun and shadow
on the ground and the air full of the scent of pine and their feet
sliding over the smoothness of the pine needles; they were
swimming in a lake, walking across a mountain meadow full
of arnica, standing together at the bow of a steamer, sleeping
together in the breathing dark of the night; they were young
together and old together, but together always and always.
Yes, he wanted to be happy, above all, and therefore it was all-
important now to stay alive; for dead men couldn't get any
of all that. He came back to Lisa grinning widely and took her
into a hard embrace.

"We'd better make up our minds right here and now that
we will have Sauerbraten for our silver anniversary," he told
her. "We'll have to pull ourselves together for just a few
minutes today, and after this is over we will have years and
years of Sauerbraten and everything else. Oh, little fool—
my little fool," he said and pressed her still harder, "I'm glad
I found you. I'm glad Gaston pushed me into this room. It
makes everything different. I don't think they will ever get
me now. I was only sounding off when I gave Adolf that
speech. I'm a very lucky man, little fool, and nothing can
happen to me."

Lisa kept her face pressed into the blue cloth of the uniform
because she was afraid to let him see how desperate she was. . . .
What if it isn't so simple? What shall I do if they arrest you
before my eyes? she thought. She did not ask what would
happen to herself, because she had forgotten herself entirely.

"What a uniform!" she muttered into his shoulder. "It
smells of mothballs. What a farce! I wish Donescu were
here. He would help us. He liked to make fun of the Rumanian
army. Of ours too."

With an effort she pushed herself away from that blue
cloth haven of Martin's shoulder and became casual. "Now
let me look at you. Don't wear that ridiculous cap if you
don't have to. Thank God you are tanned like a soldier. The
face brown and the forehead white. You must part your hair
and slick it down. Here, use my lotion. . . . That's better; now
let your eyelids droop and make tired Balkan eyes. Your eyes
are much too blue. Make them look like that, like stewed
prunes. . . . That's better. Do you know how Rumanians
salute? . . . Good. Now look at me as the Rumanians look. As

if you were wondering whether I wear a brassière. Oh, darling,
darling, you still look like a shy young German student.
You must look like a gigolo. Now kiss my hand. Come, do it.
Now I say: *Au revoir*, Captain Donescu.   And you say :
Au revoir, madame, or whatever Rumanians say, and you
bow and click your heels and kiss my hand. . . . Oh, how
funny you are! Did you never kiss a woman's hand
before ?"

"No. I'm a great Don Juan. I always kissed them on the
mouth," Martin said and gathered her up in his arms again.
"Now I am saying *au revoir* to you, I myself, Martin Richter,"
he whispered into her warm little crown of hair. "And, darling,
if I get out today I think I'll have to disappear for some
time. If you don't hear from me for a while, do not worry.
Think of me hard and wish me luck but do not worry. We
will meet again. I promise you."

"Can't I disappear with you ?"

"No. Where I'm going I can't take any excess baggage
with me."

"But how will I know how you are ? That you are well
and alive ?"

"I'll send you a message. Something very common and
simple and harmless. Let's see. For instance : Don't worry, we
have enough bread at home."

"We have enough bread at home—good. How will I get
the message ?"

"I don't know. By telephone, in a letter, through Adolf,
through some friends we neither of us know yet."

"Now I need a cigarette," Lisa said, taking herself out of
his arms. "Now we must practise." She smiled as she
remembered that first cigarette he had broken in two and
shared with her. Today the golden case was well filled
again. For a few minutes they both puffed, following their
thoughts.

"First of all you need money, don't you ?" Lisa said.

"Yes, thanks. But don't give me more than a Rumanian
captain would carry in his pocket." He made a short jab
at her chin, smiling. "I didn't know you were so practical."

"You are in for several surprises once you know me better.
I'm tremendously practical, and greedy, and calculating, and
a fraud through and through; acting Snow White all the time,
you know, but I can be as relentless as a shark—in one word,

I'm an actress. Here, put the money away. Later I'll send you more, regularly. I'll try to make very much money in a hurry. I have an idea that with very much money we could bribe some of your friends out of prison——"

Martin stiffened, putting his finger to his lips. She stood silently, holding her breath. Steps were approaching the door, stopped, became ominously quiet. Martin vanished behind the curtains. The silence inside of the room and out there began to fill with something foreboding, disastrous. Lisa made sure that Martin had become invisible; unable to bear the feeling that someone was eavesdropping out there, she tiptoed to the door and pulled it open suddenly.

"Heil Hitler," said Commissar Helm. "I was just about to pay you a call. I hope I'm not disturbing you."

"I was studying my part," Lisa said; "I—really—I'm rather busy."

"Aren't we all? Poor busy bees, buzzing around all the time," Helm said idiotically as he entered without waiting for her invitation. Lisa retreated step by step, but kept on smiling at him.

"Ah—and I bet this is the shrine where Lisa Dorn keeps those famous Parisian dresses," he said, advancing toward the wardrobe. One of the sliding doors stood open, and he began to paw through the clothes.

When Helm had left the general, Tilli had reported to him, without going into details, that the actress kept a man's garments among her own things; after some meditation the commissar had come to the conclusion that Dahnwitz was still trying to bolt—in civilian disguise and possibly with Lisa Dorn's connivance. As the orders were to handle the Dahnwitz case with the utmost caution and discretion, Helm had decided to investigate the interesting bit of news in person. And here he was now, at ten minutes past three, rummaging among the adhesive spider-webs of this feminine wardrobe.

"Would you mind explaining to me what you want?" Lisa asked with all the fortitude at her command. . . . Only the most outrageous audacity will get me out of this trap— it echoed in her thoughts.

"I don't mind at all, Lisel. I have a certain professional interest in your wardrobe. If you'll be kind enough to sit down and not disturb me I'll be through in a few minutes."

She knew that the game was up the moment he brought out that tailcoat. She stood very quietly and rigidly, with her back toward the curtain behind whose folds Martin was hiding. She could feel his warmth and even hear the very faintest sound of his breath. Everything was of a terrible and disastrous clarity, but at the same time not real at all. It was the clarity of a bad dream in which one couldn't speak, or move, or escape, and yet one knew all the time that it was a dream and couldn't be true and that it would dissolve in the end into nothing.

Helm seemed to have forgotten her presence over his find. He whistled through his teeth as he took it out and hung it over the back of a chair. Then, still whistling, he began to walk around it in a circle, thinking hard. After a while he dived back into the wardrobe and began searching for other pieces, but he found nothing. Gingerly he replaced everything he had put out of order and returned to the tailcoat. "This is interesting," he muttered. "This is truly interesting."

After several minutes of silent contemplation he came to a conclusion. Obviously, this had nothing to do with Dahnwitz. It was absurd to suppose that the general had planned to escape in an old black tailcoat that was sweated through in the armpits, shabby and shining, and that smelled as unmistakably of stale food and cigar smoke as only a waiter's coat can smell. Helm whistled again. This was really interesting. This opened up entirely new and different vistas. This linked Our Lisel directly with the underground movement to which the two stubborn old Frenchmen belonged, whose grilling had led the police into a dead-end street. In fact, the criminal police had given up the search in the hotel as fruitless and were following some misleading clues. Helm gave a little snort. As usual, it took the more subtle methods of the Gestapo to get results.

Commissar Helm felt very happy as he stood there and speculated on the importance of his discovery. The idea of grilling Our Lisel appealed to him; he rather liked to handle the questioning of women personally, especially young ones, pretty ones. There was, definitely, some pleasurable excitement in playing around with them, at first consoling them, gaining their confidence, making them soft, pliable, and then suddenly lashing out at them and cracking them. To do all this to Lisa Dorn promised to be spicier than just having a

simple, everyday love affair with her, like this stupid traitor
Dahnwitz. But, more important than the tickling sensations
this prospect gave him, Helm felt that he stood on the threshold of discovering, in one bold stroke, this most damnable,
bothersome, ever-baffling structure of secret opposition that
swept the universities and had found a hold in the rotten
minds of intellectuals and artists. This shabby old black tailcoat was the missing link between the people of the stage and
the undermining organizations of the underground. He stroked
the shabby coat most tenderly, sniffed at it, lifted it up, threw
it down again and stopped whistling.

"Did you say something?" he asked, not even looking at
Lisa.

"No. But I would like to know who put that thing in my
wardrobe," she said. Her mouth had gone dry, but otherwise
she was amazed at the amount of strength and presence of
mind that was suddenly at her command.

"Naturally, you never saw this piece of masculine attire
before."

"Naturally not."

"I was afraid you would try to tell me that, Lisel," he said
with a show of sympathy. Systematically he proceeded to
search the room for further clues. He found the leather belt
on the floor and merrily lashed the air with it.

"And this?"

"Don't be so indiscreet, Helm. You can see it's a uniform
belt. Somebody must have left it here. We don't have to
mention names, do we?"

"You smoke, Lisel?" Helm said, dropping the belt and
focusing his attention on the ashtray. There were several
cigarette stubs in it. "You smoke a lot, don't you?"

"Yes. When I have stage fright. Before I play a part for
the first time. Like tonight, for instance," she said, puffing
her cigarette.

Helm pounced on the half-smoked cigarette Martin had
deposited in the ashtray when he took the money. It was still
glowing, and a thin white thread of smoke spiralled from the
burning paper.

"You are in the habit of smoking two cigarettes at the
same time?" Helm asked. He stood frozen, like a pointing
bird dog, sucking in his stomach muscles, gripped by a growing
tension.

"Yes, I'm an addict. I'm a chain smoker when I'm nervous," Lisa said. Helm took out his gun. "Are you nervous now, Lisel?" he asked amiably. Before she could give him an answer he pushed her aside and held his gun against the folds of the curtain she had shielded all this time.

"You can come out, Richter," he said quietly. "No use playing hide-and-seek."

He pulled the curtain back, and for a moment the two men faced each other silently. Both were pale with excitement. Then Helm laughed.

"I didn't think I'd have the pleasure of meeting you again so soon, Herr Richter," he said. "And in Fraulein Dorn's bedroom, of all places."

"Go on. Shoot me and get it over with," Martin said. After the trembling fear of these last minutes, the sight of the gun pointed at him made him suddenly very cold and completely calm.

"Oh no, my dear Richter. Shoot you? That would not be very subtle, would it? I'm sure we'll have lots of fun together yet, the three of us. There must be many things you'll want to tell me. And you too, Lisel. Come here. Sit down. Let's chat."

"I have nothing to tell."

"How wrong you are, Richter; how wrong you are," Helm said sweetly.

"You don't seem to grasp the situation," Martin said. "You can't do anything to me, because I'm not afraid of you. You can shoot me, but I'm not afraid of being shot. You can take me back to prison and beat me up some more. I'm not afraid of that either. Don't you see that you've already done your worst to me? There comes a point of saturation when no threat and no pain and no suffering and neither death nor devil can frighten a man—and you're without power over people who are not afraid of you."

"Point of saturation, eh? Very well put indeed, Richter. But I wonder how well Fraulein Dorn will stand up under investigation. She is such a small slip of a girl, isn't she?"

There it is now, something said to Martin. There it is now. That's the catch, and you can't stand this; not this. "The girl had nothing to do with me. She didn't know that I was hiding in her room," he said desperately.

"I see. And you don't know her either. You didn't even

know in whose room you were keeping your clothes. Is that what you're trying to tell me?"

Martin knew that any lie he might attempt to invent would seem pathetically stupid. Helm went on gloating over the situation.

"Maybe our Lisel won't be quite as ignorant as you. Tell me, Lisel: You know Richter. Of course you know him and his organization. If you are wise you'll tell us everything you know about them. It will save you a lot of unpleasantness. My, my, what will the Fuehrer do when he learns that you made common cause with a rat like Richter? You like to be on the stage, don't you? I was always one of your most ardent admirers, Lisel; I'm such a softie—you might even bribe me into keeping this a secret between you and me. But you will have to make a clean breast of everything you know."

"I know nothing," said Lisa. She was hanging with every fibre of her being on Martin's eyes, taking her orders, her fortitude, her consolation from their intense, cold blue fires. He seemed to smile, even at this moment; balancing between now and a black eternity, he smiled. The two clefts appeared on his cheek as though cut there with a sharp knife.

"Leave the girl out of this. She knows nothing," he said.

"However that may be, it will be very interesting to put her through a little grilling, don't you think so, Richter?" Helm said conversationally, ignoring Lisa and turning his full attention as well as the muzzle of his gun toward Martin. "I think we will be generous and let you watch when we're grilling her, Richter. You're a hard-boiled brute, we know that. It did not make much of an impression on you when your sister was executed. But maybe you'll be more sensitive about Lisa Dorn."

It was a mistake for Helm to remind Martin Richter of Annemarie and threaten to do to Lisa what had been done to her. It was the one thing that called every nerve and gland in Martin's body to her defence and made every cell in his brain function with an almost superhuman clarity. When he answered, he spoke only to gain time and summon every grain of strength that was in him.

"If I had anything to tell I should have told it before. I couldn't help my sister because I have no secrets to give away. The riot in Leipzig was spontaneous. That's all I know. I don't know anything else. I don't know anything. Neither does Lisa. She has nothing to do with this. Take me, but leave her out of this."

"Very chivalrous of you, Richter, really. But every word you say incriminates the girl more. You will be surprised how much we are going to get out of her," Helm said pleasantly. He was sitting on a chair and had forced Martin down onto another, directly opposite, with the gun pointed at him.

Helm looked very surprised himself after Martin had knocked him out. He did it the way they had taught him to fight guerrillas in Russia, and it took only a fraction of a second. In that split second he ducked, hit Helm's chin hard with the top of his own head, at the same moment kicking the gun from his hand with his knee; then, as the man went slack, he crushed his nose with a hard blow that finished him. Helm slumped to the floor, and Martin picked him up again and dragged him to the door panel next to the wardrobe like a bag of limp old rags. Lisa watched him without a sound. She bent down and picked up the gun and held it out to him with the ghostlike shadow of a smile. He shook his head. Not a word was spoken between them. He opened the door and listened. The muffled backstair noises of the hotel, commonplace and harmless, wafted by. The clanking of dishes being washed in the kitchen. Somewhere an Italian chef sang in a vain, conceited voice. A door banged on another floor and a chambermaid called another chambermaid. But all this was distant, and the small grey landing outside was silent and empty. Martin dragged the limp Gestapo commissar to the door of the service elevator, with its sign: "Out of order." He opened it with the key Adolf had given him and did not even trouble to look down the black shaft as he pulled his load inside that door and let go of it. He listened, the blood now very loud in his ears; it seemed to take a long time for the body to land at the bottom of the shaft, which meant the top of the service elevator down in the basement. It was not a loud thud, rather a soft and squashy disintegration, and Martin hoped that no one had been in the basement to hear it. The top of the service elevator seemed an excellent place for Gestapo Commissar Helm to lie and rot for the time being. Martin closed the door of the shaft, straightened the sign "Out of order," and brushed his hands instinctively, as if touching that limp body had made them dirty. His head began to hurt a bit from hitting Helm's chin so hard. It felt as it had felt when he had bumped his head on a door as a child, and his mother had pressed the swelling down with the cool blade of a kitchen knife. But otherwise he felt all right now, light with exultation and a pulsing gladness. As he returned to the room Lisa was still holding the gun slackly, gazing at it with a queer expression. Her eyebrows were high up with surprise on her round forehead.

"What do I do with this?" she asked.

"Give it to me. I can use it."

She put the gun gingerly on the table between them, and he picked it up and shoved it into the pocket of his silly blue uniform.

"What did you do with him? I mean—where is he now?"

"Never mind. He's out of the way."

Lisa stretched her fingers and looked at them with great attention. "Look," she said.

"What, Lisa?"

"They're cold. But they're steady. When I have stage fright they shake, but they're steady now." Suddenly she looked full into his eyes. "You dumped him in the elevator shaft?" she asked, and the word "dumped" sounded incongruously tough and detached. "Yes," answered Martin.

"It was unfortunate," he said clumsily; all at once he was deadly frightened lest this had put an end to everything between them. "I couldn't help it," he said. "Believe me, it was the only way out."

"What did you do with him? Is he——" She swallowed hard. "Is he gone?"

"I hope so. Yes. I think there's one beast less in the Gestapo stable. I'm sorry, Lisel. Such a shock for you. But it was you or he." He waited and added unhappily: "Now you won't care for me any longer."

"Care for you?" she asked. "Care for you?" Her blood had been freezing in her body, but now it began to thaw and pulse and flow again, and she was conscious of being alive, acutely and sweetly and wildly conscious of it as never before. "Care for you?" she said impetuously. "Oh yes, I care for you, more—much more now. I didn't know, Martin, I was so frightened; I had given us up. And then you—it was like a miracle. It was wonderful, and horrible, and very wonderful.

I didn't know it. I mean I didn't know one could fight back. We can fight back, can't we? I thought it was over. But you fought us out of it. You killed him, didn't you? Oh, thank God, you killed him."

"Killed him. Yes. That's what they teach you in a war," he said sullenly. "But I still don't like it when I have to kill a man. I never will." He rubbed the painful top of his head and looked at her as if he were only now coming out of the dizzy spin. "You're a funny girl, aren't you? I think you're pretty wonderful yourself. Not a sound, not a scream, not a wrong move. What a funny, crazy little fool I've caught myself!" He stretched out his hand and touched her cautiously. "High voltage. Steel through and through. And you still care for me?"

"It ties us together, doesn't it? It's stronger than a— stronger than a wedding ceremony. For better, for worse. It makes me part of you—part of it all. Oh, my darling, we're in it together and we'll get out of it together."

"Yes, and damn quick, too," Martin said, returning from the twilight grounds of the last ten minutes to the realities of his escape. "Now there is no choice left, little fool. You'll have to get me out even if this drum-major's costume were ten times as flashy as it is."

Lisa laughed; yes, she could laugh again. There was a strange transparency about her, as if danger were the native element in which she lived truer and stronger than in the faked passions of the stage. Martin stared at her. "Come here," he said. "Come to me." She went over to him and into the gate of his arms. He held her to himself, violently. "This is good-bye," he whispered. "Good-bye. I love you, very much I love you. And I will be very careful from now on because I want to live. Good-bye. And now teach me to be Captain Donescu."

They had practised not longer than five minutes when there was a knock at the door. Lisa's heart rose in her mouth as she called: "Yes? Who is it?"

A throat was cleared out there, and an embarrassed voice answered: "It's just me. Oberleutnant Kauders."

"Who?"

"Kauders. I had the pleasure last night——"

Lisa's eyes began to dance. Martin pulled instinctively away and tried to sneak into the bathroom. Lisa shook her head, laughing softly. "No, no—that won't do, Captain," she said. "We'll let him come in and you stand here and face it. This is our dress rehearsal."

"Come in," she called, giving Martin's hand a reassuring squeeze. The door opened timidly and revealed the young flier, bowing and saluting on the threshold.

"I hope I don't disturb you, Fraulein Dorn," he said. "I tried to telephone first, but they say your phone's out of order. So I thought I'd try my luck."

"But certainly. Come in, Leutnant," Lisa said hospitably, and Kauders advanced.

"I wanted to ask you to do me a great favour," he stuttered. Then his eyes fell on Martin, and he stiffened perceptibly. "I hope I'm not intruding," he said with more politeness than tact.

"Not at all. May I present Captain Donescu, an old friend of mine? The captain is in Berlin on some sort of a confidential mission; oh, I shouldn't have said that, should I, Captain?"

Lisa had given herself that intense shove and push with which she always transported herself from the wings on to the stage. The transformation had taken place. She was acting now, and acting eloquently and with ease. She was grateful that this fool of a flier had stumbled in on their farewell; now they could try out the crazy stunt on him and see how it worked.

Kauders saluted, and Martin saluted, too, remembering— thank God, thought Lisa—to do it the Rumanian way, a little sloppily and with a fine flourish.

"Speak German?" Kauders asked very loud and in a sort of pidgin which he seemed to believe correct for conversing with foreigners.

"A little," Martin answered with a slight accent and great presence of mind. Lisa felt like applauding.

"Don't let the captain fool you, Oberleutnant," she said gaily. "He understands every word. I think it is only a diplomatic trick of his when he claims not to speak it well. I caught him several times, talking German as well as you and I do."

Thus, having built a little barrier against possible slips, Lisa gave Kauders a wink and a smile of mutual understanding. She did it because she wanted to distract his attention. She

F

did not like the way the flier scrutinized the poor uniform that had once looked so impressive on doorman George. Suddenly the smell of mothballs seemed to stand in the room as thick as a board. But Kauders wasn't interested in the foreign uniform. What he tried to find out was whether this Balkan fellow was by any chance having a love affair with the actress. He did not like the idea that a German woman like Lisa Dorn should get herself involved with a dirty and inferior Rumanian swine. On the other hand—if she wasn't too proud to go to bed with this Captain whatever his name was, then a good, clean, brave German flier had every chance of getting her too.

Kauders had awakened with a bad hangover and had spent considerable time and effort to get over it. Several strong doses of absinthe—which the obliging Ahlsen at the desk had managed to conjure up from the hotel's secret stock—together with some of the white pills had at last done the job. But he felt shaky; there was still an unpleasant taste and a disgusting tendency to break out in a cold sweat. Lying in his bed, waiting for the various stimulants to take their blessed effect, the lieutenant had taken to daydreaming. The more he dreamt and the better he began to feel, the surer he was that he would be a fool not to try at least to have a go at that actress. He was well heated up and floating on the crest of an unhealthy wave of self-assurance when he entered Lisa's room. Lisa's smile, her wink, her obvious pleasure at seeing him did the rest. Otto Kauders was only a stupid schoolboy at heart, adolescent and not more insolent than the average. But the mixture of absinthe and Pervitine turned him into a roaring lion.

"What was it you wanted from me, Oberleutnant?" Lisa asked.

"That you give me a mascot, Fraulein. But it must be something personal or it doesn't work."

"Something personal? A photo with my autograph?" Lisa asked with professional friendliness; her photo was the mascot of thousands of soldiers.

"Yes, I'd like your photo very much. But you must write something very personal on it," Kauders said. "Not just: 'Good hunting!' or 'Best wishes!' Something really personal." He would show the photo to the boys of the squadron and pin it over his bed and let them burst with curiosity and jealousy.

Lisa took one of her photos from a stack in the desk and brought
out her fountain pen. "How would it be if I wrote: 'In memory
of an unforgettable hour'?" she said, sailing away on a
little gale of exuberance. "An unforgettable hour," she
said, writing it down while telegraphing a secret message to
Martin.

"Well—thanks," Kauders stammered, overcome by the
significance of the dedication. . . . If only we could get rid of
that Rumanian, he thought; we two would understand each
other in no time. "Thanks—that'll go over my bed; but I
need a mascot, too. Something I can take upstairs with
me."

"The oberleutnant is one of our best fighter pilots; maybe
you read in the papers about him," Lisa said to Martin, trying
to bring him into the conversation.

"Indeed?" Martin said, not very intelligently.

"You do any flying, Captain?" Kauders shouted as if the
Rumanian were deaf. "No? What's your troop, Captain?"

This was a pitfall and Lisa noticed at once Martin's helpless groping for an answer. In fact, the main shortcoming
of the doorman's uniform was its lack of distinctive insignia.
There was a wealth of braid and brass buttons and even
ribbons, but no indication whatever of any troop. She linked
her arm in Kauders' and took him to the other side of the
room, giving Martin time to recover. "He's in the diplomatic
corps," she said. "Now let's see what I could give you for a
mascot."

"It must be one of a pair, you know that, don't you? I
get one and you keep the other, and when you give it to me
you must say: 'Bring this back to me.' Then I'll bring it back.
That's how a real mascot works."

"One of my gloves?"

"Something more personal, Fraulein."

"I couldn't give you one of my stockings, because I can't
get new ones."

"One of your garters would make a fine mascot," Kauders
whispered, coming close to her. Lisa pulled away, disgusted
by his hangover breath and by the proximity of his shaking
body.

"Captain Donescu," she said, "don't you think it is
time for us to leave?"

"At your service, madame," said Martin.

"Do I get one of your garters ?" Kauders whispered shakily, pressing closer. "If you're a good boy," Lisa said and eeled out of the alcove where he had cornered her. "May I come and get it ? Later ?" Kauders asked, insistent as a mosquito. "Maybe, but now we must go," she said. "Here's your photo, Leutnant. And we'll see about the mascot some other time. Good-bye."

"You don't want me to have bad luck, do you ?" Kauders said, slightly hurt.

"Of course I want you to have good luck. But I can't give you a mascot now. Some other time. Not now."

She was a bit breathless now, because they would have to take the plunge soon. A hasty glance at the clock told her that it was almost five, and at six she had to go to the theatre. Theatre be hanged ! she thought, and with this one exploding thought she blasted her entire past from her life. Her words and her obvious embarrassment had ignited a spark in Kauders' befogged brain. . . . She wants to get rid of the Rumanian, he thought. That's what it is. She wants me to come back for my mascot when she is alone. What tricks these women of the world know ! . . . Martin had meanwhile listened with utmost concentration to the blurred noises of the hotel. It was not probable that Helm's body would be found very soon. But if the devil wanted the elevator to function again, then the discovery was unavoidable and not a mouse would get out of the hotel after that.

"Let's go," he said brusquely, swept by a wave of sudden, frantic impatience. "Glad to have met you, Ober-leutnant."

But Kauders had decided not to leave the Rumanian alone with the actress. His training had deliberately and brutally beaten every shred of timidity out of his character, for timid fliers were only good to break their necks and wreck training ships. And so he pushed out his chin and said boldly: "Yes, let's all go downstairs and have a drink."

There was a moment's silence, and then Lisa said with a ring in her voice: "Yes, let's. I think that's a good idea. Let the three of us have a drink downstairs, Captain Donescu."

Martin stared at her quizzically, trying to penetrate the plan that seemed to have sprung up in her whimsical brain. . . . You plucky little fool, he thought. You dear, foolish little fool.

You comrade, you friend, you mine, you everything. . . .
Lisa was putting on her hat, and Kauders shouted at him:
"You live in this hotel, Captain?"

"No; at the embassy," Martin answered. Lisa picked up her
gloves and bag; her eyes signalled to him. He deciphered the
frantic message, and it began to dawn on him that Lisa wanted
to use the flier as his convoy. At the door there was another
stumbling-block. It did not occur to Corporal Richter to walk
out ahead of an oberleutnant. Kauders on his part automatically fell back to let the captain pass. But training and discipline
almost got the better of Martin as he stepped aside and saluted
the flier. Kauders was flabbergasted. He too stepped aside
and saluted. Lisa relieved the confusion by linking her arms
into the arms of both of them and taking them out together.
She was tightrope-walking now as she went down the stairs
with her two escorts.

The lobby was crowded, and there were uniforms everywhere.
There were even—and Martin's heart stopped as he saw it—
several members of the Rumanian Military Mission seated
around one of the little marble tables, looking every inch as
flashy as he did. If the exits were guarded, there were at least no
visible signs of it. On the other hand, the stocky fellow in the
tight blue suit with the newspaper in front of his face and placed
in a strategic spot was as definitely marked Gestapo as if he
had carried an electric sign on his head. "Shall we sit down
here?" Martin asked in much too flawless German, after he
had taken stock of the locale. The table he selected was not
too exposed and not too far from the revolving door. Pageboy Number 6 flitted over and went through the motions of
wiping the top of the table. Every pimple stood very red on
his very pale face as he did so. "Thanks, my boy. That's
fine," said Martin, who felt sorry for him. They ordered three
of the hotel's Specials, the only drink the low supplies still
permitted. It was a fierce-tasting mixture, and neither Martin
nor Lisa really drank it. The radio spilled a sticky flood of
sentimental music, moaning for Lilli Marlene, and Kauders'
thigh and knee sneaked up close to Lisa's. It made her a little
sick, but she accepted it bravely. She laughed and talked and
flirted shamelessly with the flier, hoping to God all the while
that Martin would understand her manœuvre. All of her
wanted to be alone with him, quiet and safe and close and
contented alone with him; instead she had to sit behind this

dismal little table, giving a performance for the benefit of the lobby.

"I think it is raining," Martin said. "I wonder——" and he got up and made a few reconnoitring steps toward the revolving door, as if to examine the weather. Lisa's glance was riveted on him. The rope on which she was walking was strung very high over a very deep, very black chasm, but she still kept her balance. Kauders held her back as she got up to follow Martin. "I'm crazy about you," he whispered recklessly. "You drive me crazy. Never mind the Rumanian, he doesn't understand what we're saying anyway. Why don't you get rid of him? I must talk to you alone. Where did you buy that face of yours? Don't look at me like that or I'll explode right here, on the spot. Listen, get rid of that fellow; you don't want to run around with one of those oily Balkanese."

Martin was coming back to the table. Lisa, flying at a very high altitude in very thin air, whispered back to the flier: "How can I get rid of him? I'd like to—but how? Look here—you take him off my hands. Take him out, show him the sights of the town, anything you like. Get rid of him, somehow, somewhere. Lose him on a bus, throw him in the Landwehrkanal."

Shaking all over with the excitement of his conquest, Kauders said: "You're marvellous. God, you're marvellous ! Don't worry, leave it to me. I'll get rid of him for you. And when I come back?"

"Yes. Get rid of him and come back. I'll wait for you here," Lisa said desperately. Martin sat down at her side again; she could feel him taut, not trembling exactly, but vibrating, like a string drawn too tight.

"How are you feeling, Captain?" she asked and could not keep the tenderness out of her voice. . . . I did not know you yesterday; how come that today you are all that counts? her heart asked him. . . . "Thanks. I never felt better in my life," he answered. It meant: Don't be frightened, and it meant: I love you, and it meant: Some day everything will be all right.

"Is it raining ?"

"Yes, a drizzle."

Kauders emptied his glass and took a direct course toward his goal. "You know Berlin well, Captain ?"

"Not as well as I should like, Oberleutnant," Martin said,

prompted by Lisa's foot tapping down on his. Everything had a curious lucidity, as in a high fever. He was acquainted with this condition from moments of acute danger in the war.

"I'd like to take you out and show you around town," Kauders said, giving him a wink of masculine understanding. "I know a few places you might enjoy."

"That I should appreciate greatly," Martin said with an accent that was anything but Rumanian. "Whenever you have time."

"That's it. I haven't much time. Three days' leave. That's not much time, Captain. How would you like to go on a little tour of the town with me now?"

"Now?" Martin asked. . . . Yes, now, damn you, Kauders thought fiercely. I'll get you away if I have to do it by force.

Lisa tapped a frantic message on Martin's foot.

"Good," Martin said, decoding it. "Very kind of you, Oberleutnant. That is, if madame is kind enough to give us leave—now."

"Waiter—the check!" Kauders called. Lisa was trying to keep her hands still. They had an almost irresistible urge to break matches, tear up the paper napkins, squash out one cigarette after another. She felt acutely the impression she gave the crowded lobby. It stared at her and whispered and hummed. . . . Look at our Lisel. Flirting with the two young officers. Wonder how the general likes that. The one with the burns, that's a famous flier. Who's the other one? . . . God knows. You see new uniforms every day in this hotel. Looks like a Bulgarian or a Rumanian. Do they still go around in those musical-comedy outfits? . . . Don't you know why? I heard it from one of their officers; it's a left-over from King Carol's time. The king owned some cloth factories, and he was a good business man and wanted to sell his cloth. So he made it compulsory for every officer to have twenty-three different uniforms for different occasions. It was time we came in and brought order into their rotten household. . . . Yes, if our Rumanian allies were as good in combat as they seem to be in bed—well, Heil Hitler. Heil Hitler.

At her left side, Kauders was telling about the new ME-109. At her right Martin sat, very tense, very calm, very composed. Under the table her hand searched for his and found it and held it. Suddenly he stiffened and his lips turned white. She followed his glance and went limp. It was not more than that Herr Schmidt left the desk, went over to the elevator and took off the sign: "Out of order." It had been there several weeks, causing the guests to complain and the floor waiters to swear. Now Herr Schmidt removed it and invitingly opened the doors of the elevator. Martin got to his feet. "Let's go," he said with stiff white lips. "Let's go now."

"I'm only waiting for my change. I gave him a twenty-mark bill," Kauders said, clanking his cigarette case against the glass to call the waiter. It was an eternity of two minutes before the man appeared. "There it is now," Kauders said, cramming the change into his wallet. Martin got ready to do his stunt. "*Buna seara, madame, multumesc*," he said, bending over Lisa's hand and kissing it. Good-bye, hand, good-bye, beloved, till we meet again.

Suddenly it was as if something had touched the lobby. It was like a gust of wind sweeping over a field of rye when all the haulms bend and bow before it in one direction. There was a whisper as in a ryefield, too, a rustling, humming crescendo. All heads were turned toward the men who had entered through the revolving door, for this was the Gestapo, unmasked and menacing. Lisa knew the short, small man in the uniform of an SS Obergruppenfuehrer who looked like a bespectacled, mild-mannered schoolteacher, or—Lisa thought —like a constipated mouse. This was Weyhart Wolle, Helm's superior, the powerful, dreaded chief. A compact group of four more SS men had entered in his wake. Two of them went up to the desk and seemed to ask for some information. The two others followed the chief at a little distance.

Lisa got up and stood at Martin's side. Very clearly she remembered at this glasslike, brittle moment what Martin had told her about Annemarie. The funny smell of the prison yard. That Annemarie had laughed as she went up the scaffold, that the doctor had given her scopolamin. She remembered it with such a fantastic lucidity that for one unbearable moment she became Annemarie herself. She herself was taken up to the scaffold and she knew that something had been wrong, everything had been wrong for a long time, and now it was too late to right it. And then the chief came toward them, relentless as an express train; Lisa held her smile before Martin like a shield, and the chief walked past her with a little salute, walked across the lobby and into the elevator; the two men following him went up the stairs, while of the two others one remained at the desk and one marched toward the bar. The man in the tight blue suit near the door got up with the expression of a dog eager to retrieve a big bone.

"Well, shall we go?" said Kauders, who had noticed nothing of it all.

"Yes, let's go," Martin answered.

"Heil Hitler," said Kauders, giving Lisa a bold wink. It looked funny in his naked, burned face.

"*Buna seara; auf Wiedersehen,*" said Martin.

"*Au revoir,*" said Lisa. "*Auf Wiedersehen.*"

They went to the revolving door and nothing happened. Pageboy Number 6 stood there, an ugly little urchin with the load of a great heritage on his shoulders. He gave the door a push and it began to turn. In passing Martin gave the boy a little jab, saluted and walked out. Kauders turned around, winked again at Lisa, saluted also, and followed him.

How often must I say good-bye to you, my love? How often shall I have to let you go, not knowing if I'll ever see you again? Good-bye. I'll keep my fingers crossed. Why didn't I give you a mascot and tell you to bring it back to me? You took my heart along with you. Bring it back to me. Please, bring it back.

"Hallo, Lisel," somebody said to her. It was Stetten, anxious to keep his word and get her out of the way on time. He had arrived only a few minutes previously, coming from the harassing session at the AA and trying in vain to find Helm and have a word with him about the two pending questions: Had Dahnwitz taken his exit? And had Plottke come forward with his shares? He had watched Lisa flirting with the two young officers at the same time that the chief's appearance heralded the liquidation of the Dahnwitz case. Such are life's ironical counterpoints, he thought with the cynical melancholy of a seasoned diplomat. Lisa stared at him as if she had forgotten his name.

"Oh—it's you, Baron. Hallo. How are you?"

"I'm here by proxy, Lisel. Dahnwitz wants to be excused—he can't take you to the theatre. But I have my car outside. May I take you there?"

Lisa remembered the general only as she would remember perhaps an illustration in an old magazine she had vaguely scanned in a doctor's waiting-room. She had also completely forgotten that she must play Portia for the first time tonight. She kept on staring at Stetten and through him; he was afraid the rumour of the general's end might reach the lobby any minute.

"Well—shall we go?" he asked, touching her elbow. She gathered her gloves and bag and got up, sleepwalking. She said:

"Go? Where? To the theatre? Yes. That's very kind of you, Baron. Yes, now it's time for me to go to the theatre."

SHORTLY after four o'clock the grey mist of the unfriendly day had curdled into low-driving clouds, and it began to rain. This rain gave the crowds a vague relief from the heavy unspoken apprehension that hung over them. They would stop on their way for a moment, shivering in their old yet precious raincoats, to look up into the sky, secretly hoping and praying for the clouds to remain, for the rain to pour harder, for a storm to come up and protect the city. During the past weeks many children had been evacuated from Berlin; it was a bad sign; in the meantime evacuees from other bombed towns had drifted into the city in their aimless shifting, and the horror they carried in their shattered nerves and their crazy eyes and their broken voices was like a contagious disease and made the people of Berlin sick with fear. There was much whistling in the dark. There was much talk about the new air defences, and people pointed out to one another the countless anti-aircraft guns posted conspicuously on many roofs, and the sinister grey might of the flak towers. They discussed the effectiveness of the new shelters which had been constructed hastily but with great efficiency. They felt faintly cheered by the thought that the Fuehrer had converted his own shelter under the chancellery—the best shelter in town—into a completely equipped maternity ward where women might give birth safely even during an air raid. Germans have a peculiar trust in anything German. Never having been treated as grown-up, free, and self-governing citizens, they enjoy the spurious security of children or slaves. Their part was to be good subjects, not to question or to doubt, and to obey the rules. The State then was responsible for their protection, safety, and well-being. Only during the last few weeks had it begun to dawn on them that even German flak towers could be silenced and German shelters blasted, that even German organization might break down and that even the German State was not omnipotent. And like any great faith and trust that has been misused and cheated for a long time, theirs was just beginning to simmer and boil and change into a poisonous brew of scorn and bitter contempt and hatred.

After delivering Lisa Dorn at the theatre, Von Stetten returned to the hotel to be on hand in case he should be needed for some formalities in the winding up of the affair Dahnwitz. Also, Dahlin had promised to telephone his home office and give him their final decision about the suggested deal in which Plottke's clandestine fortune was to play a prominent part. Stetten was not very optimistic about this sequel to the morning's conferences; he felt tired, worn, somehow punctured, and also not quite clean.

His nerves were on edge when he came through the revolving door, and he felt at once that a strange uneasiness was pervading the lobby. He looked around for Helm, and as he could not find him he went up to the desk and asked for him; the faces of the old men there seemed even greyer than usual, and Ahlsen sounded cramped when he answered: "Commissar Helm? I regret, Herr Baron, but I can't give you any information about Commissar Helm."

Stetten was too well trained in the diplomatic service to ask further questions. "Possibly the chief could tell the Herr Baron," Kliebert added; he was not grey but positively green in the face. "Where is the chief? Can you page him for me?" Stetten said, getting worried. Schmidt, usually so efficient and eager to serve, seemed to be in a trance and did not respond.

"I think I saw him in the bar," a gentleman who had limped by informed him. "Thanks," Stetten said, not recognizing the doctor who had been introduced to him several times. The lifeless, lugubrious figure of an old woman in a crumpled uniform shuffled up to the desk and put down a batch of telegrams. No one at the desk seemed in the mood to inquire about the latest news, but she reported it anyway. "They say

all children under ten must get out of Berlin in three days.
The Americans have a new way of killing whole towns. With
sound waves. Worse than poison gas. A man in Hallensee
went crazy and killed his four children and his mother and his
wife and himself. They say Goering is arrested. They haven't
got Richter yet," Stetten heard her croak as he left the desk.
He found Weyhart Wolle at a small table in a corner of the
bar, thoughtfully occupied with a glass of brandy and looking
sick.

"Heil Hitler. They told me you were here. I'm looking for
Helm. Do you know where he is?"

"He isn't in the hotel any more," the chief said glumly.
"Come, sit down. You're just the man I want to talk to.
You handled some preliminary steps in this Dahnwitz affair,
didn't you?"

"Yes. Did it not click?" Stetten asked tensely.

"What? Oh yes, it clicked, as far as Dahnwitz is concerned.
He died. Heart failure. You can go upstairs and pay him
your homage. He lies there as neat as a peeled egg, the
bastard."

"*De mortuis nil nisi bonum*," Stetten said, shocked. He
was used to the Gestapo variety of heart failure and to many
brutalities, but this went too far.

"*Nil nisi bonum*. Tell that to the War Department," Wolle
growled. "Let *them* take care of the trimmings. Guard of
honour, speeches, obituaries, salvo over his grave, and all
that."

"He was a good soldier, even if he made mistakes."

"That's what you think. The dirty bastard. He killed
Helm before he shot himself. Can you imagine that? Killed
him. A German general kills my best man and throws him
down the elevator shaft."

It hit Stetten in the stomach. He swallowed hard. "Give
me a brandy," he ordered quickly. Only after he had
downed it did he feel able to speak again.

"Is that what happened to Helm?"

"Yes. That's what happened. Today it got Helm. Last
week it got Schreber in Munich. In Paris it has got four since
Friday. In Norway it gets our men by the dozen; we can't
send them up as quickly as they kill them. Recently even the
Danes are making trouble. I tell you, Stetten, hardly a day
goes by without some of our men getting killed. We're

suffering greater losses in proportion than the army. Our business is much more dangerous than just being a soldier. But is it appreciated, what we're doing for the safety of the homeland? I wonder. So today it's Helm. Tomorrow it may be myself. Oh, damn the whole set-up."

"How do you know Dahnwitz did it?"

"It's clear to me that he did it. Who else had a reason?"

I could mention many, Stetten thought, but kept it to himself.

"I can figure out the working of Dahnwitz's mind as clearly as if I had seen him do it," the chief said. "'All right,' Dahnwitz told himself. 'You've caught me in a trap. But if I have to go I'm taking you with me.'"

"It isn't like Dahnwitz to throw a man down an elevator shaft. He might have shot him, yes. That's plausible. But not this."

"Sure. They're making an autopsy now, of what's left of Helm, that is. I'm sure they'll find that he was shot first. The Herr General was too arrogant to be found dead in the same room with Helm, so he got rid of him. Typical Dahnwitz."

Stetten kept on shaking his head. Wolle swished the rest of his cognac in the glass. "Well, I've got to go. Clean up the mess. Lots of work to do. Apropos, Stetten: the general's death won't be made public before tomorrow. As for Helm —he had an accident. We'll arrange for that. We don't want anything to leak out before we are ready to release the news."

"What about the hotel personnel?"

"They have their instructions. The janitor found Helm's body when they started the service elevator. He's a reliable man and will shut up."

"Listen, Wolle, I have an idea," Stetten said, hit by a sudden revelation. Martin Richter, he thought. Wasn't he believed to be hiding somewhere here? And if he were, he might have been desperate enough to do it. But not Dahnwitz. Not Arnim von Dahnwitz.

"Yes? What is it?" the chief asked. It was at that moment that something strange occurred in Stetten's mind. Why say it? Why join the hunt? Dahnwitz is dead. Helm is dead. Why involve another man in it? Let sleeping dogs lie. It might have been a diplomat's unwillingness to bring about unnecessary complications. Again, it might have been a dreg of decency left at the bottom of corruption. "About Dahnwitz's funeral: he wanted to be buried in Elgede," he said evenly.

"Don't worry," Wolle said grimly. "We'll give him a funeral de luxe. Maybe you can even prevail on our Fuehrer to shed a few tears at his grave. It would make it a bit easier for his friend Goebbels to explain the demise of four generals in one and the same week. God, do I feel lousy ! I shouldn't have taken that brandy; it's bad for my kidneys. But I needed it. After looking at Helm, I certainly needed it. Well—Heil Hitler."

Stetten ordered another glass and drank it slowly, trying to get himself in shape for the final session with Dahlin. If he had ever needed sweep, optimism, new ideas, convincing arguments, he needed them now. But all his mind would produce was one idiotic line: This is not a through street. This is not a through street. Wherever he turned he came to a dead end. This is not a through street.

He looked morosely at the noisy group of people lined up at the bar in a preposterously hilarious mood. He knew them, too. Three officers from the Rumanian Military Mission, having their fun with that little bar fly, Tilli. It seemed that there was a bet on as to the number of Specials Tilli could down without ill effect.

"*Elle est formidable, la pétite, formidable !*"

"Tilli is cheating; she pours them into the V of her dress."

"Is that true, Tilli ? Let's see if it's true !"

"Let's appoint a committee to investigate if Tilli is pouring drinks into her décolleté. I'll be president."

"*Voyons donc, mon petit cochon !*"

Tilli's laughter had the sound of a broken alarm clock, a tickling, disturbing, strident yet pathetic sound. She was all sex and noise and fun ; she poured down the drinks recklessly, and after the fifth one she actually felt as gay and abandoned and glamorous as she pretended to be. Stetten could not stand this exhibition of hilarity any longer. He called the bar waiter, paid and got up. In the door he almost ran into a little old lady in black who stood there, forlorn and bewildered, as if she wanted to enter the bar but didn't dare to. She looked like the sort of genteel old lady who had never been in a bar in her life, and she was obviously shocked by the sight of Tilli, whose arms were resting on the necks of two officers while a third one was feeding her a drink from a bottle, as if she were a baby.

"Pardon me," Stetten said, saluted the old lady and went out.

"That's Fraulein Tilli—over there," Pageboy Number 6 told the old lady. "That's the one you wanted to see, isn't it ?"

"Yes. That's Tilli. I didn't recognize her for a moment. Would you, please, kindly tell her that I want to see her ?"

"Frau Mueller, isn't it ?"

"Yes. Tell her Sim's mother. Please. Thank you."

The old lady shrank into the wall while she waited. Her pursed, wrinkled lips worked silently, and she couldn't control the nervous twitching of her face. In the pocket of the black jacket she clutched the yellow star. Tilli's laughter stopped as Number 6 gave her the message, "Who ?" she said. "Frau Mueller ? Who's Frau Mueller ? I don't know any Frau Mueller. Ask her what she wants. Can't she see I'm busy ?"

"She says to tell you Sim's mother, Fraulein Tilli."

"Who ?" Tilli said again. She put down the glass and shook off the hands of the Rumanians that were all over her. "Quit pawing me," she said angrily. She straightened her hair and pulled her skirt over her knees. "Not Sim's mother ?" she said softly. "Not Sim's mother ?"

"She's been asking for you all day long," said Number 6. "That's her, over there."

"Holy Maria, Mother of God," said Tilli, pushing the boy aside and leaving the bar. Her skin was ashen under the coarse rouge.

"It's you !" she whispered as she stood face to face with the old lady. "I didn't believe it. You shouldn't have come here."

"I know, Tilli. But I had to."

Tilli kept on staring at Sim's mother. That's the suit Knize made for her in '31, she thought. Good clothes will tell. But, God, how she looks otherwise. . . . Sim's mother nodded and opened her mouth in a grimace that was meant to be a smile. "Yes, Tilli," she said gently. "We've changed. Both of us."

"What do you want from me ?" Tilli asked.

"It's about Papa. I can't talk about it here."

"You shouldn't have come," Tilli said again. She thought it over for a moment while the eyes of the old lady did not let go of her. "Let's go to my room," she said at last with a sigh. . . . I hope I won't get in trouble through having her here. Thank God, she doesn't look Jewish, she thought. Sim did, in a cute sort of way, and Papa Baruch, too. But Mama could always pass as an Aryan. "Not the elevator," she said. "Let's walk upstairs."

As she opened the door of the monkey cage, Tilli hated her room. She would have liked to tear the photos of her act off the wall, hide the empty bottle, chase out the stale smell of cheap perfume and yesterday's debauch. She threw her kimono over a bundle of dirty lingerie and shook a heap of cigarette stubs out into the airless shaft outside the small window.

"What a nice room," Sim's mother said with sleep-walking politeness.

"Oh, forget about the room. Sit down. Tell me why you came. Come on. Relax. Do you want something to drink? . . . No? To eat? A glass of water?" Tilli said; she was afraid the old lady might faint, right then and there.

"I'm well. Don't worry about me, Tilli. You're a good child. And still so pretty," Frau Baruch said, searching in Tilli's coarsened face for the young girl she had known.

"How's Papa Baruch?" Tilli asked. "God, it's a long time, isn't it? Almost ten years."

"Yes. Almost ten years," Frau Baruch said, and there was a pause. "Papa is very sick, Tilli. That's why I come to you. You're the only one who can help us."

"You need money?"

"No, child, no, Tilli-child. I wouldn't come here for money. You know what will happen to me if I'm caught—without the star—out of bounds. I wouldn't risk all this just for money," Frau Baruch said gently. No soldier at the front, no explorer in the jungle, no test pilot in the stratosphere needed as much valour as it had cost her to make this fantastic expedition into the forbidden realm of the hotel. All the time, walking through streets she had not seen in years, among people who were not outcasts and did not know that she was branded with the yellow star, Frau Baruch had felt as if she were a ghost, invisible, returning from the beyond, floating over the places where she had once been alive. Tilli put out her hands and touched the hands of Sim's mother that were restless as the hands of people in their dying hour are said to be.

"What's the matter with Papa Baruch? What can I do for him? Visit him? It's not easy, you know."

"Papa has a cancer of the stomach, and he can't die. We can't get medicine, Tilli, we can't get a doctor. There are no Jews left in Berlin. Maybe there are a dozen or two, but we don't know them. We're the last Jews. You don't know what that means! There's no one to help poor Papa. He lies there and screams with pain. By day, by night, he screams many hours, until he is too weak to scream. He faints for a while, and then the pain wakes him up again and he screams. If he could rest! If he could sleep! But we have no medicine. I don't want to complain to you. I don't want to bother you. But, Tilli, you were always such a good, kind, helpful child. I had to come to you. Remember when Sim had scarlet fever? A grown-up man and scarlet fever! You fought with the doctor when he wouldn't let you into the room, and you stayed with Sim and helped me nurse him, and you played the clown and made fun with him all the time. Sim never laughed so much as he did when he had scarlet fever. He talked about it so often."

"And I didn't catch it, see," Tilli said; "there was nothing to it. I had it as a child, and you don't get it twice." She smiled softly as she wandered back into the past; she could hear the clicking of the stones as she played dominoes with Sim on his bed table and spoon-fed him his milk mush, and teased him because he had grown a red beard during the sickness. Kaiser Barbarossa she had called him.

"You cared a lot for Sim, didn't you, Tilli-child?" Frau Baruch said. "I know much more about you than you think. He talked so much about you. He was so much in love with you, he couldn't keep your name out of the conversation for half an hour. He asked me whether I would mind if he married you. 'You will marry her whether I mind or not,' I told him. 'Go ahead and marry her and don't ask questions.' But Papa was against it. You know how Papa is; he wanted Sim to marry a Jewish girl. He picked daughters-in-law all the time, but Sim didn't even look at them. He wanted you. Maybe Papa was right. Where would you be today if you had married Sim? But I didn't see that far. I only wanted Sim to be happy. He would have been happy with you." Suddenly she was afraid of having said the wrong thing. "You won't hold it against Papa that he didn't want Sim to marry you?" she asked anxiously. "If you could see his suffering, Tilli-child—it is worse than what Job had to suffer."

Tilli shook her head. She had loved Sim, and she had always liked his mother. She hadn't cared much for Papa Baruch, and he hadn't cared for her at all. . . . Why doesn't he make an end of himself, if it's that bad? she thought.

"He is too weak," Sim's mother said as if she had asked it aloud. "We haven't even a window to jump out of, we live in a basement. You can't imagine how weak he is. He has asked me to kill him, not one time but a thousand times. But how can I kill him? I am a coward, Tilli. Maybe I am a coward. I can't take a knife and cut his veins. I could never kill a chicken, how can I kill my husband? If we had medicine, yes. If I could make him sleep—and sleep myself——"

"Can't Rosa do something? Can't she get a doctor to come? She knew many doctors through her work, didn't she?"

Frau Baruch stared at Tilli, her mouth worked again silently and the twitch in her face grew stronger.

"Rosa? Don't you know about Rosa? They sent her to Poland," she said at last.

"When?"

"It's seventeen months and twelve days now. We've never heard from her. We hope she is dead."

Leave me alone, Tilli thought rebelliously. I don't want to know all this. I don't want to hear about all this Jewish misery. It's your misery, not mine. I have my own problems, oh, haven't I! My life isn't all honey and sugar either.

"I don't want to take up your time," Frau Baruch said with the sensitivity that comes with suffering. "I only came to beg you for some sleeping pills. I remember you used some Veronal once in a while. I didn't think it was good for a young girl like you. But I remembered it in my need, and I told Papa I would find you and beg you for some. It wasn't easy to find you," she said with a shadow of a smile; "but you'd be surprised how many people are kind to us old Jews—when they dare, that is. I got your address at the last place where you lived. I haven't seen Papa since this morning. It's very bad that he is alone, screaming with pain, all day long, all day long. But I promised I would bring him some sleeping powder so that he could sleep a few hours. I couldn't come home without it, you see that, Tilli."

"But I haven't got any Veronal. I—I'm tired as it is—and I have to stay up late anyway. I'm sort of—sort of a social hostess in this hotel. Look after the officers who come on leave, you know. No, I don't take sleeping powders any more."

"I see. But couldn't you get some? I can't, but maybe you could get them in a pharmacy——"

"I might ask the doctor to write me a prescription. They're terribly fussy now before they let you have anything like that. I suppose they need a lot of medicine for our soldiers. But I might try and talk to the hotel doctor."

"Tilli, Tilli, if you would do that for us! If Papa could sleep! Oh, my good, good child, I knew you wouldn't let us down."

When Frau Baruch had started out on her expedition, she had promised herself not to complain, not to cry, not to make a scene. She had been beyond crying for a long time. At the lowest bottom of the well of suffering there are no tears, there is only a frozen, paralysed dryness.

"I brought you something, too," she said and tried to smile and behave like the fine old lady she was. "I thought you might like it. It's a picture of Sim when he was three."

"Thank you. That's sweet of you," Tilli said and took the photo. It was a faded snapshot of a baby, sitting on a lawn, with a big teddy bear in front of it. While Tilli looked at it without any emotion, a chain of thoughts began to reel off in her mind. . . . Yes, I think I can get Veronal from the doctor; maybe I can get as much Veronal as she needs. Enough to put them both out of their misery. Poor devil, poor Mama Baruch. It's terrible what they're doing to them. I'm glad Sim didn't live through it all. It's better the way it is. They would have sent him to Poland too. Now let's see. What about Rosa? What about it? If I get them the Veronal that's a very great thing I'm doing for them. I'm sticking my neck out a mile against the wind. They can do something for me, too, can't they. Did she take all her shoes along to Poland? I'll bet she didn't. I'll bet she didn't have any use there for those nice high-heeled pumps she bought just before—before the thing happened to Sim. It's not very nice to ask for her shoes,

is it ? No, it isn't nice. But, hell, there are many things that
aren't nice in this world. Nobody is so damned nice to me
either. I'm sure if Mama Baruch knew I needed shoes she'd
be only too happy to give them to me. If I had known they
sent Rosa to Poland I could have bought them long ago. Sure,
I'll get them the Veronal and I'll give them money, on top of
it. Of course, if they have enough Veronal they won't need
money any longer . . .

"I'm sorry to hear about Rosa," she said. "But maybe
it's only half as bad as you think. Some day you'll hear from
her and everything will be all right."

"About the Veronal, Tilli," Frau Baruch said. "I have
a long way to go home. I'd like to get there before it's
completely dark." The way stretched ahead of her beset with
dangers, like a dark moor she had to cross.

. . . I liked Rosa almost as if she were my own sister, Tilli
went on, following her trend of thought now with the per-
sistence of a hungry shark. We're very much alike in many
ways. Same size, same taste. We could always wear each
other's dresses and everything.

"How much Veronal do you think you could get ? It will
take a lot to kill the pains and make him sleep."

. . . Did Rosa take all her things with her ? They don't allow
them much luggage when they take them to Poland, I understand.

"If he could sleep tonight; you don't know what it would
mean. If he could be without pains for a whole night——"

Tilli gave herself a last push and took the jump. "Tell me,
Mama Baruch, don't you have some of Rosa's things left ?
Dresses, hats, shoes ?"

"What ? What did you say, Tilli-child ?" Frau Baruch
asked, at a loss. "Rosa's things ? No, there's nothing left.
We—we had to sell them piece by piece. You know, even
two old Jews like us have to eat. I kept a lock of her hair.
That and the photo I gave you are all that's left of the
children."

"Well—it doesn't matter," Tilli said, and Frau Baruch
looked at her, wondering what to make of the inappro-
priate remark. Tilli sagged a notch or two on her spine
as another hope went up in smoke. She pulled herself
together and patted Frau Baruch's thin, emaciated hands.
"I'm glad you came to me; I really am," she said clumsily,

and under the mask of grease paint and hard reckless living
there appeared for a moment the face of the girl she
had been twelve years ago. She couldn't have expressed
what it was that caused the transformation. That someone came to her for help, that someone trusted her to be
kind and do the right thing. It was a nice compliment,
in a way, wasn't it? She pushed the shoes out of her
mind.

"Wait here; lie down a little, be comfortable, and don't
worry," she said. "I'll go and see how I can get something
for our Papa. And don't get impatient and don't be frightened.
I'll see that you get home safely."

All right, sucker, she told herself as she went out to find
the doctor. Go ahead and be noble. You're a veritable Maria
Magdalena, aren't you? Soon you'll go barefoot, too. Go
and violate the drug law, put your head under the axe to help
an old Jew. And he didn't even want me to marry Sim.

"Feeling better now?" the doctor asked as he limped into
Geoffrey Nichols' room. It was the hour between dusk and
darkness, but Nichols had not turned on the lights. He was
sitting on his deck chair in the loggia, listening to the rain,
the rug pulled up to his chin, his cold hands resting quietly
on his knees.

"Yes, thanks. Quite well," he said.

"Did you rest after the drops I gave you?"

"More or less. I was sitting out here, thinking." The doctor
fished under the rug for Nichols' wrist and checked his pulse.
It was thin and unrhythmic, but not much worse than
usual.

"Think you are in good enough shape for your broadcast?"

"Of course."

"You had quite a bad attack this noon, you know."

"Yes. But I feel really well, thank you. I had a bit of an
excitement this morning, but I'm perfectly well now."

The doctor switched on the light and examined Nichols'
face. "I'll give you a little shot to pep you up for the broadcast," he said. He put his kit down and brought out the
syringe, broke the ampulle of Coramin and carefully sucked

the clear liquid through the needle. Nichols peeled off the rug, got up and came into the room, closing the wooden door to the loggia. He pulled up the sleeve of his housecoat, and the doctor drove the needle into the pale flesh. "Now lie down for a few minutes," he ordered.

Nichols stretched out on his bed and watched the doctor packing up his paraphernalia. "Stay a few minutes, Doctor," he said. "There are a few things I wanted to ask you."

"Not very long, though," the doctor said, pulling a chair up to the bed. "I've got to look after our poet. He started one of his famous four-day drunks this morning and needs medical care and the admonitions of a friend, or he'll break every piece of furniture in his room, and his neck too."

Nichols chuckled. "It's his easy method of running away from himself," he said.

"Johannes Koenig seems to be proud of it. 'I get drunk, at least,' he told me. 'But Nichols does it when he's sober.'"

"Meaning I do what?"

"Accept things as they are, I suppose."

"I did a bit of thinking today," Nichols said, looking up at the ceiling. "I tried to clear up some fundamental issues; it appears I've been driftwood for a very long time. Today I began to wonder about the current—whether it's as strong as I thought."

"You're not a very healthy man, Nichols; I don't believe your heart would stand swimming against the current."

Nichols sat up and fastened his gaze on the doctor. "How long would you say I can go on living with this heart of mine, Doctor?" he asked. "I know that's the sort of question doctors detest. But please don't camouflage the answer."

"Frankly, I don't know. I don't know, Nichols. Maybe you'll have your coronary embolism tomorrow. Maybe you'll live to be seventy. What's the difference? Maybe I'll fall and break my neck on the stairs and maybe that perfectly healthy pageboy who always brings you the paper will be killed in an air raid tonight. In times like these death becomes unimportant and commonplace, Nichols. There's a lot of most unspectacular dying going on everywhere."

"Have you seen many people die, Doctor?"

"Yes, many. I was in the last war, you know. I'll get into this one too."

"I never saw anyone die. It's rather a handicap for a writer. Tell me, Doctor, how is it ? Is it bad ?"

"Yes, bad enough. But of course there are degrees. If you want someone to tell you that death comes with wings and music and that all you do is to walk through a cypress gate, you'd better ask Johannes Koenig. He's a poet. I'm a doctor and I can only say that it's bad to die. But mind, Nichols. Death isn't ever as bad as life. No comparison. No comparison at all. Anyone who can stand the hazing and skinning life gives you, can take death like a pleasant laxative."

"Odd. I never looked at it from that point of view," Nichols said and lay back again. The injection began to take effect, and he felt at ease. He smiled up at the ceiling as he remembered something. "I seem to have frightfully overrated the pleasure of being alive, ever since I was a boy of twelve. You know, I won the hundred-yard dash at St. Swithins, and fell down in a dead faint five yards beyond the tape. I never made a dash since."

"An endocarditis, of course. But with good care you can live to be seventy."

"Yes. That's what the sages of Harley Street declared. It seems to be an international slogan. But it's curious what such a dictum will do to a boy."

The doctor fiddled with his kit and pretended not to listen. It was rare for an Englishman to make confidences about himself, and he was anxious not to disturb Nichols.

"The only fight I ever had after that was the fight against my own heart. Kind of a sporting proposition, you know. I couldn't swim, I couldn't sprint, I couldn't join the crew, no soccer; they didn't even let me play cricket. The only sport I had was to bring my heart to heel, knock it down, win out against it. Other boys simply lived. But if I managed to live, it was something to be proud of. It sounds easier than it was, really. No games, no fun, no cigarettes, no tea, no coffee. No excitement, no excesses of any kind. I lived inside of a cocoon, but I lived. When I fell in love I thought that would be my end, it was such an outrageous excess and excitement. I was afraid of it and tried to take it only in small doses. Naturally, the girl got tired of me and soon chucked me. I survived even that. Great mercy, how proud I was of myself when I had kicked even love out of my life. There's nobody as absolutely selfish and asocial and arrogant and, of course, lonely as a sick man who insists on staying alive."

He closed his eyes, and the doctor hoped he would rest for a little while. He got up and tiptoed to the door; but Nichols began to talk again.

"I was in Vienna for some treatments when the war started. They took me prisoner and made this simple little deal with me. No broadcast—no medicine. I accepted it because I had made up my mind to live to be seventy. I had my own war, and I was going to win it." He opened his eyes and gave the doctor a round, friendly grin. "And after all this you come and tell me that life isn't worth the trouble of living, Doctor?" he said wryly.

"It's not how long a man lives. It's what he does with his life that counts in the final summary. Short or long—that's only relative. What you do with it is something absolute," the doctor said, speaking more to himself than to his patient. Nichols thought this over for a few minutes.

"Yes," he said then. "Right, Doctor. That sums it up rather neatly, doesn't it ?"

After the doctor had gone, Nichols remained lying on his bed, thinking. From time to time he chuckled, amused by the pictures that his mind reeled off for him. Shortly after six Adolf had visited him and given him a complete description of Martin Richter's successful escape. It was a beautiful joke, and it was his joke, his idea, his inspiration. Lying on his bed, he went through every move of it, savouring the irony of it, the audacity, the mischievous triumph of having snatched the fugitive away under the nose of the Gestapo. . . . They kill their intellectuals, but they scrape and salute before a doorman's uniform, he thought, laughter running warm through his body. I did it, he thought. I'm sick and weak and a coward—but I did it. . . . I made a dash again and I won again, he thought. The only thing that took away from his enjoyment was that he couldn't share the joke with anybody. . . . It ought to make for a rather amusing chapter in my memoirs, he thought. Except there will hardly be time to write them. No, hardly, after tonight, he told himself, still laughing softly. . . . He felt exceedingly well, and the Coramin injection was only partly responsible for it. He had felt sorry for himself quite often, even before he had been a prisoner of the Nazis. But he didn't feel a bit sorry for himself tonight.

He closed his eyes, resting for a few minutes under a thin cover of half-sleep filled with pleasant pictures and smiles. The sound of the door which was cautiously opened woke him, and he sat up with a start.

"It's only me, Mr. Nichols," Tilli said timidly.

"And what gives me the unexpected pleasure?" he asked, unable to keep the sharpness out of his voice. A visit by Tilli was always disturbing, but never more disturbing than just now.

"I'm looking for the doctor. I thought he'd be with you before your broadcast."

There was nothing Nichols had to say to that; he closed his eyes again. Tilli looked at his drawn face, shifting her weight, stalling; this room with the sick Englishman was such a quiet haven to her. She would have liked to stroke his hair or something, but did not dare; their relation was not given to tender little caresses.

"You don't know where he is? The doctor, I mean."

"No, I don't."

"But you had an attack today; Number 6 told me. You shouldn't be left alone," she said.

Nichols opened his eyes reluctantly. "Thanks, Florence Nightingale," he said. "I don't want company."

"You hate me, don't you?" Tilli said quietly, making a step toward the bed. Nichols did not look at her and yet saw everything: breasts and thighs, throat and arms, the whole tired, threadbare, shopworn and yet challenging temptation. "Hate? No—it isn't as simple as that," he answered with a sigh.

"It's not so complicated either," she said, plucking the rug up to his shoulders and straightening it absently. "You are a man, and you need a woman once in a while, and you hate me because I'm the only woman you can get and because you need me. You see?" she ended; her hand on top of the rug remained resting warm on his chest. It was a common hand, not small, not slim, with short fingers and a greedy-looking thumb. Yet somehow there was a childish and innocent expression about this hand. Nichols shoved it aside.

"Oh, Tilli, through what experiences you must have gone before you became so amazingly clearsighted about the complexity of the relations between the sexes," he said, amused yet also struck by the truth in her analysis.

"You always talk over my head to make me feel ashamed," Tilli said plaintively. Nichols felt the very faintest stir of pity for her, just as in moments of their strange intimacy he sometimes felt a faint stir of joy or consolation.

"Look here, Tilli," he said elaborately. "I didn't choose you for a companion; you were thrown into my life as part of a deal I detest. Even you must understand that this cramps my erotic style. So don't let's discuss it any longer." He wanted to be left alone with himself and his decision. Her presence made dim and muddy what ought to have remained tranquil and crystal clear.

"A deal you detest? Well, have you ever stopped to think how I feel about this deal?" asked Tilli.

"I can imagine how you must feel about a cadger like me who can't give you any of the rewards and small attentions to which you are used from other gentlemen. I only hope the Gestapo pays you well for snooping in my cabinets and in my mind," he said, impatient and embittered now.

"The Gestapo has nothing to do with you and me. I like you. You're different," she said. It sounded sleepy and yet urgent. Nichols tried to push it aside.

"Don't let's get emotional, my dear," he said; Tilli paid no attention to the irony but followed her own trend of thought.

"I always thought writers are curious people. But you're not a bit curious. You take me for granted as I am. You never stopped to ask how I got there."

"If you don't mind, Tilli, I've heard too many girls of your kind tell how they got there," Nichols said; and then, after a glance at her face, he added, softer: "All right, Tilli. How did you get there?"

Tilli began to smile. "Do you know Lisa Dorn?" she asked, and Nichols had trouble to follow the abrupt detour of her little mind.

"You mean the actress? I saw her picture in the papers. Why?" he asked.

"Our pictures were in the papers the same day—a few years ago. Lisa Dorn was the girl who handed flowers to the Fuehrer. I was the girl whom they drove through the streets with a sign around my neck saying: 'I slept with a Jew.' That's why she's now the sweetheart of the nation and I am what I am. You're a writer, Mr. Nichols—now go and write that story!"

After Tilli had ended there was a palpitating quietness in the room. Nichols sat up and stared at her in amazement; he could feel his heart again. Now that he wanted to see her face she had turned it away from him and was hiding it behind her hands.

"Go on, tell me more, Tilli," he begged, at a loss for the right words.

"Sure, I slept with a Jew," she went on, and now that for the first time she spoke about it, there was Sim again, and there was the day they had taken him to a concentration camp, and there was—much too clear and much too close— the postcard announcing his death and the little cigar box with his ashes that was all that came back from that camp; and there was Papa Baruch screaming with pain in some rotten basement, and there was Mama Baruch in her fine old knize suit, waiting for a lethal dose of Veronal, and there was Rosa on her way to Poland, and there was she herself, Tilli, the gayest bar fly in the hotel. She got up and began pacing the small room; she would have liked to cry but had forgotten how it was done. All she had was that dry, hot, angry despair inside of herself and that stinging urge to make Mr. Nichols understand her.

"Yes, Mr. Nichols, that's how it all started with me. That's how they began to put the pressure on me and make me do all they wanted. Then you go down and down and down—like falling in a bad dream. With Lisa Dorn it went up and up and up—and no pressure at all. But wait and see. Some day, maybe, they'll hang a sign around her neck, and it will say: 'She slept with a Nazi'—and that's going to be worse than having slept with a Jew!"

Her bitter, imploring desperation surged over and hit Nichols like a huge breaker, sweeping him out of his calm. "Oh, Tilli!" he said. "Oh, Tilli, why did you never tell me?" She began rubbing her hot, dry eyes and turned towards him. "Well, why did you never ask me?" she replied. Nichols, struck by regret and sympathy and the sorrow for all that could have been and was irretrievably lost, put out his hand to her.

"We could have been friends, Tilli," he said, clumsy with pity and sadness. Tilli perked up at once. She grabbed his hand and snuggled her cheek against it for a moment. She pushed her hair back, took out her handkerchief and wiped her dry eyes, and then she began to smile again. She sat down on the chair near his bed, crossed her legs, and her body assumed its inviting attitude all by itself. "Well, it's not too late to become friends, is it?" she said. . . . Oh yes, it is, Nichols thought. He, too, began to smile. Life remains absurd to the last breath, he thought. That of all the things I am going to leave behind, this little whore will be the one from whom it is hardest to part! What irony! What a sublime joke! . . . Tilli, practised in reading men's faces, remarked with feeble triumph:

"You see? You do care for me; you just didn't know it yourself. From now on everything will be much better—for both of us."

It was such a complete, transparent moment that she forgot everything—even her need for new shoes. But just then Nichols' glance, gliding along her legs and down to her feet, discovered the holes in her shoes, those holes which she so miserably and shamefully had tried to hide from everybody.

"Oh, Tilli, oh my girl!" he said gently. "Oh, Tilli—your shoes!"

It startled her out of her dreamy mood; she pulled her feet under the chair in a spontaneous movement and asked angrily: "Well, what's the matter with my shoes?"

"Poor, poor shoes!" said Nichols. "They've got holes in them. They're going to pieces. You need new shoes, Tilli." He was full of pity and he meant not only her shoes; he meant everything; all of Tilli and all of himself. She began to blossom out in a great, warm radiance; her face opened up like a flower, a pink lily floating softly on the quiet waters of his pity.

"Why, Mr. Nichols!" she whispered. "That's the nicest thing any man ever said to me."

And then the luminous moment was gone, the lights turned out inside. Nichols remembered his broadcast, and Tilli her quest for Veronal. But even after she had left, the room seemed turbulent, filled with strange new currents. The rain was beating thinly upon the little roof of the loggia, from which the copper sheeting had been removed a long time ago. Nichols stretched out on his bed once more, trying to concentrate. . . . Now let's see where we can find a toehold in this moronic manuscript, he told himself as he pulled the pages under the lamp on his night stand and began to study it once more.

". . . Do our enemies really believe the morale of the German people can be broken by air raids? Do they tell you that Germany is sinking? That the German people are getting tired of the war? Do they believe this country is like a groggy prizefighter whom a few hard punches will knock out? Do they really and truly think the German people will give up the fight before they have won a total victory in this total war? No, no, never! Don't believe it. Germany is as strong, nay, stronger and more determined than she was in the spring of 1940. . . ."

They are wonderful, these Germans with their declamations, he thought. They leave holes in them big enough for a man to put his fist through. This ought to be a good show tonight.

At five minutes past seven the three technicians from the Deutschlandsender rumbled in and began to rig up their console and string their line and fill the room with buzzing activity. Wiedemann arrived a few minutes later, wildly excited, as usual. Poor Herr Wiedemann, although he had nothing to do but sit and listen, suffered violent attacks of stage fright before each broadcast.

"Calm down, my dear fellow, calm down, for God's sake," Nichols told him. "A broadcast isn't as important as all that."

"Don't underrate yourself, Nichols. Yours is a very important broadcast, and it carries a very grave responsibility for me."

"Do you really believe in propaganda?" Nichols asked, floating happily on a wave of exuberance and Coramin. "I don't. No, my dear chap, I don't believe that propaganda has any value. Ever been to New Zealand? No? But maybe you know that the native Maoris were very bloodthirsty cannibals until the middle of the last century. Well then, before each battle the warriors of the feuding tribes spent some time making terrible faces at each other. It was developed to a fine art, which each young warrior had to study diligently; Hakka they called it. Can you imagine anything sillier than two fierce, savage tribes of cannibals sticking out their tongues and making faces at each other in the hope of frightening the enemy into surrender? That's what all propaganda is: making faces at each other. But I'll tell you something. In New Zealand there is no report to the effect that the one who could make better faces ever won. It was always the cannibal with the bigger war club and the stronger arm who in the end cooked and ate his enemy."

"Yes; and *we* have the bigger war club," Wiedemann said, bewildered and confused by some intangible mockery in Nichols' lecture. "If you're not just telling me a fib."

"If you will excuse me now. I must dress," Nichols said, amused, and retired into his bathroom. He shaved, brushed his hair back, slipped into his dinner jacket. Ordinarily this was rather a strain on his heart, but tonight he was oblivious of it; it was amazing how unimportant this sick heart of his had become.

Captain Schreber had meanwhile arrived, one of Goebbels' men; he was the actual director of the broadcast, a bouncing ball of a man, spreading kindliness and good cheer, both somewhat cramped tonight. There had been a terrible accumulation of bad news all day long and the Deutschlandsender, after chewing it thoroughly, suffered from indigestion and constipation. The Propaganda Ministry, losing its head for once, had given divergent and confusing directions, a few blunders had been made, and there was a whispered rumour that Goebbels' sphere of influence was going to be clipped. Like most Germans, Captain Schreber was overworked, creaking under the strain of too long hours and too little sleep, combined with poor nutrition and a constant gnawing, chafing anxiety. Making a mistake was dangerous for a man in his position. It might cost him not only his job, but also his head. Yet, in the growing confusion and bewilderment of recent weeks, it was almost impossible to know what was a mistake and what wasn't, who was in and who was out. In other words, whom to fawn upon and whom to kick in the shins.

"Well, is our star in voice tonight?" he asked, bouncing around Nichols, patting his shoulder and trying to warm him up for his task. The microphone was tested and all preparations made in an ensuing miniature bedlam. It was as if with these five men the whole nervous outside world, pregnant with catastrophe, had broken into Nichols' cloistered cell. Barking and quarrelling, irritation and impatience. The sour smell of badly washed bodies and Schreber's finger-snapping, nail-biting, hair-tearing attempts to appear jolly. Only five minutes before the beginning of the broadcast did the clamour subside. Nichols, who had remained calm and curiously bent over himself, got up and straightened the pages of the manuscript.

"Everything ready?" Schreber asked the technicians. They nodded, taking their places at the controls.

"Ready, Nichols?"

"Yes. Ready, Captain."

"And don't forget to raise your voice when you say: 'If ever the day should come——' you know where?" Wiedemann implored in a hoarse whisper.

"Right."

Schreber watched the hand on his wristwatch. Nichols stepped behind the microphone. Silence. Attention. One minute to go—fifty seconds—forty . . .

Only during those last ten seconds before he began to speak did his heart give him trouble. It was like a fierce, small animal rearing inside of his chest, ready to leap.

"Attention! GO!"

" . . . As on every Monday we bring you an old friend, our guest and your compatriot, Geoffrey Nichols," Schreber with his thick accents waded into the announcement. "With the discerning and understanding eyes of a writer, Geoffrey Nichols is observing the everyday life of Germany and reporting to you at first-hand what he sees and what he thinks about us. Here is Geoffrey Nichols, speaking from Berlin to England."

Schreber stepped back, and Nichols brought the microphone up to his own height. . . . Now let's see what faces we can make, he thought.

"Once again I am speaking to you, an Englishman to Englishmen, to warn you against the propaganda lies your press and your government are spreading. Germany is as strong as ever. . . ."

. . . From Berlin to England. England. Where is England, what is she in this hour? This fortress, built by nature for herself against infection and the hand of war—that's Shakespeare, isn't it? This happy breed of men, this little world . . . No, I don't know England as she is today, but she must still be as Shakespeare saw her—or she would have quit long ago—

this happy breed—this little world—how does it go on? This blessed plot, this earth, this realm, this England. Thank you, Shakespeare, old man, now I know her again. Are you listening to me, you over there, you happy breed? Please, listen, don't turn off the radio in disgust, have a bit of patience, I have something to say to you. I have spoken into a vacuum, many times, every time. I didn't think of you as you really are, not as definitely and determinedly as I ought to have thought of you. Not so that I could see your faces and hear what you had to tell me, not so that I could walk inside of your minds. I never cared for England the mulish way Englishmen are supposed to care for her; yes, I am an uprooted expatriate, but, taken all in all, I'm of the same breed as you. . . .

There was a light fog over the channel, and the water was choppy with hard little wavelets, but a few hundred feet above the air was clear and pure, translucent with the radiance of the rising moon. Over there was England. This blessed plot, this earth, this realm, this England. From over there they came, small and black and swift, like moths passing against the gleaming disc of the moon. Through the fog and the water and the moon-soaked night he could see England now, the country that was his, the people he had known long ago and the new people brought up in this war whom he did not know; except that they were England and he was England too and so they were made of the same stuff. Solid, durable, indestructible material. Dry-lipped, frugal, stolid, humorous, unassuming; dignified in their eccentricity, sober in their rampages. So gallant that they never thought, much less spoke, of gallantry. Born decent, as you were born with eyes and hands and feet. This happy breed—indeed, happy breed. . . .

Such were the thoughts that flowed vaguely through Nichols' mind during the minutes it took him to rattle off the hollow phrases of the manuscript. Captain Schreber shoved his wrist with the watch under his eyes, and Wiedemann signalled him frantically to slow down. There were seven minutes more to go on the broadcast; he dropped a page he had finished to the floor and tore into the next one, slowing down and raising his voice.

"Do our enemies really believe the morale of the German people can be broken by air raids? Do they tell you that Germany is sinking? That the German people are getting tired of the war? Do they believe this country is like a groggy prizefighter whom a few hard punches will knock out? Do they really and truly think the German people will give up the fight before they have won a total victory in this total war?"

Geoffrey Nichols took a deep breath and flung himself high and wide into space. "Yes, yes!" he called out. "This is a sinking ship, it's going down! Keep flying, keep coming, keep hammering at them. All this is true! Hit them—hit them hard—they're almost finished—a few more blows and we've won!"

He had counted on the shock, and he had counted correctly. It took Schreber and Wiedemann several seconds before they were able to co-ordinate their actions to the unexpected and unbelievable; enough seconds for him to send his message and vindicate himself once and for all. To make their confusion complete, the air-raid sirens began to shriek just then; there was one on the roof of the hotel, and its screaming was so loud and sent such shivers of vibrations through the walls of the building that everything was drowned out in the infernal noise. More and more sirens, a frantic chorus of wails and screams and shrieks, a symphony of panic. Nichols held the microphone close to his mouth and kept telling the truth to England, while Schreber and Wiedemann yelled at each other, yelled at him, tried idiotically to tear the microphone away from him, to pull him away from it. One of the technicians jumped into the mêlée and shot his fist into Nichols' face; it was like looking into a flashlight while something exploded inside of his head. Then the blood began to flow lush and almost pleasantly from his nose, his legs gave way under him and he hit the floor. The sirens howled madly, stampeding the city into fear and flight.

The second before he went under, Nichols saw the five men in the room doing jerky jumps, a grotesque danse macabre. One of them spat every vile name into his face, another one—and it got too dark now to recognize him—was kicking his head as he lay on the floor, and one shouted: "What's all the excitement for? I took him off the air the moment the alarm started."

Then there was blackness, shot through with streaking green, yellow, and orange stars, and Geoffrey Nichols had begun to travel homeward. . . .

G

THE air raid was on in all its fury. Blasts and explosions, the insane, shattering noise of the barrage, the monstrous voice of destruction. Hail of shell and shrapnel and cascades of broken glass; blue, yellow, orange, red flames bursting into deadly giant flowers, geysers of dust and debris shooting high up into the sky. Walls crashing, pavements melting in the ferocious heat, mains and pipes and tracks torn from the ground like bloody twisted guts. And over it all the mobile dome of searchlights, the annihilating fireworks of tracer bullets and cannon bursts, where, thousands of feet above, the air was turned into a compact battleground for the fight of mythical monsters. It was a Wagnerian vision, loudly and fully orchestrated, and mounting to its inevitable conclusion, the ultimate twilight and fall and annihilation of the iron-clad Teutonic gods.

The people of Berlin, huddled in their insufficient shelters, felt very small and terribly frightened. They had gone through air raids before and had taken them fairly well. But this was different and horrible and of a merciless finality. Being small people, they did not realize their own responsibility for this; they were not aware of having unleashed the tearing beasts of war themselves, of having set off the fires that were consuming them now. Ignorant and petty, they were still concerned with their own small lives and anxious over what was to be their own share of the damage in the wholesale catastrophe. Their sons, brothers, husbands were at the front, or prisoners, or wounded, or killed. Their children grew up into strange creatures, lacking some of the human sensibilities, as if some vital nerves had been cut out of them. Their health was poor, their lot was hard, their joys were scarce. And so, huddled in the shelters, they kept on worrying about the small, trashy things that they had amassed and cherished. Would the house still stand? Would the upright piano, acquired through years of saving, be ruined by water? Wouldn't the dog go crazy in this racket? Would the china break? Would the gas stove still function afterwards? Would the walls crack and the neighbours discover the hoarded food in the larder? Would this and that and the other thing come to harm? And, great, almighty God in heaven, why does this happen to us? Who is to blame for it and how can we get out of it—if we ever get out at all?

The air-raid shelter of the hotel enjoyed a special reputation; in fact it was on account of this bomb-proof shelter that some of the wealthy and privileged of Berlin had given up their residences and moved into the hotel. The shelter gave itself the airs of a rathskeller, with painted beams and vaults, benches and tables. Drinks could be ordered, and a gramophone, turned on full blast, was doing its best to drown the menacing uproar outside. But somehow the spurious cosiness and faked atmosphere of the place made it the more sinister, the longer the raid lasted—and it seemed to last forever.

At first the people down there behaved as well as people always behave in public, when it takes more courage to give way to one's innermost shattering fright than to keep up a show of being cold-blooded and fearless. One or two card games, transferred from the smoking-room to the shelter, were stolidly pursued. Gauleiter Plottke and his wife, whose farewell dinner had been rudely interrupted, had rushed with their children into the shelter at the first wail of the sirens. They were quibbling as usual. "Why did you have to get us into town just today?" Frau Plottke nagged. "Why? We were perfectly well off in Karinsee, but, naturally, you have to chase us to Berlin just when there is the worst air raid we've ever had."

"I didn't know there would be an air raid, did I?"

"You ought to have known. What sort of a Gauleiter are you, if you don't even know what the Tommies are planning?"

"Too bad they forgot to send me a postcard this time. Anyway, instead of shooting off your face you should be thankful that I'm getting you and the children to Switzerland before things get worse here."

"Oh, I should be thankful, should I? Well, why didn't you think of it before today, when they're blasting Berlin off the map? Why didn't you send us last month? Frau Goering and Frau Goebbels, of course, they went away weeks ago— but then, they have clever husbands, while I'm married to an imbecile."

"Shut up and don't make a spectacle of yourself," Plottke growled, and Frau Plottke shut up reluctantly. He still hadn't confessed to her what had happened to his parcel of French chemical shares. Glumly he considered the probability that

after this raid the morning train for Switzerland might
not be able to depart, for lack of tracks or because the station
might have disappeared altogether.

In an effort to keep up the morale and give a good example,
he poked his children in their ribs and told them to sing something. Soon a few hapless people gathered around and joined
in, very loud and very slow and very sentimental. Herr
Schmidt, returning from the personnel shelter where he had
herded the pageboys, muttered an angry and embittered
counterpoint. . . . Look at the Herr Gauleiter! His brats can
sing, they're well off. They're in this bomb-proof shelter and
tomorrow they'll get hustled off to where it's nice and safe.
And what about my children? Why are my children stuffed
away in a flimsy basement, in a creaky old slum house that
might come down any moment—if it hasn't come down
already? Great God, what about our children, Herr Gauleiter?
Is this what you call: No more class struggle, no more
differences, one Reich, one will, one people, the common welfare
before individual welfare? Don't make me laugh! Your
brood gets everything and mine can croak; you stay home and
grow a fat belly and I am just good enough to be used for
cannon fodder. . . .

Von Stetten and Dahlin had found two chairs in a corner;
Dahlin talked and Stetten listened, smoking one cigarette
after another, his lips compressed into a thin line.

"This raid is your answer," Dahlin said. "It corresponds
exactly with the apprehensions my home office expressed to
me over the telephone this afternoon. Why should our banks
take a parcel of French shares in payment for our good
ore?"

"Because we offer them to you at a fantastically profitable
rate," Stetten said, tiredly. "They were 126 before we occupied France. They're still quoted at 60. We offer them
to you at 36. The Société Anonyme Chimique de Lyonnaise
is as good as ever; after the war these shares will soar sky-
high and you will rake in an enormous profit."

"Right. If the R.A.F. didn't exist. *If*, my dear Von Stetten.
You're giving me a good sample tonight of what the R.A.F.
can do. If the R.A.F. razes the Lyons plant, as it probably
will some nice day, these shares will have the approximate
value of toilet paper. I'm a simple man, I say what I think.
We don't sell our good ore for toilet paper."

"Don't be so nervous, Dahlin. We can talk about it to-morrow. This is not the moment——"

"I am *not* nervous, damn you!" Dahlin roared; it was his first air raid, and he was taking it badly. Stetten lighted another one of his precious, smuggled cigarettes. . . . This deal is dead and buried, he thought, and not the slickest magician in the Foreign Office can bring it back to life. A full-dress occupation would be the only means to persuade Sweden that we are her friends. . . . He had a bitter taste in his mouth. He knew that the High Command had neither the means nor the inclination to embroil itself with another recalcitrant country. A muffled blast which made the walls shiver and the floor rear up put a period to his glum speculations.

Farther down, pasted to the wall, the banker Vander-straaten clung desperately to Professor Mazhar Cevdet Onar. "Listen," he whispered after each detonation. "Listen, that was a close one, listen." He was pale, sweating, trembling, a sorry mess of a man. He had suffered a shock in the bombing of Rotterdam three years before and had never got over it; a shock severe enough to drive him into the Nazi camp. And here he was *with* them, cornered, doomed, lost. From the frying pan into the fire. From the rain to under the spout. He had tried to save himself and had got himself ever deeper into peril. He had tried to get off easily, but there was no getting off easily in this present world. "Listen," he moaned; "listen to that, listen!" Mazhar Cevdet Onar made notes in a little book with the fatalism of the true believer in Mohammed and also of one who has kept his best trumps for the end of the game.

"You never hear the one that hits you," he said in French; it was cold consolation as the bursts of bombs came closer and the shelter shook in short hard spasms. The Plottke party sang louder in a desperate show of fine spirit.

"Listen to them! Listen to those howling dervishes!" Vanderstraaten moaned. "Look at them! Look at those obnoxious people! And yet the Germans always go around asking the world why nobody loves them!"

"You don't like the Germans, Mynheer Vanderstraaten? How remarkable! But you collaborate with them. Me, I like them very much," the professor said delicately. "I have great admiration for many of their fine qualities. But I refuse to collaborate. That's the difference between us."

"Listen!" groaned Vanderstraaten, clutching the Turk's arm. "This is unbearable. They'll kill us all. Why, oh why must I be in Berlin tonight? Listen, they're close now. Listen——"

As the raid lasted and mounted and the planes came on, wave after wave, and the bombs dropped closer and closer to the heart of the big, sprawling city, more and more people crowded into the shelter. Soon there were not enough benches and chairs, and they crouched on the floor and huddled on the stairs which led to the door, while new arrivals stumbled in and picked their way across the legs and arms of the others. The Rumanians, expelled from the bar, entered in one body, bringing bottles with them to nurse their high spirits along. They were so preposterously gay and silly, so demonstratively unaware of the danger, that everyone hated them.

Three mad-eyed people who were rushed in from the street brought a gust of panic with them. A badly dressed man and two women, they were obviously not the kind that belonged to the hotel. They had been overtaken by the raid on their way home, after leaving a sick child at a hospital. The younger of the two women was hysterical and could not stop babbling. Searching for cover, she had got stuck in the melting asphalt of the pavement, and paralysed, unable to run away, she had heard the bomb whistle overhead and seen it hit the house in which she had wanted to seek shelter. Her words did not make much sense, but they were so fraught with naked, crazy horror that they broke the thin shell of well-mannered self-control in which the guests of the hotel were hiding. Her whining hovered, long-drawn out and ghastly, like a suffering animal's howl, over the rising clamour of voices. It was as if this inhuman lament made the bomb-proof walls vulnerable and transparent, so that the people in there could stare through them and see what was happening outside and above. The man was ashamed of his wife's cries and shouts. "Shut up," he told her. "Shut up, shut up, you!" But she went on and on, getting shriller and shriller. The older woman, possibly her mother, did not say a word, only rocked back and forth, on her old knees, from which blood was trickling; she had been cut wading through the broken glass that covered the streets knee high. Suddenly she got up, stretched out her haggard arm and demanded loudly: "Stop the music! Stop that devil's thing! A sin and a shame it is to play music at such a time. Pray we shall, not make music."

For the last five minutes no one had thought of changing the record on the gramophone, and it had repeated over and over and with plaintive insistence the soldiers' song about Lilli Marlene standing under the lantern. "She is right. Stop the gramophone!" Plottke commanded. But the moment the music stopped, the sudden vacuum filled itself with an inferno of thuds and blasts and bursts; it made the raid and the danger and the horror so real that Frau Plottke began to scream: "Turn on that gramophone! Let's have music, for the love of God, let's have music!" By now the shelter roared, whined, screamed, laughed drunkenly, prayed monotonously, sang defiantly, whispered desperate pleas; a high voice asked for a doctor, glasses and bottles rocked and rattled and broke, the gramophone kept moaning for Lilli Marlene. Up above, outside and all around and everywhere was the *crump-crump* of distant bombs, the horrid whistling of others close by. There was the icicle-like sound of shattered glass, the dull enormous crash of crumbling walls. And in the breathless, sudden, ominous silence before the explosion, the clicking of chips could be heard and the brief, monotonous calling of hands from the table of the persistent poker players.

The hotel doctor and Oberleutnant Kauders arrived together at the peak of the raid's second wave.

"Get down there, get the hell down there; don't be a god-damned fool, and take cover," the doctor said, angrily pushing the remonstrating flier down the steps.

"But I have a date with her. Are you sure she isn't in her room?" Kauders asked shakily. Between the two raids he had managed to make his way from the nearest underground station to the hotel to keep his date with Lisa Dorn, but he was badly rattled.

"Perfectly sure. She's in the theatre, and you can bet your life she won't return before the raid is over."

"But she told me she'd wait here for me. Why did she go to the theatre?"

"Because she's an actress. It's her place of occupation."

"Why didn't she tell me that she had to go to the theatre? I would have gone with her," Kauders said stupidly. The doctor left him and waded toward the hysterical, whining woman; without much ceremony he grasped her arm and gave her an injection. She yelled once, high and shrill. "Shut up," said her husband. "Shut up or I'll have to beat you." She stared at him without recognition, and he put her head on his lap with an embarrassed, coarse tenderness. Soon she began to cry, and after a little while she grew quiet. Kauders strode over the tangled limbs of the crowd; the older woman made space for him at her side without interrupting her prayer. He shrugged and sat down on the floor, leaning his back against the wall and stretching his legs in front of him. The fury of the raid seemed to subside, and for a few minutes there were no more bombs falling in the vicinity. Plottke announced loudly: "*Sieg Heil!* We sent them home with their tails between their legs!" His bowels felt loose and chilly,; he dried his face and disappeared into the emergency toilet which was one of the assets of this de luxe shelter.

The last ones to arrive down there were Tilli and Sim's mother. Tilli had her arm firmly linked into the dazed old lady's arm as she led her down the steps. The two of them had stuck it out in Tilli's room as long as possible, but Herr Schmidt, in his authority as an air-raid warden, had sternly ordered them into the shelter.

"I shouldn't have stayed so long. I shouldn't have come down here with you," Frau Baruch whispered wretchedly. "I should have gone home. I shouldn't be here. I should be at home. I should be with Papa. Oh, please let me go."

"Don't be crazy," Tilli said. "How do you think you'd get across the town in a raid like this? Be quiet. Easy, easy. Here you're as safe as in Abraham's lap. Guaranteed bomb-proof. Come on. Don't be such a rabbit."

Frau Baruch shrank into herself, trying to make herself small, invisible if possible. What terrified her was not so much the horrors of the bombing as the density of the crowd in whose midst she found herself after years of utter isolation. To make up for Frau Baruch's cowering, Tilli acted brazen and aggressive. "Come on, here, would you let us through, please?" she said, steering the trembling little bundle of fear along.

"Would you please push up a little?" she asked a pale young girl sitting on a corner bench. "There's still some room left. Thanks. Come on, sit down," she said to Frau Baruch and forced her into the narrow space.

She hitched herself up on the edge of the table, but was

discovered by the Rumanians, who, by now, were totally and completely, although rather charmingly, drunk. They picked her up with great Rumanian cries of joy, carried her into their own corner and placed her on the lap of their senior officer. Left thus alone, Frau Baruch's trembling grew uncontrollable. She held her hands tightly clenched in the pockets of her jacket. The left one held the tube of Veronal, the right one clutched the yellow star. That was how Gauleiter Plottke, returning from his trip to the toilet, found her.

"Excuse me," Frau Baruch mumbled, paralysed with fear, and got up to make way for him.

"It's all right; I can sit somewhere else," the great man said with a politician's shop-worn friendliness. But Frau Baruch, muttering terrified apologies, made an effort to disappear, creep away, hide in a mousehole, erase herself. He saw only her back, and it was, possibly, the meek and frightened subservience in the bearing of this old, tired, Jewish back that caught his attention.

"Why don't you stay here ? You aren't afraid of me, are you ?" he asked, slowly walking around her to examine her. A little strength and dignity came back into the old woman now that she had to face the worst.

"Thank you, Herr Gauleiter," she said, quietly looking into his eyes. Plottke stared at her for a moment, and then he slapped his thighs.

"I thought I recognized you. Frau Baruch ! The Jewess Sarah Baruch," he said. "And how does Frau Sarah Baruch get in here ? I'm asking you how you dare to come in here !" he inquired, and his voice grew louder and louder. "This is unbelievable ! This is preposterous ! This Jewish impudence surpasses everything ! You dirty Jewish swine, how did you get in here ? Answer when you're asked."

Frau Baruch's wrinkled lips worked, and at last they produced a small sound. "The air raid——" she mumbled. A few people had become interested in the reason for the Gauleiter's shouting. The young girl on the bench said petulantly: "Ach, let the old Jewess go. It's not worth getting angry, Heinrich. Come, sit down here." But the Gauleiter was streaking along, unappeasable as an irritated hippopotamus. All the pent-up fear of the last half-hour, all the fury he had carried with him through the day exploded and struck out at the defenceless old woman.

"Let her go?" he raged. "Let her go, this vermin, this bad smell, this piece of dirt? Don't you know the law, you, Frau Sarah Baruch? How dare you break it? How dare you leave your district? Where do you get the nerve to push yourself into the same shelter with Aryans? Why don't you wear your yellow star? Leave me alone!" he shouted as Von Stetten, who stopped behind him, muttered a few calming words into his ear. "I don't care a damn what impression I make upon our foreign guests. All I care about is to get this town cleaned up; but they're like rats, these Jews—chase them from one hole and they crawl out of another. Can we never get rid of them? But I've caught you, Sarah Baruch, and you'll get your punishment and you won't feel like gallivanting around in this hotel when we're through with you, I can promise you that."

Suddenly Tilli shook off the hands of the Rumanians and came over, placing herself between the crushed tiny figure of Sim's mother and the roaring, trumpeting Gauleiter. She still held a half-filled bottle in her hands, and she had drunk just enough to have reached the aggressive stage—the stage in which soldiers and sailors pick a brawl and girls of Tilli's kind feel like telling the truth, once and for all.

"Listen to me, Schnucki," she began under her breath. "That's enough. It's enough, Herr Gauleiter, and if you don't lay off this miserable little wretch of a woman I'll tell you a story. I'll tell everybody a story. If you have forgotten how you took off your cap and scraped and bowed before her, I haven't! It was 'gracious Frau Baruch' here and 'thank you, Herr Baruch' there when you were nothing but a stock clerk at Baruch's Department Store. Remember when they caught you stealing skins from the fur storage? You weren't so big then, you cried and whined and promised to be a good boy. And Sim went to the old man for you and asked him to give you one more chance and keep you employed. What a chance he gave you, poor Sim, what a chance! When your gang came to power, you killed Sim—yes, that's what you did; you killed him, not the straight way, as a decent murderer kills a man, but by your own crooked methods. You blackmailed him into signing his name under a contract that made you the owner of Baruch's. And then you sent him to the concentration camp and had him killed there. That's how you started, Herr Gauleiter, that's how you earned your first hundred thousand,

and that's how you went on from there. You've blackmailed
and cheated and swindled and murdered your way to the
top, step by step. I sometimes wonder how you can sleep.
I sometimes wonder what your dreams are like, Herr Gauleiter.
I wonder if Sim comes at night and visits you and shows you
the hole in his back where the bullet went in. He visits me,
often, and shows it to me.

"Listen, everybody, listen to me," she called out, very loud
now, for the air raid was rising to a new pitch, as if it had held
its breath for a brief pause and came roaring in now with
doubled strength. "Your Herr Gauleiter is a common thief
and a murderer. He has cheated everybody, he even cheats the
party and the Reich; he has sent hundreds under the axe and
some day, soon, he'll die under the axe himself. I'm laughing
at you, Schnucki; go ahead, glare at me, yell at me, shake your
fists at me, have me arrested, have me killed, too. I don't care.
I don't care. Why should I care ? I cared for Sim, and you
killed Sim. You broke up everything I had and threw it in the
dirt. I had two brothers, I cared for them, but they froze
to death in Russia. I cared for this one and that one, but
they're all gone and I am what I am. I cared for the Englishman—now he's gone too. Listen to the bombs. Listen,
listen! It's over and finished with all of us. Why should
I care ? Your game is up, Herr Gauleiter; I'm not afraid of
you; you're a rat in a trap yourself. You're a rat in a trap
and you won't get out, no matter how much you run in circles.
Oh, I wish a bomb would come down right now and make an
end of you and me and the Jews and the Aryans and of everything. I wish I were dead, except that I should hate to be buried
in the same grave with a rat like you——"

She came out of her mad, self-destructive, nihilistic trance
and stared, almost surprised, at the bottle in her hand.
"There!" she said as she flung it into Plottke's face with
an oddly nonchalant gesture; it hit with a dull plop against his
forehead, splashed some darkish liquid over his sputtering
face and his uniform and broke with a crash on the floor.
Tilli suddenly flung her arms around Frau Baruch's frail,
trembling person, dropped her head on her shoulder and burst
into convulsive sobs. "Come on, Mama, let's go, let's get out
of here," she said brokenly; a narrow lane opened before them
as they went to the stairs and up the steps and out of the
shelter, Plottke only made a brief commanding movement

with his head, and one of the ever-present Gestapo agents slipped after them to arrest them. Plottke wiped his face with his handkerchief.

"Poor girl," he said with a laborious smile. "Drunk and crazy from shock. Some people simply can't stand an air raid. They go crazy. She belongs in an institution."

All through this scene the bombs had fallen, incessantly and always nearer, in a steady, mounting, rising, growing, inescapable crescendo. It was as if the fears, the hatred, the wrath, the despair, the consternation, and the hopelessness of the doomed country were compressed into the crowded space of this shelter. Voices surged and rose and fell, faces grimaced, fists threatened; Plottke lowered his head and pushed it out against the menacing crowd like a cornered bull in the ring. He could not understand what they yelled at him, the bursts were too close, too frequent, too deafening, but he knew what it was anyhow. He knew what a mob was; he had been part of the mob himself, and the party had taught him to fight *in* it, and *against* it, to sway it, to use it. He knew by instinct what the mob would do to him and his like, once they had lost their power. . . . To hell with them all, he thought in a blind rage. I'll go to Switzerland tomorrow and keep all my money and be out of it all. . . . A lovely vision flashed by: the chalet at the shore of the lake, white walls, a red brick roof, an old walnut tree, and he was a nice retired official in a comfortable grey flannel jacket, playing with the dog and feeding crumbs to the birds. And at the same moment he also knew that he would never get away, never, that he would have to pay for everything; the hair stood on end at the nape of his neck, and there was a coldness as if the axe were coming down even as he thought of it.

Suddenly Otto Kauders began to talk. He had been sitting next to the praying old woman all the time, just as oblivious as she was of the goings-on around him. As the ground beneath them lost its consistency and became fluid, rocking in waves like the sea, rearing, shaking, shivering, the flier began to perspire. Sweat oozed from his pores, covered his burned skin with stinging salt, dropped in great, heavy beads on to his hands, ran in streams from his armpits and his loins and down the backs of his legs. He took his head between his arms and began rocking back and forth, summoning all his will-power to hold on to himself. But he couldn't. His nerves

snapped and broke, those over-worked, over-strained nerves
of a stupid, immature, animal-dull hero; it was like a dam
bursting, like a flood sweeping him away, it was like
falling again, falling and falling and falling, and he was
stripped of all strength and couldn't hold onto himself any
longer.

"I can't stand it," he groaned. "I can't stand it any longer,
stop it, hear me; stop it, it's unbearable, it's inhuman; stop
it, you swine, stop it, this is too much, too much, who can
stand such a thing, no, no one can stand it, I can't stand it,
I can't——"

"Come on, come on," the doctor said to him. "What's
the matter with you? Have you never been in an air
raid?"

Kauders gazed at him with his white eyes, that were glazed
with abject horror. He shook his head, his mouth hung limply
open.

"Air raid?" he said in a queer sing-song. "Yes. Many
air raids. But not like this. I was always upstairs. Fighting.
Three thousand metres above. Duck in a cloud. Keep on his
tail. Let go of a burst. Give it to him. Get it, too, sometimes.
But give it to him good. Never like this. It's fun upstairs.
But this is terrible. It's terrible, it's terrible!" he cried, and
his voice cracked. "You know something, Doctor?" he
whispered with a queer secrecy. "I never knew it. Never
knew how a bomb sounds when it comes down. Never heard a
bomb. I'm a fighter—I can't stand it down below——"

He stopped as another one came down, howling directly
overhead like an evil, malicious, scornful animal. The sudden
silence, the breathless second, the knowledge that this was it,
that this was the end—and then the deafening roll of the
explosion, tearing at the roots of the world, clouds of dust,
settling slowly, the acrid smell of destruction, the choking
fear; and afterward the surprised realization that they were
still alive and the shelter was still standing and the planes
still coming in again and again.

Yes, my boy, thought the doctor. This is how bombs sound
when you're on the receiving end of it. That's the bill we pay
for our glorious blitz. That's what you young daredevils
cooked up for us. . . . The flier was talking again, he was crying
now, sobbing like a child. The doctor picked up his limp,
clammy left hand and pushed the sleeve back. "The swine,"

Kauders sobbed, "dropping bombs on us. Women, children, civilians, all bombed. My father, my mother, dropping bombs on them. They'll kill my little dog at home too, the swine. Kill everybody down here—no fight—I can't stand it, stop it, I can't stand it, I can't stand it, I can't stand it, I can't stand it——"

He screamed now, unbridled, galloping off into the mad relief of a nervous breakdown. The doctor wanted to push the needle into his arm before Kauders could stampede the whole shelter into a panic, but the flier broke away from him and stumbled up the steps. "I can't stand it here, let me out, I can't stand it, I don't want to die in this rat hole, let me go, I can't stand it——"

The roaring, the whistling, the silence, the burst. And with the next bomb the lights went out. Black. Nothing. In the darkness there was one long, high scream: the flier's sobbing. The old woman was praying monotonously: "Forgive us our debts as we forgive our debtors. . . ." The howling, screaming fall of the next bomb. And in the second before it dropped, in the deadly quiet, Vanderstraaten's voice, strangely calm: "That's the end. We are all trapped. Not one of us will get out alive."

THE air raid was over. Berlin began to crawl out of holes and shelters, to count the casualties, dig out those buried under debris, line up the stretchers, call for the ambulances, amputate smashed limbs, pull sheets over the dead; close dangerous streets, evacuate toppling buildings, cart wounded to the hospitals, bandage, nurse, console, and record; Berlin also began to cry, to wail, to scream, to run in circles, to go insane, to flee, rush, escape. A stunned population stared up into the flaming sky flickering with the restless flares of the conflagration and making a farce of their efficient blackout. They were numbed, dazed, amazed at being still alive. Also, they were convinced, now that they had lived through it, that they could not face another raid; that it was more than human endurance and fortitude could stand. That, surely, nobody could be expected to survive another night like this; and yet, in the dark undertow of their minds, they were equally convinced that this was only the beginning, that from now on every night would be like this one, and that the superhuman was demanded of them.

Go back to work, keep the milk trucks rolling, the market stalls open, the streetcars running, the telephone buzzing. Mend the pipes and mains and wires; remain at the work benches of shops and factories, manufacture planes, shells, tanks, trucks, ammunition; print newspapers, keep the theatres going, take your baby for a walk, cook, feed the family, wash the laundry; make the trains run, repair the powerhouse, stay at the switchboard, sing over the radio, sell stamps, carry mail, bake bread, open the store; dress, clean your teeth, shave, sleep, smile, talk, eat. Attend to the enormous task of making the normal, the day-by-day life, go on amidst the most sinister and cataclysmic abnormality.

Self-pity is one of the predominant traits in the German character. Their capacity for suffering is outweighed by their uncontrolled drive of being sorry for themselves. They harbour a provincial, narrow-minded belief that sufferings, pains, misfortunes, and hardships are something special, reserved for Germans only and unknown to the rest of the world. They are like the man who thinks that nobody's toothache ever hurt as much as his. Their exaggerated concern with themselves makes them callous toward the other members of the human family. They are forever presenting the same old bill, carrying an eternal chip on their shoulders, a permanent grouch in their hearts, and an unhealed sore of one sort or another on the body of the nation. The urge to dramatize themselves, romanticize themselves, to play the tragic lead in a drama, is at the root of the ease with which they can be swayed into war. They are the ham actors of history, forever brandishing swords, going into self-analysing soliloquies, aiming guns and swearing revenge at the drop of a hat. In a way, war has not much reality for them because it is only a consequence of this pose and attitude; like the actor, they never really expect to get hurt in the fray. Not since the Thirty Years' War of the seventeenth century had Germany seen the real face of war in all its murderous ugliness. The German armies were always sent to fight their battles on foreign soil; if they could not win the war there, they surrendered rather than have it carried into their own country.

But after the all-clear of this night, when the people came crawling out of their shelters, they saw for the first time, and felt and experienced and began to understand, what it meant to be in a war. They saw what other nations had seen through to the bitter end and what, indeed, had been inflicted upon them by the Germans; and there came to them a dawning of comprehension why these other, more mellow nations hated war: the holocaust, the rape, the senseless chaotic mess it was; dead children, women gone insane, old men burned to charred ghosts, young men crippled; mothers killed and torn away from their brood, the roofs blasted, the walls torn down, even the room in which they had warmly and safely lived hanging open now like a ghastly stage over the abyss of the gutted street; their lives a shambles and the menace of coming horrors hanging over them. It was the first serious lesson for an immature people that had refused to grow up and live sociably with the rest of the human family.

The destruction that engulfed them made them furious, boundlessly sorry for themselves, smarting for revenge and crazy with fear. But it also planted in their subconscious a seed, a revelation, an idea which might take root and grow and bloom in years to come: That war was not only a word, or a speech, or a song, a fanfare, a flag under which to march to glory ; but that it was real and evil and horrible and infernal and that they wanted none of it for the rest of their lives nor for future generations. . . .

The hotel was still there, although a fire had eaten into the two upper floors of the new wing and a bomb had damaged its façade. The concussions had cracked some of the sumptuous pillars in the lobby, the glass roof had come down in shatters; there was not a window left intact in the building, and a hot draught blew billows of dust and smoke in from the street. Another bomb had dug itself into the pavement near the back entrance, and the explosion had done considerable damage in the personnel shelter and flooded the wine cellar with the contents of broken bottles and burst barrels. But the fire had been checked, the personnel shelter been evacuated, and with some effort the hotel's own generator had even been coaxed into giving enough electric power to keep the emergency lights functioning.

In the dust and smoke and the choking smell of fire and explosives, a shapeless crowd milled around the desk, shouting, pushing, gesticulating, swearing: those who wanted to get away from the accursed city at all costs, those whose rooms were burned out, those whose belongings were destroyed in the holocaust. Ahlsen was a nervous wreck, unable to cope with the situation. But old man Kliebert had summoned the forsaken dignity and presence of mind of a former mayor and, supporting himself as best he could on shaking knees, he tried to clear up the muddle. Schmidt stood like a rock in the clamouring uproar. "Sorry, there won't be any trains leaving in the morning," he repeated, the receiver clamped between ear and shoulder and using both hands to handle the crowd. "Sorry, there won't be any trains leaving, Herr Gauleiter. . . . Sorry, there won't be any trains, Herr Dahlin. . . . No, sorry, Herr Vanderstraaten, there won't be any trains. . . . Sorry, I can't give you any other information. . . . Yes, I'm trying to make a connection with the air line. . . . No, sorry, Frau Plottke, you will have to wait like everybody else, and there simply won't be any trains leaving. . . ."

"The animals are trying to get into Noah's ark," Von Stetten said to the doctor, who was bandaging the head of one of the pageboys who had been hurt in the personnel shelter.

"What's that?" he asked, concentrated on his task.

"The deluge. They hope to get away and wait for the dove with the olive branch on top of some Mount Ararat. One might also say that the rats are leaving the torpedoed ship."

"There," said the doctor, making Number 6 comfortable on a stretcher and proceeding to the next case. The stretcher-bearers inched forward in a slow procession, carrying the gravely wounded out to the ambulances and leaving the slightly injured in the doctor's care. Another line of stretchers was in the meantime moving down the service stairs and out through the debris of the back door, their sad, silent load immobile under sheets and blankets; for even in the midst of catastrophe the hotel held stiffly and proudly to its reputation for tact and discretion. The doctor left the Slight Concussion and bustled over to a deep chair where he had deposited a Nervous Breakdown.

"How do you feel now, Oberleutnant?"

"Fine. If I could only get something to drink——"

"I'll see that you get something," the doctor said and bustled on to a Fractured Arm. His hands were warm, his mind clear, his fingers sure and nimble, and the stiff leg did not seem to hamper him in the least. He was happy tonight, was the doctor. At last he belonged, he was busy, an important person, a man greatly needed and appreciated. Merrily he inhaled the stench of disaster in which he felt at home as he had not been at home since another disaster, twenty-five years ago, had torn him out and thrown him onto the trash heap, flower, fruit, root and all.

"Ah, here you are, thank God. I've worried myself sick about you," Von Stetten said, rushing to the revolving door, which miraculously had remained undamaged and through which Lisa Dorn entered. She was hatless, and her hair hung down in great disorder; she had a smudge on her face and looked dishevelled, but not frightened. There was rather an intangible radiance about her, as if she were giving off light. Yet her eyes were red and smarting from the smoke and glare of the burning streets through which she had passed; in the dim light she peered at Stetten and through him.

"Worried about me? Why, Baron?" she said absorbedly. Her gaze searched the lobby, trying to penetrate the shambles, and reluctantly returned to him.

"You are a very valuable property of the State, don't you know that?"

"Am I?" she said, with a fleeting mockery in her voice. "Am I? Really, Stetten?"

"Yes. If only so much as the tip of your little finger were hurt it would be a great national loss," Stetten said. He tried desperately to find a transition from their usual banter to the sad event he had to bring to her knowledge.

"Never worry about me. I'm tough," Lisa said. "We had a wonderful performance, all through the raid. We kept them in their seats, yes, we did, and our theatre still stands. They even sent us home in one of their old buses. But what happened here? It doesn't look too good."

"That's why I waited for you. Your room is burned out. Gone. Kaput. You can't sleep here; they don't know what to do with all their guests. I thought I might take you to my apartment. It seems to be intact. I'm a trustworthy bachelor, you know——"

"My room? Burned out?" She smiled a little. "All my Parisian dresses? What a pity!"

"I'm afraid so, Lisel. There's something else I must tell you——"

"Looks like a third-class waiting-room after an earthquake," she said, still searching the lobby. There were people on stretchers waiting for the ambulance; others slightly injured, in the doctor's care; others, unharmed, had fallen asleep exhausted on chairs and sofas and yet others began resignedly to curl up on the beds and mattresses the hotel was improvising on the floor of the lobby, in the bar, in the empty, unused Yellow Pavilion. All elegance had gone out by the broken windows, and the hotel was nothing but an emergency station, a bivouac close to the front lines.

Lisa went to the desk where the crowd was giving up its siege and receding. Herr Schmidt was in the process of peeling off the hotel uniform. "Did you see Oberleutnant Kauders? Is he around somewhere?" she asked. Stetten, who had followed her, said, baffled: "Kauders? The young pup who had a nervous breakdown? What's he to you, Lisel?"

"I had a date with him," Lisa said, and Stetten could see that she was miles away. He shook his head wonderingly. . . . Women are funny animals, he thought. . . . Schmidt attended to the last of his duties before leaving the hotel and becoming a soldier once more. "Oberleutnant Kauders is over there, in that chair behind the pillar. He seems to be resting, Fraulein Dorn. And here is a letter for the Fraulein and a dozen roses. They're a bit wilted, but I had no place to keep them, seeing that your room burned out, Fraulein Dorn. And I'm sorry about Herr Koenig, but I couldn't do anything with him. You know how he acts when he's a bit under the weather. In his bed, like a log. I tried to get him out of his room and down to the shelter, honestly I did, but I couldn't. So it happened."

"What happened?" Lisa asked, with the wilted roses dangling from her hand.

"He got burned pretty badly; the ambulance took him off just before you came in. Not much hope for him, Fraulein Dorn."

"What a pity!" Lisa said; there was hardly any emotion in her voice. She carried the roses with her as she walked quickly across the lobby; the letter was tied to them with a bit of wire, but she did not seem interested in reading it. Kauders slept; his mouth was open, and his head looked like that of an unfinished doll before the hair is put on. Lisa shook him, and he woke up. It took him a few minutes to find himself and to recognize her, and then he pulled himself together with an almost audible snap.

"You're a nice baby," he said. "You stood me up! I thought you would never come."

"Well, here I am. There was an air raid, you know."

"Yes. Here you are, and that's the main thing. You know what you promised me. Now we can——"

"Tell me first: did you get rid of him?" Lisa asked. She had asked nothing else since the moment this stupid boy had taken Martin through the revolving door out into freedom; all through the performance, all through the raid, through the drive home, through the flaming inferno, nothing but: Did you get rid of him?

"Rid of whom?"

"But you know. That Rumanian. Captain Donescu. Did you get rid of him?"

"Oh, him! And how I got rid of him! Took him first to Kathi and made him a bit tipsy; I hoped he would stay there with the girls, but he stuck to me like a burr. Finally I managed to lose him in the underground."

"Where?"

"In the underground. Station Potsdamerplatz. Jumped on a train and left him standing on the platform. Clever, what?"

"Very clever. Oh, you're wonderfully clever. I really didn't think you were as clever as all that. Left him in a crowded station—in the underground—why, that's marvellous! I think—I think I must give you a kiss for it," Lisa said, pressing down an urge to sob or laugh or make a fool of herself. She had to hide her face somewhere, let off steam, do something. She dropped the roses, put her arms around the boy's neck and kissed him, kissed fervently his obnoxious, naked face. "God Almighty," sighed Kauders, who was not used to such high-voltage kisses and went limp under their impact. He was still collecting his countenance, shaking like a leaf, when Lisa walked away from him and forgot his very existence in the same moment. Stetten had picked up Dahnwitz's wilted dozen roses; it gave him a queer feeling to know that the roses were still there while the man who had sent them had been dead for many hours. "The letter, Lisel," he reminded her gently.

"What? Oh, yes, the letter. It's from the general, you know; I know by heart what's in it."

"I think you'd better read it."

Martin got away, she thought. He got away, but where is he now? If something happened to him in the air raid—but no, nothing can happen to him, nothing will, nothing must. . . . She saw him as distinctly as though he were standing before her. . . . I'm a great hand at surviving. The statistics are in our favour. . . . Lean, sparse, purposeful, flame of a blowtorch, man-arrow. Life had whittled him down to the core, nothing was left but the essential, the true, hard, innermost kernel, and this kernel was invulnerable. The urgency in Stetten's voice reached her nerves at last, and she turned away for a moment from the dear vision, left it alone and returned to the devastated lobby of the hotel.

"What did you say, Stetten? Did—did anything happen to Arnim?"

"Read the letter first."

She opened the letter and read it. It shocked her, but it did not reach her. It only touched her with a small chill and a detached regret, and there was a faint stir of gratitude and a dim pity. She even smiled as she thought: All my old men are leaving me tonight. Stetten, who had been ready to catch the fainting girl in his arms, was disappointed but also impressed. Brilliant countenance, he thought. Good pedigree, after all. "Poor Arnim," he said. "Poor Arnim," Lisa repeated. Kauders sailed up to her and put his arm in hers. "Lucky my room didn't burn," he said, trampling in on her mood. "Lucky there's a bed left where you can stay tonight, darling."

"Leave me alone," she said, shaking him off.

"But, Baby—you promised——"

"I've just received a very sad message; leave me alone, Leutnant," Lisa said, shoving him away.

Her whole attention was focused on Pageboy Number 6, whom she recognized only at that moment. He was lying on a stretcher, his head was thickly bandaged, and he was making some grotesque signs to her. She went quickly over to him and knelt at his side.

"Adolf, you poor boy, are you badly hurt?"

"No. I'm fine. The main thing is that we have enough bread at home."

"He's a bit delirious. Concussion," remarked the doctor, who took the expression on Lisa's face for consternation.

Adolf nodded his aching head and collected all his strength. "My father phoned me right after the all-clear," he whispered. "He said they're all well there. And there's enough bread at home." He closed his eyes and bit his lips. "I'm not a sissy," he mumbled. "I'm just damned dizzy, that's all. I want to go home."

"A bit delirious. But he'll snap out of it soon," the doctor repeated. Lisa kept kneeling at the side of the stretcher, holding on to Adolf's soiled, scratched hands. "It's all right, Adolf, it's all right," she said. "It's all right, you're all right, everything is all right now." She had gone through all the danger, the fear, the tearing anxiety, the raid, the seven hells of this day and this night without cracking up; but the joy, the relief, the happiness that suddenly struck her made her feel faint. She groped in her mind, tried to get a hold of herself, to line up her thoughts and plan her next step.

"Where do you live?" she asked the boy.

"Reinickendorferstrasse 84," he mumbled. "My father says they didn't get any bombs in the neighbourhood; I want to go home."

"Can he go home, Doctor? Or is he badly hurt?"

"He'll simply have to go home. There's no space in the hospitals for such light casualties. The question is how to get him there."

"Never mind. I'll get him home. I'll take him home myself. Of course, I can, I'll get a car somehow. Reinickendorferstrasse 84. At last my Red Cross training will be good for something." Adolf grinned dizzily; his hands were clutching hers like the claws of some half-tamed little animal. . . . I'm coming, Martin, Lisa thought. I'm coming to you. I'll be with you. I'll be with you once more before we have to part again. . . . Every hour, every minute she could still spend with him were of a fantastic, unbelievable, almost unbearable

preciousness, as time can only be in the face of death. . . . I'll
hold your hand, I'll look into your eyes, I'll touch your hair,
I'll hear your voice, I'll talk to you and you will talk to me;
we are still strangers, but it is very important that we learn to
know each other better. So much time, Martin. The night is
not over yet, and there are hours and hours and hours for us to
be together before you have to leave me, and leave me again
and again. Reinickendorferstrasse 84. Maybe a cellar. Maybe
a shack. Maybe a ruin. It will be our paradise in any case,
Martin, my beloved.

"Stetten, you must be a good Samaritan and let me have
your car and chauffeur to take this boy home. Reinickendorferstrasse 84, that's not so very far, is it ? We'll get through somehow. I'll drop you off at your place first, and then I can go
on in your car, can't I ?"

"Nonsense, Lisel. You stay at my place with me, and my
chauffeur can take the boy home afterwards; doesn't that
make better sense ?"

"No, it doesn't. I'd—I'd rather be left to myself tonight;
you must understand that, don't you ? And I'd rather keep
myself busy and pretend that I'm doing something rather than
sit and brood——"

"At your command, Lisel," Stetten said correctly. It
sounded like the ghostlike echo of Dahnwitz's way of talking;
the caste was stronger than the individual. "But where will
you sleep ?"

"I won't sleep. This is no night to go to sleep," Lisa said
impatiently. Kauders pushed his shaking body into the fore-
ground. "I protest," he said. "I won't let you go out on the
street; you'll stay in my room if I have to carry you there
bodily."

Lisa simply brushed him aside. "Don't be a pest, Kauders,"
she said, holding Adolf's struggling fingers firmly and assur-
ingly in hers. "Lie still, Adolf, I'll take care of you. Oh,
Doctor, I think the boy is fainting."

Herr Schmidt had completed his change of costume.
Now he was a mouse of a civilian and in the morning he would
be a soldier. "Well, good-bye and see that the hotel is still
here when I come back. *If* I come back," he said, handing his
keys, his cap, his register to old man Kliebert. He looked once
around the lobby. "It's not what it used to be," he muttered.
"I wonder if it will ever be the same—afterwards?"

His glance took in the revolving door, through which at that moment the telegraph woman entered—men's shoes, ragged uniform, steel helmet—as calmly as if she had not gone through hell and fire to deliver her wires. "Telegram," she said, holding her pad up to him. "I'm not here any longer," Schmidt answered. Kliebert signed and scanned the single telegram she put down. "Telegram for Kauders, Oberleutnant Kauders!" he called out.

"Kauders—here," the flier answered with military snap, clanked up to the desk and read the wire.

"Oh, damn it all!" he cursed when he was through with it.

"Bad news?" the doctor asked with a trace of pleasure. His own telegram had not arrived. Maybe it never would.

"Got to report for duty immediately. Oh, damn it and curse it and confound it! They don't give a man time for anything. Three days isn't too much, is it? But no, they've got to call me back just when I get going. My bill. I'm leaving. And how the devil do they think I'll get to the field in this mess?"

Nobody asked the telegraph woman for news, because the blazing, blasting, burning, catastrophic news was self-evident; but she reported it anyway. "They say eighty thousand are dead tonight. They had to put the Fuehrer in a strait jacket. Stalin says if we kill all the Bonzen we can have peace. In France they're having a revolution." She shuffled toward the door with her queer, automaton-like motions, and stopped half-way, as if she remembered something else. "And they didn't get Richter," she said. Suddenly a strange transformation took place in her face. It twitched and moved and came to life as by a strange magic. "And they didn't get Richter," she said, and her voice, too, became the voice of a living human being and began to ring. "And they didn't get Richter. And now they won't get him, ever; no, they won't get him. They won't get Richter."

There was a baffled silence as she disappeared, and Herr Schmidt said: "Plemplem. Not quite right in the attic."

As he walked toward the door, he stumbled over the picture, the Fuehrer's heroic-looking image, that had come off the wall again. He gave it a good kick that sent it out of his way. "Let someone else have you, for all I care!" he muttered as he left the hotel.

Otto Kauders paid his bill and clicked his heels in taking leave from Lisa. He had pushed his nervous breakdown away back into his subconscious together with that awful moment of baling out, together with all the shocks and jarring fears and damages he had suffered; he was a hero again, a thoughtless machine with perfectly functioning reflexes, but with its wires worn thin and its final disintegration close at hand and inevitable.

"I have my car outside, Lisel, if you please," Stetten said. He held the door open for the doctor, who transported Pageboy Number 6 through the narrow lane in front where the debris was already cleared away. The boy slept now under the influence of a sedative. The doctor bedded him on the seat, and when that was done he looked at his hands. They began to feel empty again, now that everything was done, all bandages made, all casualties attended to. His great night was over. He fastened his eyes on the burning sky. His leg was very stiff now; he was a lame man, out of step with the times. . . . Well, there will be more air raids, he told himself, and there was more hope than apprehension in it.

As Lisa walked out through the revolving door she knew that she left everything behind that she had been, up to this day. No more Parisian dresses, no oranges with her supper, no milk for breakfast, no extra rations, no privileges, no favours from the heads of the crumbling party. . . . Oh, Martin, you took me out in the nick of time, she thought. And if it should happen that we have to fall, at least we will fall together and on the right side of the barricades. She left all yesterday behind, and everything was a great, hard-to-attain tomorrow. She wanted to take a deep breath, but the air was hot and bitter and tasted of fire and smoke and dust. Stetten helped her politely into the car, and she placed Adolf's bandaged head on her lap and leaned back.

"As soon as I know the details about poor Arnim's funeral I'll let you know," said Stetten.

"Yes, please. That's very kind of you."

"At what address can I reach you?"

Lisa wondered for a moment if in this destroyed city there was still such a thing as an address. "As long as the theatre is still standing, I suppose you'll always find me there," she said. Stetten gave no answer, and when she looked at him he had fallen asleep in the deadly exhaustion that was the lot of an old-school German diplomat.

"We'll first drop Baron von Stetten at his place and then we'll try to go through to Reinickendorferstrasse 84," Lisa told the chauffeur. With a little smile she wondered whether this shiny, long Mercedes car of the Foreign Office had ever before touched the proletarian quarters where she was going now. Slowly, laboriously, the car picked its way through the gutted streets of the ruined city. The sky was bright with fires, but above its black ceiling of smoke and dust there was somewhere the first trace of the coming dawn.

Somewhere in the destruction of this night was the hope for better days. Somewhere in this burning Sodom and Gomorrah lived the Ten Righteous Men for whose sake God would forgive all the wicked.

"I'm coming, Martin, please, wait for me," said Lisa Dorn.